TOWN OF TRIALS

A COLDWATER CHRONICLES THRILLER

D. R. YOUNG

DRYWRITES.COM

First edition

ISBN: 979-8-9931410-2-2

Ebook ISBN: 979-8-9931410-3-9

CONTENTS

"A gem cannot be polished without friction, nor a man perfected without trials."

- Seneca

1

HEART ON FIRE

Flames ate at the hundred-year-old wood of the Coldwater County courtroom.

They crawled up the judge's bench where Otto Chapel's high-backed leather chair spun lazily, empty. The chair's armrests were blackened and curled, wrapped in fire. Legal pads were knocked to the floor, caught one by one, and turned into glowing ash.

John Chance crouched behind the overturned prosecution table, arms shielding his face from the heat. He held one arm around Sarah, the new, young blonde staff attorney. She pressed her face into his shoulder, trembling.

But John's shadowed eyes weren't focused on her. They were staring into the space Annaleigh had occupied moments before—the same area now fully engulfed in flames.

The fire had erupted during Coldwater's most crucial cross-examination.

John risked another glance around the table's edge, searching for her. Smoke billowed across the floor like fog, rising in random plumes. Through it, he glimpsed shards of his surroundings.

Chairs in the jury box overturned as townsfolk scrambled to safety by diving over half-walls, tripping on benches, and vaulting over others to reach the exit. The fire's roar and the boiling wood swallowed their screams.

Another plasma arc streaked overhead, forcing John back into cover. Sheriff Dane Parnell and Deputy D. Clyde Brothers ducked low behind pews, pistols raised but useless.

Too much fire and smoke.

No clear shot.

Then, through the haze, he saw something that only existed in his nightmares.

In front of the witness stand, a crumpled body lay where Annaleigh had been standing. White shirt, dark pants, charred fabric sticking to blackened skin. No movement. No rise indicating breath.

Zero signs of life.

John's throat tightened. The lump there felt like stone.

No. Not her. It can't be her, he thought.

The sight pierced through his eyes like a knife. He couldn't look away, couldn't blink.

This is the last time I come to court unarmed.

Memories slammed into him. His living room last spring, Wesley Raith's forearms glowing white-hot, fire flickering off his fingers as he lost control. John had grabbed those arms and felt the searing heat on his face. He'd smelled his own flesh burning—the most unforgettable aroma.

This situation was undoubtedly worse. Annaleigh was in serious trouble.

The thrum that had filled the room—the low, electric pulse behind each lava sphere—abruptly ceased. The rain of flames stopped, leaving only the crackle of burning wood, the wail of the injured, and the panicked scramble of the fleeing.

"Stay here," he told Sarah, voice rough. She nodded, eyes wide and watery.

He vaulted the table, shoe soles melting and slipping on the red-hot hardwood. Heat licked his legs. He leapt through the fire and dropped beside the body. Shaking hands reached for the shoulder and flipped it.

Dark pants, white shirt—at least, what remained of it. Charred collar, burned sleeves. Face covered by soot and shadow.

John's breath left him.

"Annaleigh!"

The scream burst out—raw, broken, echoing off the blazing walls. He stared down at the body, willing it wasn't her, hoping the smoke cleared, wishing his eyes stopped watering so he could see more clearly.

Behind him, Parnell shouted something. Orders, maybe. John couldn't hear it over the roar in his ears.

He couldn't take his eyes off the body.

Around him, the courtroom kept burning.

2

DUAL SHADOWS

The midnight moonlight shone on John Chance's dashboard, illuminating his cozy little mobile office.

He sat low in the Sheriff Department's Chevy Caprice, the same make and model as Sheriff Parnell's, except for the decal on the doors and the hideous shade of brown that wrapped the outside. As Coldwater's newest detective—and only detective—inherited the unmarked car from the previous occupant.

Three months sitting in this car, and it still doesn't feel right.

A constricting holster wrapped around his shoulders, holding the semi-automatic pistol close to his ribs. He still hadn't gotten used to walking around every day carrying a loaded weapon. An odd mix of power and paranoia, to be sure.

He sat parked on the edge of the back parking lot of Hank's Three Pump, watching the bar's back door, the other half of his life wouldn't leave his mind—or sight.

Folders and legal pads cluttered his dashboard. He used the steering wheel as a desk, jotting down notes on the cases he'd handle as a prosecutor, being careful not to accidentally honk the horn by pressing too hard with his pen. Spare clothes and his courthouse loafers were neatly stacked in the backseat. Judge

Chapel would not look favorably upon John wearing his black boots into the courtroom.

Heavy eyelids covered eyes that kept shifting. Three Pump's door. Legal pad. Door. Case folder. Door. Lather. Rinse. Repeat.

Late nights watching entrances, exits, and alleys had taken their toll. Constant action and late nights had worn him down. He'd lost weight and hadn't slept eight hours in a row since law school. Fatigue wears on everyone.

John was no exception.

He had one aim, one goal, one purpose: to find and capture the fugitive Kenneth Roy Atlee. Taking free time to slow down and lose focus wouldn't help him accomplish it. He had chosen to have it all, at least in the form of simultaneous careers, but his decision gradually destroyed him from within.

September's late surge of heat had finally waned, and the early fall nights dropped into the low 60s. The leaves, however, eagerly held to their green, desperately resisting the shift to orange and red.

This suit jacket will soon pull double duty. Keep me warm and hide the gun.

Since officially joining the department, John had numerous chances to improve his first stakeout. That failed mission resulted —through no fault of his own, of course—in alerting Mayor Cameron Raith to John's less-than-covert presence.

Former mayor.

Luckily, the Caprice had a dashboard-mounted switch to turn the headlights—and high beams—on and off. No more stomping on the floorboard, at least when he wasn't driving his trusty 1972 pale green Dart.

With John's attention divided between his court work and the bar's back door, his shadowed peripheral vision failed to notice an approaching figure. The passenger door swung open, and a tall, thin figure slipped into the seat. John's head jerked, and his right hand went into his jacket, fumbling for the pistol's handle.

"You look tired, babe," Annaleigh said, curling the corners of her lips.

John relaxed, exhaling. "No rest for the wicked." He eased his hand from his jacket and draped it around her. He leaned in and gave her a kiss. "You don't need to keep checking on me."

"You need to start locking your doors. I'm worried about you —you put in almost a full day at the courthouse, then wind up out all night, too. And, it's no rest for the *weary*? Not wicked."

John glanced upward.

"Oh, your eyes still bothering you, sweetheart? They looked like they spasmed for a sec. I'd hate to have to take you to the hospital for exhaustion *and* a bloody nose."

"But, I don't have a bloody nose—"

"You will if you roll your eyes at me again, mister."

"Don't worry about the nights," he said, ignoring the sarcasm. "I'm getting closer. I know it. Then all this will be over."

"When you do get him, things have only started. We've got to impanel a jury, prepare for trial, sentencing, all that. But, luckily, it means you don't need to spend every night watching a new door."

"It's the same door a lot of the time," he chuckled. "Hard to get leads when nobody will talk, Annaleigh. So, all I can do is retrace his steps. He's bound to show up at one of his old joints. Parnell thinks Kenneth's gone for good, but... I'm not so sure."

"You can't rely on your hunches all the time, John."

"I'll rely on whatever it takes to stop him for good."

She handed him a brown paper bag and a thermos. "I brought you something. Chips and a BLT, minus the T, of course. Just the way you like it." She tapped her painted nails against the side of the metal canister. "And hot chocolate. It's getting chilly out there. I honestly don't know how you made it this far in life with your palate. You don't drink coffee. Or tea. And, who eats a BL sandwich anyway?"

He unfolded the top of the bag and sniffed deeply, catching the scent of bacon inside. "Made it this far because of the love of a good woman, it seems. This bacon smells delicious."

"Don't get weird, your mom made it. I'm just the messenger... but she'll be glad you approve." She extended her hand to grasp the door handle. "Now, you start eating while I hop out and take a quick peek inside. It'll speed things up a bit, and then you can come home with me—"

"What?" His head snapped around to look at her, eyebrows furrowed. "Absolutely not."

"I'm a big girl. I can take care of myself."

"Oh, I know what kind of girl you are. Especially when the lights go out." He smirked. She blushed. "But... if he's in there and he sees you—"

"Come on, I know the bartender. We had a great conversation that one time, at least when I wasn't getting hit on by drunks."

"Thank you for bringing me a snack. Believe me when I say this, I love—" Her eyes lit up with anticipation. "—having you here. But you need to go. It's not safe."

Her shoulders slumped as she lifted her cheeks. "I'll wait up for you," she whispered, planting a kiss on his cheek. "Don't be too late—the lights will be off when you get there."

A frown wrinkled his lips after she softly closed the door. He wanted her in the car with him. He longed to be anywhere she was. At least he had something to look forward to. Through the rearview mirror, he watched her climb into her red Chevy Cavalier and drive away, shaking his head and sniffing the bacon once more.

"I don't deserve you, Annaleigh Stanton," he mumbled. Two bites later, as he chewed, he snatched the mic from the police-issued CB radio mounted under the dashboard.

"Clyde? You around?"

After a few seconds, the radio crackled to life, and a familiar voice came through.

"Yes, sir, Detective Chance. Ears are on."

John sighed and lowered the mic below his chin. He lifted it back to his lips as one side curled upward. "How long are we gonna keep that one up, *Deputy?* Don't know if I'll ever get used to you calling me that. Can we switch to channel 7?"

"Copy."

John turned the CB's dial and switched to a private channel—one that wouldn't be broadcast over the main dispatch line. He waited a few seconds, giving Clyde time to do the same. His finger hovered, about to activate the mic, when Clyde's voice came through the speaker.

"What's on your mind, John?"

A small smile crept across John's lips, appreciating Clyde's choice of names. "Pretty sure Annaleigh thinks I'm crazy."

"You've been dating the girl for what, three months now? Of course you're crazy... crazy in love. Every man who's ever been in your position goes nuts at first, too. Happens to the best of us."

"Not what I'm talking about, Clyde."

"You'll have to fill me in then, champ."

"Every night I go out doing... this. Chasing a ghost. Prioritizing him."

"Ah, I hear you now. After seeing the hours you've been keeping, can you blame her? Usually, this is the honeymoon phase of a relationship. Honeymoons are typically spent with your significant other, right?"

"That's your take? Everywhere I go, no one's on my side."

"It's not about sides." John felt Clyde's kind eyes piercing him through the radio. "*You* chose to be both a lawyer and a detective. But you also chose her. Don't forget that."

"I think it's almost three jobs, to be honest. There's the courthouse, the station, and then, this... the hunt."

"Four, really, but don't ever tell anyone I said love is like a job." He chuckled to himself. "Seriously, though, everyone's on the lookout for Kenneth, and not just us. The whole town, John. We'll find him."

"It feels like it's my whole purpose now, and not just the job. It's been three months, and nothing. I'm... I'm failing."

"Nonsense," Clyde scoffed. "You found the guy who robbed

Emerson's Jewelry. You figured out the high school kid stole money from under old man Waldren's nose at the hardware store. I'm sure there's been more, but that's on top of all the extra moonlighting. If I had to judge your first few months as a detective, I'd say they've been pretty successful."

"More successful than the last guy? I feel bad how it ended, but Mumber didn't set that high a bar."

"You only saw him at the end, but Hollis Mumber was a solid investigator, John. Once, he was like you—young, eager, cocky—though about a foot shorter." He chuckled.

"And wider," John chimed in.

"Father Time comes for us all, that's for sure. But from my point of view, you two are cut from the same cloth. You both want to do a good job. Time changes us all differently, though. Maybe Hollis lost sight of that after a while. But you, John, you're free to chart your own course. You can set that bar as high as you want. I've got faith in you, kid."

"Your pep talks are always appreciated, Clyde," John said, rolling his neck and keeping his eyes locked on Three Pump's door. "And, I know that one of these days, Kenneth will be exactly where I expect him. Something in me says tonight's the night."

"Is that why you're parked in the brush behind Three Pump? You think he's drinking his sorrows away?"

John's brows raised as he broke eye contact with the rear entrance, looking around. "How did you... Clyde... where are you?"

"Who do you think is covering the front door, kid? We're a team. I've got your back. Or in this case, Three Pump's front." A warmth grew inside John that momentarily beat back the fall chill in the air. "Now," Clyde continued, "if we only knew what vehicle he drove these days. We all know about his yellow pickup, but didn't see that parked here when I did my lap around the lot. He's probably sporting different wheels now."

"You did a lap? And I didn't see you?"

"What can I say? You were staring at that door so hard, I thought you were trying to open it with your mind."

"That'd be some trick."

"These days, feels like something like that's getting more and more possible."

A cool breeze blew through the detective's open windows, ruffling John's hair. He inhaled the fresh air, faintly scented with the smell of beer drifting from the bar's cracked-open windows. He pulled a notebook from his side up to his steering wheel, where he could read it while still monitoring the joint's exit. He keyed the mic.

"Since I've been watching, the bartender comes out on the hour with a bag and throws it away in the dumpster. Aside from that, it's been pretty quiet back here. Anything happening out front?"

"Naw. Watched a few people go in, all did double-takes when they saw me. Maybe that'll work in our favor, though. If word gets around inside that I'm out front—"

"He'll have no option but to come my way."

"And we can bring him in together. Like I said, I've got your back."

The outdoor light shining on the back entrance went out, drawing John's attention.

"Hold up, something's happening back here. Based on the usual patterns, we're not due for another trash run for another twenty minutes, but somebody just turned off the back light." The door swung open, and a man stepped out into the shadows, carrying what looked like a plastic trash bag. "Never mind, Clyde. Not sure why the light went out, but he's just carrying another trash bag."

The bar's dumpster sat about twenty feet away from the bar's back door, near the far corner of the building, beside a protrusion that John assumed to be a walk-in refrigerator. The man, still cloaked in shadow, moved toward it. He reached the dumpster and paused, head twisting. The large, burly silhouette shifted, first thinning then widening back to its original shape.

He's turning. Is he looking at me?

In a quick move, the man dropped the trash bag and bolted to the side, disappearing behind the bar.

Shit.

"Clyde! It's him—I think! Took off on foot around the west side of the building."

Without hesitation, John heard Clyde's siren start its wail, and red and blue flashing lights lit up the front parking lot.

John started the Caprice's engine and floored the gas pedal. The tires spun and kicked up dirt and gravel as he sped out of his parking spot to the building's front, in time to see a car rush from the lot with Clyde's marked cruiser right behind.

"We've got a live one," Clyde's voice blared over the police radio. "Switching back to main."

John skidded onto the road, chasing after Clyde's tail. Without taking his eyes off the road, he reached down to his radio and spun the knob all the way to the left, resetting it back to channel one.

"This is Detective Chance. Kenneth Roy Atlee has been seen fleeing Three Pump in a beige Ford Taurus station wagon. Plates are unknown at this time. Deputy Brothers also in pursuit. Heading west."

A familiar voice crackled over the radio, brimming with confidence.

"Sheriff Parnell here. Bring him to the square. We'll be waiting."

3

BLINDSIDED PURSUIT

John kept Kenneth's taillights in sight—two red eyes glowing through the night. Clyde's cruiser chased between them, lights flashing but siren off, like a silent predator closing the gap.

Kenneth drove quickly but steadily at first, heading toward town. Once the courthouse came into sight, he peeled left into residential streets. John muttered a curse under his breath and pressed the radio button.

"Suspect now heading south down Henry Street. Clyde is maintaining pursuit. I'll take Saline. Clyde, when you reach Newberry, attempt a PIT on the driver's side—try to force him to turn right. I'll be there and will block him in."

Clyde's voice cracked again. "Copy."

"Same here," Sheriff Parnell echoed. "We're headed your way."

John floored it, passing Henry and drifting into the turn down Saline Street, one street over and parallel to Kenneth's and Clyde's paths.

The neighborhood around them had been quiet—porch lights on, kids' bikes in driveways—an otherwise normal scene that suddenly felt fragile.

Through the gaps between houses, he saw Clyde's cruiser surge ahead, closing in on Kenneth's rear quarter. Clyde drifted left, then right—a perfect PIT setup. Kenneth reacted as expected, swerving to avoid contact.

Exactly where John wanted him.

When Kenneth swerved right onto Newberry to avoid Clyde's cruiser, John skidded out from the side street and blocked the intersection. Kenneth's headlights flared bright, tires squealing as he jerked the wheel.

The station wagon fishtailed, hit a curb, and slammed into a young, sturdy maple at a yard corner. The crash caved in metal and shattered glass. Kenneth's wagon jerked once, then stabilized, hood folded, steam escaping from the radiator.

Kenneth flung open the driver's door and sprinted across the lawn, jumping a low chain-link fence as if it were nothing. John slammed his cruiser into park, grabbed the portable radio from the seat, and gave chase. Mid-step, he clipped the radio hook onto his belt and hooked the mic to his breast pocket.

"Foot pursuit—southbound through yards off Saline and Newberry. Male suspect. Dark coat. Heading toward Marlowe. I'm chasing."

John cleared the fence in one bound, boots pounding the grass and the radio's curled cord bouncing like a spring across his chest. Kenneth had already made it two houses ahead, cutting through flower beds and hopping over another fence. John's vision wavered—peripheral edges blurring into black tunnels.

God, running was the worst. He hated it. Always had.

The world shrank to objects directly in front of him. Everything else blurred into shadows. If he pivoted to take in the full scene, he'd surely trip over something.

"Suspect crossing Marlowe—through backyards toward Lee," he barked into the radio. "Need units to block streets."

Static. Then Parnell's voice, calm but urgent. "Clyde's circling to you. Foley and Taggart en route."

John clenched his teeth and pushed harder, taking long strides to catch up. He cleared another fence, landing awkwardly with a jolt in his knees. Kenneth still pulled ahead—a big man, but quick and desperate.

Darkness pressed in. No streetlights back here—only porch glow and the random floodlight left on overnight. John realized too late he should've grabbed a flashlight. A beam really would've been helpful.

Too late now. Keep him in sight, and it won't matter.

The radio on his belt jostled, almost coming loose. He hastily slammed one hand on it to keep it steady, then grabbed the mic with his other hand.

"Crossing Lee, towards..." He glanced around but couldn't remember the next street name. He had done his best to memorize the street map, but the rush of adrenaline surging through him only aided his feet. His mind clouded as he tried to recall the map between steps. "...whatever the next street west is."

He listened as he ran.

No radio traffic. No response.

Kenneth turned right and pushed through a hedge. John broke through behind him.

"Pursuit headed north, towards College... I think. Maybe Franklin. Anybody read me?"

Between the footsteps and heaving breaths, he heard silence from the radio. No acknowledgements, no fragments, just silence. Not even a pop or a click.

Maybe it broke?

He hoped units would close in, even without updated positioning. The longer he chased on his own, the higher the likelihood he might lose sight of Kenneth.

Unless the others predicted the chase's path, backup was a gamble. Kenneth bounded around the corner of a brick ranch house. John closed the gap to ten feet—close enough to hear the man's ragged breathing ahead.

Gotta take him down. Push him from behind. Knock him off balance. Hold him at gunpoint. Wait for backup.

He couldn't shoot the man. Parnell had withdrawn the shoot-to-kill order weeks ago after pressure from the new mayor. "No more Wild West in this town," the mayor had said. "We need to reinstate order from chaos."

The new mayor apparently had little experience dealing with those members of society who could burn it all down with one snap.

Five feet away. Almost in reach.

John lunged, arm outstretched, fingers grazing Kenneth's back.

One more step, then he could shove him down—

An arm shot out from behind the corner, wearing some kind of uniform sleeve, fast as a snake. It cracked across John's forehead, snapping his head backward.

The world tilted. Pain bloomed white-hot.

John crumpled.

And everything went black.

* * *

"WHAT THE HELL HAPPENED?"

John's eyes fluttered open, squinting at the night sky. He lay on the ground, pain throbbing in his face and on the back of his head.

"Cussin' don't make you cool, *Detective.*" Clyde's slow, smooth twang echoed in John's head. "Glad to see you're back among the living."

John shushed him and rubbed his eyes. "Say I'm not cool a little softer, please, my head's killing me. The next time somebody tries to take your head off, you're allowed to cuss. I give you permission."

"If I recall, somebody did try to burn me alive not too long ago. Still healing. Didn't have to stoop to such language."

John stopped rubbing his face and checked his palms for

blood. He inched up a brow at the deputy. "Pretty sure one slipped out on you."

The man's lips curled into a sly grin. "Maybe a little one."

"How you feeling, son?" Sheriff Dane Parnell knelt beside John and gripped his shoulder. "Come on, let's sit you up."

As John sat up, he craned his neck and winced in pain. "God, I was this close... an arm's reach behind him... did we get him?"

He looked around at grim faces. Clyde glanced downward. Parnell twisted at the hip, avoiding eye contact.

"When I pulled up, I saw Kenneth chugging that way." Clyde pointed towards the front yard. "I gave chase, and we ended up a couple of houses away. He set off to the left, but then..."

John glanced around nervously. "Then, what? What happened?"

"Well, something caught my eye, and I got distracted. A fire started in the bushes to my right—the opposite direction where Kenneth was headed. Not sure how, he was nowhere near it. No one was. I had to stop and put it out before the house caught. Those innocent folks don't need their house burned down for this. I'm sorry, John. He got away."

"He got away? Seriously?" John let out an exasperated sigh.

Clyde rose to his feet with a solemn expression and retreated a few steps away. "Look, I'm sorry—"

"He radioed for backup, John," Parnell explained, while standing up and resting his hands on his belt. "But by the time we got here, Kenneth was gone. That's when we heard the call about an officer down... about you. Abandoned everything to get to you."

"Heard? From who?"

"From me." The smug voice of Deputy Cason Foley made John release another deep sigh. Foley looked back at him, expressionless. "It's my fault."

Confusion washed over John's face. "What's your fault?"

"Your ass on the ground. I knocked you out."

John blinked, soaking in the confession. "You? You did this?

You let him escape? You mother—" He surged to his feet with a burst of adrenaline. He made it one step before stars clouded his vision. He wobbled, falling to one knee. A strong set of arms caught him.

"Taggart, ease him down gently," Parnell commanded.

Deputy Dallas Taggart, Coldwater's newest deputy, guided John back to the ground. The man's bushy red hair and beard brushed against John's shoulder as he lowered him.

"Thanks, Dallas," John murmured. "Maybe you could take a shot at him for me? Revenge by proxy?"

Taggart chuckled. "Sure, but maybe I'll wait until he's not expecting it."

"All right, everyone, settle down," Parnell barked. "Foley, explain yourself."

"I heard John's...uh, Detective Chance's locations over the radio, but then it went quiet. I guessed and headed here to try to cut them off. Thought I could get in front of the chase. Got to this corner, heard someone coming, figured it was Mr. Atlee, so as soon as he rounded the corner, I swung. Didn't realize it was the detective until he was already down."

"Bullshit, Foley," John said, looking up in disbelief. "I relayed my position the entire time."

Taggart unclipped John's radio from his belt and inspected it. "Looks like your channel got switched somehow. You were talking to nobody, bud."

"See?" Foley said, arms open wide.

John squinted and pressed his forehead, grimacing. "It still doesn't explain everything. Kenneth was right in front of me, close enough to touch. There's no way he ran past without you seeing him."

"You calling me a liar?" Foley challenged. "Your memory is probably tricking you."

"I wonder why," John mumbled.

"Is this true, Deputy?" Parnell asked. "You didn't see anyone else until the detective came around the corner?"

Foley shifted his feet. "Absolutely, Sheriff. No one else."

As John sneered, something pulsed around Foley's head—a vague lavender ripple that disappeared as quickly as it had emerged. John's face stiffened, uncertain of what he'd seen. He looked at Clyde and Parnell, wondering if they noticed the same flash of light. They showed no reactions.

"Did anyone see that?" John asked, pointing at Foley with a wobbly finger. Everyone else looked confused.

"See what?" Parnell asked.

"I'm not sure how to describe it. It was a purple.... thing. It flashed. Right behind his head."

"The only purple I see is on your face, young man," Parnell drawled. "That bruise is really gonna hurt tomorrow—"

"No, really, I saw something. I know it—"

Foley flicked his head around, as if some insect buzzed around him. "Maybe you saw a lightning bug. Or maybe you're seeing things. I sure as hell don't." He crossed his arms. "Real sorry about hitting you."

"That sounded sincere," John quipped. "Whatever, man. Something was there. I know what I saw." John rubbed the back of his neck. "But, there's still maybe a one percent chance it's the blunt force trauma talking."

Clyde's hand grabbed John near his armpit and pulled him up.

"C'mon, I'll get you home. You can see Doc Jensen in the morning. But if we don't get some ice on that face, it might never stop swelling."

4

COURTHOUSE WELCOMES

Annaleigh's heels clicked across the courthouse vestibule, the echo bouncing off the faux marble tile that had seen every secret Coldwater ever tried to bury. She balanced two coffees—one black, one with a reckless three sugars—and checked her watch.

8:27 a.m.

A hint of a smile curved her lips as she remembered when she and John used to walk in together. He'd wait in the parking lot for her to arrive, eager to steal a few moments alone with her. She'd known about his plan from the very beginning, but she didn't dare reveal that to him.

Why ruin a fun thing?

With him working double-duty in split careers, their shared jaunt from the parking lot now happened much less often. Even though he slept at her place most nights and worked with her at the courthouse every morning, he would stop on his way in to brief Sheriff Parnell on his stakeout from the night before. There was no briefing for John today—he'd kissed her and hopped in the Dart to get a full workup at Coldwater Memorial.

The bailiff, Harlan, waved Annaleigh through security with the lazy grin he reserved for locals.

“Mornin’, Counselor. I hear new blood is starting today?”

“Yes, sir, she starts at nine. Hopefully, I can get a few things done before she shows up.”

Harlan whistled. “Seems sharp, that one. But, don’t worry, miss, I’m sure she won’t outshine the boss.”

Annaleigh stopped mid-step. “What do you mean by *seems* sharp? Do you know her?”

“Yes, ma’am. We met when she got here, arrived about ten minutes ago. I already sent her upstairs to wait.” He flashed a simple smile again. “Don’t worry, miss, I told her not to touch anything.”

She didn’t know why, the situation dug into her like a splinter. She glided up the stairs to the upstairs prosecutor’s office.

Sarah Sinclair stood by the window, sunlight cutting across a charcoal suit that looked more expensive than Annaleigh’s first car and blonde hair twisted into a knot so precise it looked engineered. When she turned, her warm and professional smile carried with it a hint of overconfidence.

“Annaleigh Stanton?” Sarah crossed the room, extending her hand. “I’m too early, aren’t I? Sorry… bad habit. I wanted to make a good first impression.”

“Don’t mention it. Early is perfect, and eager is appreciated. And, just call me Annaleigh, okay?” She handed Sarah the three-sugar coffee. “Big city lawyers like it sweet, I think.”

Sarah’s eyebrows lifted, pleased. “Aw, you remembered! St. Louis isn’t big, but I’ve heard a lot of people call it a big little city, if you know what I mean. If you tell that to anyone not from around here, most people hear *Missouri* and then stop listening.” She sipped from the cup, her eyes closing for half a second. “You got the sugar just right. You’re a dangerous woman, Annaleigh.”

Annaleigh laughed, but it sounded thinner than she intended. Something about Sarah’s voice—low, unhurried, with that river-city lilt—made her uneasy. She cleared her throat.

“Tour first, paperwork later?”

“Lead the way.”

They returned downstairs, weaving through the corridors like a slow parade. Annaleigh pointed out the quirks: Judge Chapel's hatred of clicking pens, the stenographer who cried at every sentencing, the one stall in the first-floor restroom that locked from the outside and trapped a public defender for four hours last spring. Sarah absorbed it all, asking questions that were never obvious, never pointless.

On their way back toward the stairs, they peeked into the empty courtroom. "The big stage," Sarah murmured. "Pretty fancy for a small jurisdiction. But, I'll bet it's seen its share of crazy."

"And then some. This whole town has." Annaleigh's voice caught, wrapped in memories of mayors, corruption, and flames. She shoved it down. No need to weigh down the newbie on her first morning. She led the way back to the staircase.

"I couldn't help but notice this on our way down," Sarah said, her eyes drifting to the faint scorch mark, barely visible. "The texture's different, like it's been painted over. But... looks like a handprint. Some kind of ghost story?"

"Something like that." Annaleigh forced a smile. "Coldwater's full of stories. I'm sure you'll hear them all over time. Some of them, probably more than once, depending on who you're talking to."

They ended up in Annaleigh's office—really a corner room filled with ambition. Sarah's eyes fixed on the framed photo of John shaking hands with the Sheriff at his official swearing-in ceremony.

Sarah tilted her head. "So that's the famous lawyer who became a detective? Turned down the St. Louis prosecutor's office to stay home and work here, right?"

Annaleigh's pulse skipped. "Sounds like you know a little about him."

"By reputation. Word spreads fast there, especially in the circles I hung out with. That job was a highly sought-after spot—

all of us 'muni' prosecutors wanted it." Seeing Annaleigh's blank expression, Sarah added, "That means *municipality.*"

"Oh, I know what it means. I just didn't realize it was such a competition."

"There was a frenzy when we heard about it. The guy they finally chose? I'd seen him in court—the guy couldn't argue his way out of a paper bag."

Annaleigh smirked. "Water under the bridge? Now that you're here?"

"Completely. Speaking of being here, when we spoke before, I don't think you answered my question of *why.*"

"Why what?" Annaleigh's response came a bit too quickly.

"Why hire me? If he's working in this office, too... are there going to be enough cases for all three of us?"

"Two-and-a-half." A half-hearted smile curled Annaleigh's lips.

Sarah straightened. "I'm new, but I assure you, I know what I'm doing. I have two years of experience and can handle everything from filing to plea deals, even filling in for you down in court if you need it. You can count on me to contribute in a meaningful way—"

"No, no, you misunderstood. The half is not you." Although Annaleigh's cryptic statement caused Sarah to jump to the wrong —but expected—conclusion, maybe it wasn't kind to play tricks on the poor girl on her first day. "It's John," she said, pointing back to the picture. "He's going to be splitting time between here and the Sheriff's Office, so I'll need someone who can help out with the small stuff when he's not here. And... someone who doesn't mind the third chair when he is."

"No issues with that at all. Annaleigh—I'm up for any challenge you can throw my way," she said, smiling broadly. "So... is he coming in today?"

"Probably a bit later, he's at an appointment right now. And, by the way, he didn't come home just for the job." Sarah leaned in, patient. Annaleigh heard herself say it before she meant to. “He came home for me. We’re... together.”

The words floated between them like a dare.

Sarah’s expression remained unmoved. Not a blink, not a flinch. Only a gentle, almost affectionate smile. “That’s wonderful,” she said. It even sounded genuine. Too genuine. Like she’d rehearsed it. “I mean, really. From the stories I’ve heard, he seems pretty cool. Can’t wait to meet him.”

Annaleigh waited for some hint about those stories or more reasons why Sarah would be so interested in John. Nothing followed. Sarah turned to the stack of files on the desk, reaching for the top folder.

“Is this the Emerson Jewelry case? I imagine jury selection can’t be far off,” she said, seamlessly.

Annaleigh automatically corrected her. “Seated them at the end of last week.”

Sarah nodded, flipping pages with ease. She hummed the chorus from Cecilia, by Simon and Garfunkel, under her breath. The same melody John muttered when he thought no one was listening. Annaleigh’s stomach sank.

“How did you—” she stopped herself.

Sarah looked up, innocent. “How did I what?”

“Nothing.” Annaleigh distracted herself with her cold coffee. “Just doesn’t seem like your first day. You’re prepared.”

Sarah’s eyes lit up. “I read up on every Coldwater case before I accepted the job. Wanted to know what I was walking into.” A small shrug. “Professional curiosity.”

The room suddenly felt smaller.

Professional curiosity? Right.

“Every case?”

“Even stopped by the Sheriff’s Office to review the blotters, for cases that might not have even gone to trial, just in case.”

Annaleigh’s eyes narrowed. “You... already went to the Sheriff’s Office?”

My new hire's first field trip was to my boyfriend's work? I thought she said she didn't know him.

Her phone buzzed on the desk, snapping her out of her own thoughts. Only John called her desk phone directly—everyone else had been trained by Genie to call the main line routed to her desk.

Annaleigh picked up the receiver, then put it back down.

Sarah noticed, of course. "Speak of the devil?"

"He'll live." Annaleigh's voice sounded strange in her own ears.

Sarah's smile softened, almost kind. "I'm not here to step on toes, Annaleigh. I'm here to help, especially if we can bury Kenneth Roy Atlee so deep he never sees daylight again." She tapped the photo of John. "At least, as soon as he can catch him."

Her fingers lingered on the photograph a second longer than necessary before she turned away.

"You know about Kenneth Atlee? If I didn't know better, it sure sounds like you've been in town for more than a few days."

"His name kept coming up in my research," Sarah said over her shoulder. "Read all about it."

"In your research...?"

"I'm trying to play my part and do it well. You know, be ready for anything on day one."

Annaleigh watched her walk to the window, sunlight crowning that perfect knot of hair, and felt the first cold twist of something she didn't want to name. Jealousy, maybe. Or a warning.

Either way, she worried this feeling wouldn't fade away quickly.

Her phone rang again. This time, she answered.

"Hey," John's voice sounded rough. "You good over there? I don't usually get a hang up."

"Barely." She glanced at Sarah, who examined the courthouse lawn as if it held secrets. "New attorney started early."

"Smart ones always do. Pretty sure that's what I did." A

pause. "Annaleigh, is everything okay? I know this tone—it's the same as when I wake you up after I come in too late."

Annaleigh forced brightness into her tone. "Never better. But, call me as soon as you hear from Dr. Jensen."

"On my way there now."

She held the receiver to her chest and then hung it up.

Sarah turned back, all business again. "Care to walk me through the evidence chain in the jewelry case?"

Annaleigh nodded, her throat tightening.

Outside, the bells from a nearby church rang nine. As if on cue, Genie Glitter's heels clicked up the stairs with baked goods in her hands, ready to start her day and feed the new hire.

Annaleigh followed Sarah into the bullpen, the smell of expensive coffee and a stranger's perfume lingering behind them both.

5

CONTEXTUAL GLOWS

The morning sun blinded John, despite wearing a pair of dark sunglasses. He slowed the Dart and guided it toward the shoulder, turning into the Gas & Barn.

He eased up to a pump, then shoved the nozzle into the car's green hip for a quick fill-up. The smell of gasoline wafted up to him, and even though he knew better, he inhaled it.

Everything in moderation.

On the other side, a balding man filled up a shiny new pickup. John leaned against his door and had no choice but to overhear their conversation as the gallons flowed.

"...we haven't been over to visit in ages." The wife's voice from inside the pickup irritated John instantly.

"Yes, dear, I know," the man replied. "Things have been busy."

"You mean *you've* been too busy to see my mother."

"What do you want me to say? There's always something I've got to get done. Besides, she hates me."

"No, you're the one who can't stand her."

The man paused, trying to think of an answer that wouldn't land him sleeping on the couch for a week. "Wait? This weekend? Can't. Gotta mow the yard Saturday—it's gonna rain on Sunday.

I'm not sure we'll have time to drive all the way up to Farmington and then back afterward."

"Don't worry, we'll have time. We can go when you're done."

Another pregnant pause from the man. "I don't know, dear. I'll need to take a shower and clean up afterward. There's no way we can make it in time for lunch."

"Great news, then," the woman said. "Because I already told her we'd be over for dinner."

John attempted to hide his smile, knowing the man had been beaten.

The man sighed. "Sounds great, hon." His tone wavered between sarcasm and defeat. "Can't wait."

A soft purple afterimage hovered around the man's trucker hat, fading like heat off asphalt. John did a double-take. The gas pump clicked, signaling a full tank. Dazed, he hung up the nozzle, flicking glances back at the man.

The man got in and slammed the pickup door shut. Subtly, John angled himself to catch another glimpse through the window, hoping to see it again. Whatever it was.

He didn't.

John blinked, clearing his vision, certain he saw... something.

Or did he?

The concussion. Sure. That explained it.

That's the logical reason he's begun to see colors and watch as they wisp away into the air.

* * *

JOHN RUBBED at the band-aid stuck inside his elbow. He had never been a fan of needles. Yet, in the three months since his showdown with Wesley Raith, where he caught blood and bone shrapnel in his face and eyes, he's been stuck with more of them than he could count.

With each blood draw, he'd look away while a young and

eager Coldwater Memorial Hospital nurse lied to him. "It'll only pinch for a sec."

Sometimes he'd get lucky when an older nurse entered the room wearing a scowl. She'd do the job and leave within thirty seconds. No lies attempted. No words at all. Menial tasks came naturally to them after years of practice.

The young ones, though, rarely find a vein on their first try, then painfully dig and jab, with nothing more than a hollow "sorry". Oddly, those nurses always entered the room with a smile. How ironic.

Dr. Abigail Jensen, the internist in her mid-thirties who moonlit as the town's coroner, walked in with neither a scowl nor a smile.

"The test results are *that* good?" John asked.

Jensen pulled over a rolling stool and sat beside John at the examination table. She flipped open a folder, skimmed its contents, closed it, and looked up at him.

"I've got two pieces of good news and... some other news. Which would you like to hear first?"

"Give me the good, and we'll take it downhill from there."

She nodded. "The first bit of good news is that, according to the scans, there appears to be no lasting head trauma. Take it easy for the next few days and come back in if the headaches persist."

"So, seeing colors will be temporary?"

"Most likely. We ruled out detached retinas, as those would appear as streaks of lightning, which is not exactly what you described you're seeing. At this point, my advice would be to just give it some time."

John crossed his arms. "One down. You had more good news?"

"Yes, I do," Jensen replied, casually patting the folder on her lap. "You've been a trooper with all the tests—"

"So many needles," John muttered.

"—and I apologize for how long it took to get an answer, but I'm glad to say we've finally identified the anomalous chemical that kept showing up in the results. It's a compound called Picloram."

A flat expression washed over John's face. "Am I supposed to know what that is?"

"No, and I didn't recognize it either. I kept telling you that we've been waiting on the state lab in Jefferson City to come back with some results. That's only half right. The truth is, they gave up some time ago. They sent the sample back marked 'unidentified contaminant' and moved on—"

"Gave up? How long ago? What have we been doing all the time?"

"Slow down, I swear I'll explain everything. I wasn't about to let this lie, so I personally drove a vial to Mineral Area College myself. Dr. Franklin in the chem department ran it on their Hewlett-Packard GC-MS. It took him all of thirty seconds to figure it out."

She tapped the pages.

"Picloram is a pyridine-based herbicide. It's the kind of stuff ranchers spray on thistles and locust trees. Has been registered since the sixties and is probably on every co-op shelf in the county."

"A weed killer? In my blood? From my point of view, doc, that sounds pretty bad."

"That's mainly why nothing flagged it. Hospital tox screens check for drugs, heavy metals, and possibly some more common pesticides, such as DDT residues. Picloram doesn't even register on those panels. Plus, the mass spectrum doesn't match the structures in the textbooks I usually check. I searched for exotic poisons and rare metabolic disorders—turns out I should have looked in a farm journal." She leaned forward, her voice softening. "The level isn't huge—point-zero-eight parts per million—but it's definitely there and shouldn't be. Its half-life in soil can be ninety days, maybe longer in wetter conditions. In the handful of documented cases I found, if discovered in a person's blood, it usually clears within a couple of weeks... unless something locks it into the tissue. In your case, it bonded with your red blood cells, which is highly unusual. That's kept it from deteriorating naturally."

John stared at the floor. "Wesley's hands... the fire... his blood... do you think that... ability... is in *me*?"

"Let's not get ahead of ourselves. I'm not quite ready to say this explains the... um, abnormalities you witnessed in that boy," she said carefully. "You absorbed a much smaller dose. That might be the only reason you're sitting here still... normal."

"Normal enough to see colors?"

"Yes, John," she scolded. "You're still normal. I'm not convinced your vision issues are related to the Picloram. Concussions can also present in similar ways."

"Wait, so was that the good news? If so, we don't see eye to eye on what 'good' means, doc. Is there also bad news, then?"

"Sorry," she laughed. "That was both the good and the bad news. Everything got a little muddled there."

The tension in John's shoulders eased. He exhaled, letting them drop as a wave of calm washed down his spine.

"At least it doesn't sound like it's a death sentence," he admitted.

Jensen sat up straighter at John's words. "I don't think that's anything you have to worry about right now," she said. "I'm confident that we'll figure this out."

For a moment, the outline around her medium-length dark hair blurred into a shimmering violet veil, then snapped back like a lens refocusing. John's eyes narrowed.

"There it was... I saw it again. Right behind your head."

"As I said before, you have to give it time. It should go away on its own. You took a pretty hard fall last night."

"Doc, no offense, but you just found out there's weed killer in my blood and I'm seeing colors... and you don't think I have anything to worry about?"

Her eyes shot left, then back. "No. Whatever risk you have is minimal, due to the concentration levels. I'll continue to do more research, but don't be worried, John. Because, at this stage, I'm not."

Once again, the air around her head shimmered with a fleeting, ethereal lilac glow, retreating before he could blink and remember it. He rubbed his lips with his fingers, uncertain if he should speak up again.

She handed him the report. "Keep this, you might need it for your case. And John, when you finally catch Mr. Atlee, if you can get me even a single drop of blood, voluntarily or not, I want to run the same panel. Something tells me his numbers will look like yours."

John stood. "Doubt it," he said quietly. "They'll be worse. Thanks, doc."

On his way out, he stopped at the nurse's station, determined to test a theory. He leaned one hip against the counter and knocked on it with his knuckles, catching the attention of two nearby nurses.

"Morning, ladies," he said with an easy smile. He nodded toward someone refilling a small refrigerator. "Rhonda, are those the little bottles of orange juice everyone's been talking about?"

"They sure are, darlin'," Rhonda replied, barely glancing up. "You want one? Got two left."

He observed her head. No flicker, no shimmer. Just fluorescent shadows and tired eyes. He glanced past the open refrigerator door and confirmed the presence of two tiny bottles of orange liquid.

"Naw. Thanks for the offer, though." He turned his attention to the younger nurse, sitting behind the desk. "Hey, Tammy, a couple of nights ago, I swung by Scoops—happened to see you and Dallas sharing a hot-fudge sundae. You two looked pretty cozy. Are you officially an item now? If so, maybe we could double-date, you know, with me and Annaleigh? I'm sure she'd love it."

Tammy, stretching casually for a pen, froze mid-reach. Her

cheeks flushed brightly as she forced out a laugh that sounded unnaturally high.

"What? No. That wasn't me—I mean, yes, it was me, but it was just ice cream. Dallas and I are friends. Everybody's making it something it's not."

John hadn't verbalized the additional details he'd seen that night—that he saw them kissing in that booth, too. But the instant the lie left her mouth, it happened.

A quick, electric purple shimmer rippled around her head, then disappeared in half a heartbeat.

His pulse quickened, but he kept his expression neutral. He pushed off the counter, surrendering with both hands.

"Understood, my fault. Small-town gossip then. Catch you later, ladies."

He walked away, mind racing.

Truth? Nothing. A lie? That strange flash.

He couldn't fully explain it, but he had the perfect idea to further develop his newfound gift.

6

TESTING THE LIGHT

The single bulb in Annaleigh's living room lamp cast a soft light that dimly lit the room, creating long shadows across the bookshelves and the worn-out couch. She'd kicked off her shoes the moment she stepped inside, trading dressy flats for socks and the day's tension for peace and quiet.

John's arrival was imminent. She waited, patient, the quaint two-bedroom house smelling faintly of cedar from the candle she'd lit on the coffee table.

When the knock came, she opened the door wearing shorts and one of his old law-school hoodies stolen from him a month ago. He looked like he'd carried the whole day home with him—tie loosened, shoulders a little hunched—but when their eyes met, and lips touched, some of that weight lifted.

He followed her inside and slumped onto the couch. She slid in beside him, crossing her legs and leaning onto him until her head settled in the familiar hollow of his shoulder. His arm wrapped around her, fingers resting lightly on her sleeve, rolling the fabric between them.

She allowed the silence to linger for a moment—comfortable, not empty—then tilted her head slightly to catch his face.

"Remind me never to hire someone smarter than me again."

"Too late. Already did." John clearly responded too fast.

"What? You think she's... never mind. Nice answer. Had that ready to go, did you?"

"Wait... you weren't talking about me? Because I thought—"

"I didn't hire you, genius. I just told Gamble that he should." She smiled—then Sarah's too-calm grin flashed in her mind. Hers faded.

He pulled her into a tight embrace. "No, no, no. I only meant that she's... um, the smartest staff attorney you've hired."

"She's the only one I've hired," she said dryly.

"I'm not digging myself out of this hole, am I?"

"It's possible, but it will definitely require more effort."

He planted a series of unhurried kisses on her neck.

"Does this help at all?"

"Yes. Less talking. More kissing," she said as she arched her head and pressed her lips to his in an open-mouthed kiss. After a few seconds, she pulled away. "Are we okay, John?"

"I get the feeling we're about to be really soon—"

"No, I mean, are things okay with us? You only spent a few minutes at the courthouse today, and honestly, it wasn't the first time you've done that. When you said you were going to split your time, I thought it might be... more evenly divided."

A deep groan escaped John, and she ran her fingers through his hair to soothe him. She knew he didn't want *this* conversation. But her mind couldn't leave things alone.

"I—I don't know," he said, exhaling again. "He's still out there. It's on me to catch him. I feel like if I don't get him..."

"It's not only on you. It's on all of us."

"I'm the only detective in Coldwater, Annaleigh. It's literally all on me."

Her shoulders drooped. "You say it like you're alone, on an island? You're not, John. You have support."

"Where's all this coming from? Because I wasn't in the office enough? Look, I'm trying, I really am. But, it seems like there's something else on your mind."

"No, I'm fine." She knew she'd answered too quickly.

He twisted his neck, and his chin bumped the top of her head.

"What... are you doing?" she asked.

"Nothing, just trying to get a better view of you. Come on, you don't sound like you're fine. You still sound annoyed, like when I called earlier." A sly grin spread across his face as he rested his hand on her leg. "I mean, you're still *fine*, don't get me wrong—"

She nudged his midsection with a playful elbow but said nothing.

"Look..." He breathed in slowly, as if weighing his words carefully. "A while ago, you said something pretty important to me, and I know I didn't exactly say it back—"

"Didn't exactly? John, I said I loved you, and you basically said 'thank you'."

"So it *is* bothering you?"

"No," she sighed. "That's not what I meant." She closed her eyes and squeezed his arm. "I had a big head start on you. It sounds weird, but I feel like I've known you longer than you've known me. That's why I wanted to say it. I know you'll say it when you're ready." She lifted her head off his shoulder and kissed him on the neck.

"I'm not purposefully staying away from the courthouse," he said. "Once I catch him, I swear, I'll make sure my time is split 50-50."

"Maybe third that and include time for your little side project."

"I... uh... yeah. Definitely."

"Definitely, what? It's almost as if you don't want to find out who your father is. John, if you'd let me, I'd love to help—"

"I'm pursuing a few leads."

"Leads? That's amazing. You haven't mentioned leads in a while. Really great news, John." A series of stammers escaped his mouth. Annaleigh continued. “That’s what I thought. Like I said, it sounds like you’re not really looking.”

“I am, but...”

“But what?”

“Something’s been bothering me. I know it shouldn’t, but it does. He’s in Coldwater. He’s *been* in Coldwater—this whole time. I’m not exactly hiding in a corner. This whole town seems to know me, and yet he’s done nothing to reach out. My mom’s playing coy, saying that it’s my journey, or whatever. I don’t know why he wouldn’t come to me.”

She nestled her head against his shoulder again, allowing her arm to rest on his thigh, and rubbed his knee with her thumb. “Whatever it is, I’m sure there’s a good reason. That doesn’t mean you should stop looking. This is important to you. To me, too.”

“*You’re* important to me, Annaleigh.”

“Then maybe let me help you. And maybe come into the office more often. I’m starting to worry that if a big trial comes up, you won’t have enough time to contribute. I still haven’t seen you do anything in court but accept a plea deal.”

“I know, I know. But the new girl’s there, things can be different now. If I’m not there to help, then Sarah can.”

“Oh, yeah. *Sarah.*” As soon as the name escaped her lips, she realized it carried more venom than she intended.

“Whoa. Trouble brewing already between you two?”

“Sorry... it’s that... she did something today. I’m not sure how much to read into it.”

“She seemed friendly when I was around. Eager to help. Seems to know her stuff. What’s so bad about that? She’ll probably outdo me pretty soon.”

“Well, she does have several years of experience, and she isn’t working part-time as a detective.”

“Ouch.”

“But, besides that, there’s something about her. I haven’t quite figured out what it is yet.”

“You were with her in the morning, not me. Maybe she’s

different when it's just you girls." Annaleigh cleared her throat. "Women," he said, quickly correcting himself. "Between Genie and the *several years of experience* from the great Sarah Sinclair, I'm outnumbered."

Hearing him say her name aloud made her stomach churn. Sharing him with the Sheriff's Office was one thing, but the way Sarah talked about John and the strange similarities between them... it felt like the story being told was incomplete and hidden from her.

"You two haven't met before, have you?"

God, did that sound too crazy?

"Her? No, first time was today. Why?"

Good. Not too crazy.

She sat up and twisted around to face him. "It's weird—she talked about you like she knew you or something. Apparently, you're some kind of big hit up in St. Louis."

"I'm a hit? What?"

"The talk of the town, or something. At least in some places. All because you turned down the job."

His head tilted up and down, lips full. "Oh."

"And," she dipped her chin, fiddling with her fingers, "you two hum the same song."

"I hum?"

She snapped her head up, brows furrowed. "The fact that you don't realize you do that is odd, if you ask me, but that's not the point—"

"What song?"

"That Cecilia one."

"Oh, yeah, great song. Totally catchy. I hum it? Interesting." He leaned closer and lowered his voice. "I think I've got the cassette in the Dart. I could teach it to you, if you feel left out—"

"Come on," she urged. "Be serious. You two have *really* never met before?"

He reached up and placed his hands on her cheeks. "No, I swear. Not before today. Look, it's just a silly song. It's got a fun melody. I'm sure tons of people hum it and don't know it. Whatever this is… I'm yours. You're mine. If that's what you're worried about."

"So… you don't think she's pretty? Her and her perfect little blonde bun?"

"What? No, of course not—"

"Now I *know* you're lying."

"Here's the thing," he said, chuckling. "I can see how other guys would find her attractive. But you're hot, so you win. Satisfied?"

She crossed her arms and slouched a little. She wasn't naive. She understood what he meant.

It meant he thought Sarah was attractive but didn't want to say it.

He leaned in and, with a strong grip, straightened her up and kissed her lips. "My turn."

"Your turn for what?"

"Twenty questions."

"Twenty? The way you were kissing my neck, I thought you had other plans for tonight."

"Oh, that magic will *definitely* happen afterward. But I'm a detective now. Asking questions is in my nature."

"Your nature? How many minutes on the job do you need to have before it becomes your nature?" She smirked. "Fine. Shoot." She slapped his thigh, startling him. "Wait, Mr. Detective, sir. I didn't really mean to say shoot. I surrender… wouldn't want your *nature* to get the wrong idea."

"Very funny. Let's start with some easy ones. This might seem odd, but just go along with it. How long have you worked at the Prosecutor's Office in Coldwater?"

"This is where you're starting? Fine, a year. You know that already. Please tell me all these questions aren't going to be about things you already know?"

He stared at her, waiting for something to happen. His eyes

scanned around her head, as if he spotted something floating in the air.

"Lose something?" she asked.

"Don't worry, it's nothing. How many staff attorneys have you worked with during that time?"

She looked up, doing the mental math. "Three, I think? One guy was here when I started, then Gamble went through a couple more before you arrived... so that's four, including you. If you can really call yourself a staff attorney, based on your *nature*."

"Okay, quit poking the nature—it didn't do anything to you. How many of those three were women?"

"None."

"So, besides Genie, you've never worked with another female attorney your entire time in Coldwater?"

"Well, Genie's not an attorney—"

"Annaleigh—"

"Then, no."

"What about your time at Cobb County?" His neck leaned forward, still intensely focused on her.

"No. None there either. John, why are you looking at me weird?"

"I'm not," he said, waving his hand. "Don't worry. It's fine. How many female attorneys were in your graduating class at law school?"

"A bunch. I don't know the exact number... are you going to tell me what these questions are all about?"

"Were you highly competitive with those women?"

"What? I mean, I wouldn't say *highly*—"

His eyes flared. One side of his mouth curled upward, starting a smile, then vanished as he scrunched his eyebrows. "Oh, come on now. I swear there's a point to this. So, maybe not highly... what about mildly competitive, then?"

"Sure, John. We were competitive with each other."

"For grades... or for guys?"

She scoffed. "I'm not sure what that has to do with anything—"

"What I'm getting at, hon, is that it's been years since you've worked with another woman attorney. And... the last time you did, even then, it wasn't really a team situation, but either friendly fire or actual opposition." He paused, then looked at her with a set of kind eyes that she hadn't really noticed before. "So, maybe you've got your defenses up with Sarah."

Damn. He's got a point. Maybe this jaunt as a detective will make him a better lawyer, after all.

"No, that's not even close to reality—"

His eyes flashed again as something appeared above her head. She instinctively reached up and patted her hair.

"What is it? Is there something on me? Is it a bug?"

"Sorry, it's... nothing. You're not jealous of her, are you?"

"Me? Jealous? Why would I be?" His eyes darted up again, but he remained expressionless. "Oh my God, John. *Why do you keep looking at the top of my head?*"

He ignored her question. "Listen, whatever you're feeling, you don't need to worry. It doesn't matter if your new girl's a smoke show or not. She doesn't hold a candle to you."

Her pulse spiked. "I'm not sure why you think I'm jealous, but to make sure I heard you right... YOU THINK SHE'S HOT?"

He gulped, finally coming to terms with the words he'd said without apparently thinking them through.

"No... I meant... she's... you're... come on, you know what I meant."

Annaleigh slumped against the back cushions of the sofa, huffing and crossing her arms. "Whatever."

He scooted closer, lifting her chin with a finger. "No one compares to you, Annaleigh. No one. Not in my eyes." He kissed her forehead and softly rubbed the back of her hair.

"Your broken eyes can only see half of me, so I'll take it with a grain of salt. But, I'll take it." She closed her eyes and melted into him. "And, for the record, I'm going to need a lot more of *this* before you get to those other plans of yours."

He placed another kiss on the top of her head and rubbed her shoulder. "You name it. I'll do it," he whispered.

She craned her neck, enjoying his touch. A soft moan escaped as he moved his hand up from her waist.

Her eyes snapped open.

"So, do I have anything in my hair or not?"

7

CRACKS IN TRUST

"Thought I might find you two here."

John slammed the door of his ugly brown Chevy Caprice and walked over to a wooden picnic table. Sheriff Dane Parnell and Deputy D. Clyde Brothers sat on opposite sides, eating chili dogs out of small paper baskets.

"Ah, Detective," Parnell said with a smile. "Care to join us?"

Clyde finished scooping up a forkful of chili, wiped his mouth, then gestured to a spot on the bench next to him.

John eased himself down. "If you don't mind, I was hoping to get some advice... from both of you."

Parnell wiped his mustache with a napkin, then straightened the short hairs with his fingers. "What can we do ya for, young man?"

"I wanted to ask about the other night—the chase and... about Foley. Has he said anymore about what really happened?"

"Indeed, I've talked to him," Parnell said, nodding his head. "His story hasn't changed. He swears he didn't see anyone else—just you. Claims Kenneth must've been farther away from you than you remember."

John smacked the table. "That's horseshit!" Clyde's lips parted, but John raised a hand to stop him. "I know, cussing. I'm not cool." He turned back to Parnell. "Sheriff, Foley's lying. Plain and simple."

"That's one heck of an accusation, John. It was a pretty hectic situation. Maybe you're both right, from your own perspectives. Why don't you tell me what you remember?"

John collected himself before visualizing the scene in his mind. "I chased him. Over fences, through yards, in the dark. He had a head start, but I closed the gap right as he was rounding the corner of that house. Then Foley took me out." He leaned forward, elbows on the tabletop. He feigned reaching into the air with his hand. "I was that close, Sheriff. Close as you are to me. There's no way Foley didn't see him."

"You really did hit your head pretty hard," Clyde said, taking a sip of lemonade. "I know you like to reimagine the scene in your head to reassess it. Maybe your recall is off because of the accident."

"Accident?" Another sigh escaped John's mouth before he could catch it. "Look, Foley stalked Annaleigh and then lied about it when she caught him. You really don't think he could be lying about this, too?"

Parnell's eyes flicked between John and Clyde. "Having overactive feelings for a girl is understandable. What I find hard to believe is that one of my deputies would knowingly assault my detective."

A fleeting lilac corona, shapeless and trembling, appeared around Parnell's head, then vanished into nothing. John stared, stunned that Parnell might utter a falsehood.

"You really believe that, Sheriff? God's honest truth?"

With pursed lips, the Sheriff's head bobbed up and down. Another distortion appeared around his head, then vanished.

Interesting. It even works without hearing the words.

"That may be the company line, sir, but if that's the case, let's revisit some other situations," John said, flashing a sly grin. "Something else has been bugging me for a while... the night Wesley Raith escaped from custody." He nodded at Clyde, trying to build a silent coalition. "Custody, might I add, where he was under the watchful eye of Deputy Cason Foley."

Parnell looked down. "Oh, I remember that day. Vividly. "

John paused, reflecting on the losses of that night. The death of Deputy Amos Hinkle and the serious injury to Detective Hollis Mumber. A debilitating wound that led to Mumber's early retirement and John being offered the job.

"We all do, Sheriff, but as you told me, our protocol states that the deputy must keep an eye on the holding cell at all times."

"We've been through this, *Detective*." John's brow lowered at Parnell's slight emphasis on his title. "But, there's no way to prove Foley's story. It's possible that when Raith did his fire-thing, it didn't shine those bright lights every time. The boy could've melted the lock without Foley seeing anything out of the ordinary."

John bounced his thumb at Clyde and himself. "You didn't see what we saw, Sheriff. Wesley never lit up without some kind of light at the same time... and whatever the hum. If Foley did see it, he should have heard it."

"It's still speculation. I have no way to prove anything you're saying... besides Foley's word."

"Fine," John said, gesturing with his hands. "Let's assume anything is possible, and Foley didn't see it. And he didn't hear it. What happened after Wesley melted the lock?"

"According to his statement, he was knocked out when Wesley kicked open the cell door and didn't wake up until you and I were kneeling beside him."

John's lips curled into a half smile. "The entire time? He claimed he was unconscious... from when the cell door knocked him out until we arrived?"

"Yes, John. These are the facts. You know all of this. I'm not sure what you're trying to prove here," Parnell said. He lifted his glass to take a drink.

"Then, how did he radio for help?"

A loud gulp escaped from Parnell's throat, followed by several coughs. Once he caught his breath, he lifted his chin and looked at John over the bridge of his nose.

"What are you trying to say, Chance?"

"It's no trick, Sheriff. If Foley was knocked out when Wesley broke out of the holding cell... and then didn't wake up until we were with him, how do we explain hearing his voice over the radio calling for help? That's the reason we all rushed to the station. He told us everything was on fire. How did he know? How could he do that while unconscious?"

John paused, watching Parnell remember the scene, then added the words he'd been dying to say. "Unless he really wasn't knocked out. It's possible he was part of Wesley's plan all along. It's a pattern, Sheriff. It's Foley's history. And, I've... got concerns."

Parnell bit his cheek. "Well, son, maybe I should, too."

* * *

JOHN ENTERED THE SMALL, windowed lobby of Crossroads Auto Repair and found the place lifeless.

No cashier sat behind the counter, no customers waited in the three dilapidated chairs placed against the windows. Only a garage sale flyer from last spring hung on the bulletin board.

John pushed through the employee-only door into the work bay and spotted a man leaning over the engine compartment of a four-door sedan, beneath an open hood.

"I'm looking for Wade," he said firmly. "Is that you?"

"Who's asking?" The man didn't even lift his head from the engine.

John moved his suit coat aside and flashed the badge on his belt, even though the man still wasn't looking. "Detective Chance from the Coldwater Sheriff's Office."

The man tilted his head back and stretched his neck. "Chance, eh? Heard about you."

"Don't doubt it. All kinds of stories tend to spread around

this town." John offered a polite smile, hoping to break the ice. "Hope it wasn't all bad."

"It was."

John scanned the area to ensure they were alone and let the insult drift away, unanswered.

"I'm looking for someone. Been asking around. Oddly enough, when I ask about this person, most people point me to you. Why do you think that is, Wade?"

"My direction? Is that so?" The man set his wrench down on a greasy rag draped over the edge. "If you knew who I was, why'd you have to ask?"

The man's features looked familiar, though John couldn't quite remember why. They hadn't met before, but maybe he'd seen the man around town?

"When I ask about Kenneth Roy Atlee's whereabouts, why is the most common answer this body shop?"

"No clue."

The lie revealed itself in a fleeting indigo ripple.

"Nice try, but if you tell the truth, I'll do my best not to charge you as an accessory."

"I always tell the truth, *Detective*." Wade's mouth sneered at the corner as a violet wisp curled upward.

"I know you're not, so stop screwing with me. I have a special talent for knowing when people—like you—are feeding me bullshit."

"Must be tough to be you, then, swallowing bullshit every day."

John's mouth opened slightly, realizing the trap he'd set—and then fell into it himself.

"Look, drop the act, Wade. I've got multiple witnesses who say he's been here. I'm guessing you know where he is. Tell me, and I'll be on my way."

The man rubbed his greasy hands together and leaned against the front grill. "No worries, I got all day. Told them I wouldn't be finished with this clunker until tomorrow. Under-promise, over-deliver, amiright?" He crossed his arms and smiled, proudly showing an empty tooth socket.

"Has Kenneth Atlee been to this shop recently?"

"No."

An orchid blur flickered above his head.

John rubbed his forehead. He had been around town, jumping from lead to lead, questioning everyone he saw. For the most part, the members of the Coldwater community were honest.

Mostly. At least about the big stuff.

He'd only seen a few glows around town when questioning witnesses. Each time he pressed in and called people out on their deceit, it produced enough clues to move him to the next place. A Coldwater-sized jigsaw puzzle, one piece at a time.

But this guy, this slimy, greasy, puny man… he had no desire to say anything that wasn't bile and lies. John had seen so many colored wisps that he wondered if the Picloram had a sense of humor all of its own.

"Have you seen Kenneth Atlee in the past few months?"

"Nope."

The glow flashed again.

These vague, open-ended questions weren't getting John the answers he needed. As he looked at the man's smug face, he thought of a different tactic.

"Let's take a step back. I give you a name, and instead of asking who the man is, you simply deny seeing him."

"Well, of course, I've seen him. You guys have posters up in every store around town."

"Is that so? Didn't see one on your board out front."

"Oh, you didn't? I swear I hung that up, just like the Sheriff asked me to."

Shimmer.

"So we agree on what the man looks like. Have you seen him today?"

"Can't say that I have."

Flicker.

"How about yesterday? Did you see him yesterday?"

"Nope."

Flash.

This man is actually incapable of telling the truth.

"The day before that?"

"Don't remember. It's hard to keep track of everything."

"Any other employees working today? Perhaps their memory is a bit better?"

"My daughter sometimes works up front after school, but no, I don't have other employees you can talk to."

John smiled confidently. "You see, I get to ask the questions. You can answer honestly, or, as you have been doing, lie through the gap of your missing tooth. But here's the best part, Wade—you don't get to tell me who I can or can't talk to." He leaned in, glaring at the man as if he were a hostile witness on cross-examination. His heart raced, but he kept his eyes glued to the mechanic, hoping he'd break.

That is, until the rear door to the shop opened and a familiar voice shouted from across the bay.

"What the hell are *you* doing here?" Deputy Cason Foley strode in, wearing civilian clothes—the first time John had seen him out of a deputy's uniform.

"I'd ask you the same question," John shot back. "You're interrupting my interrogation."

The deputy chuckled and glared. "I don't care what you were doing. It's over now."

John's forehead lowered as his lips pinched together. Why did Foley think he could barge in and stop his questioning? Off duty, no less?

"This man has material knowledge of the location—"

"This man is my dad, you ass," Foley shouted, cutting John off. "And whatever business you had with him is done."

John's eyes flicked between the two men, now realizing their resemblance. In all his previous conversations, no one had mentioned that the man named Wade from Crossroads Auto Repair was Wade *Foley*. At least then, John might have made the connection.

"Your father?" John shook his head. "Knowing that, I would've expected the family of a Sheriff's deputy to have a little more respect for the law. Maybe, you know, actually tell the truth when asked questions by a detective."

Wade scoffed. "When a real detective shows up, I just might."

"Times up," Cason said, pointing to the lobby. "You can go back out the way you came in."

The Foley men stood shoulder to shoulder, a united front against John. With Cason here, John had zero chance of getting useful information. He painted on a fake smile.

"Thanks for your time, sir. Cason, we can talk about this further... with the Sheriff."

"Looking forward to it," Cason replied, cheeks reddening.

John spun around and moved back toward the lobby door. He pushed it shut behind him and noticed a young woman, maybe sixteen or seventeen, standing behind the counter. He looked back at the shop door, where the large employee-only sign covered most of the small window.

If John couldn't see inside, he guessed that Wade or Cason probably couldn't see out, either.

"You must be Wade's daughter. Didn't see you there when I came in. I'm Detective Chance from the Sheriff's Office."

"I know who you are," she said softly. "Got here a few minutes ago, but I heard you two in there. Thin walls. Sorry about my dad. He can be pretty stubborn. I'm Daura."

"Nice to meet you, Daura... look, I'm trying to find a pretty dangerous guy. I'm sure your dad means well, but I think he's not telling me everything he knows. How about you? Have you seen Kenneth Atlee around here?" He pulled a folded piece of paper from his jacket pocket and held it up to her. "This guy."

She squinted at the photo, then snuck a glance at the shop

door. She leaned forward, wiggling her fingers, urging John closer to the counter.

"That guy gives me the creeps," she whispered. "Always comes in, asks me to go to the forest with him. Says I'd like it. Gross... like that would ever happen. Mentions it a lot with Cason and my dad, too. 'Meet me *at* the forest.' 'We'll talk about this *at* the forest.' No idea what it means, but he weirds me out. So, yeah, he's been around here."

John's heart leapt into his throat. A solid lead. "When did you see him last?"

"Today, before I left for school, in there, talking to my dad. This isn't going to get him into trouble, is it?"

"I'm not after your dad, Daura. But, if it turns out he's done more than talk to Mr. Atlee, like if he's helped him in some other way, I can't promise anything. But, as of right now, he's not in trouble. Do you have any idea where Atlee went after he left?"

"He said something, right as he was leaving. I heard every word... thin walls, remember? You sure my dad's not going to be in trouble?"

"Tell me where Kenneth went and I'll do my best to forget the *wonderful* little conversation I just had with him."

She peeked again at the shop door, then pulled out a piece of paper, jotting something down.

"He's got some kind of warehouse. He gets shipments there sometimes. Said he was going to be there all day." She slid the paper across the counter. "Here's the address. Now, please go. Before my dad sees you. And remember, you didn't get that from me."

8

CONDITIONAL SURRENDER

John killed the engine a block early, behind the skeletal silhouette of the old grain silo.

The sky had turned bruise-purple, and the air smelled of rust and river water. Life in Coldwater's industrial district had a different feel. No residences, no shops, no gas stations. An island of infrastructure, devoid of everything but darkness and isolation.

He stared at the scrap of paper on the passenger seat.

Warehouse 7, North Dock Road.

The looped handwriting, written in purple ink and slightly smudged from the handoff, belonged to a sixteen-year-old high school student who, somehow, knew more about the location of Kenneth Roy Atlee than all the other residents of Coldwater combined.

She appeared genuine. She also looked frightened. He'd have to note it mentally and deal with it later. A key point: no glow appeared around her head when she pressed it into his palm.

That's the reason he believed the intel was solid.

His radio crackled. "John, you there? Expected you back a while ago. Check in." Parnell's voice echoed in John's lonely cruiser, stripped of its usual country niceties.

"Sheriff, I'm code-fifty-one. Need you here to look at something. I finally found that picnic table you were looking for your niece. Bring Clyde and Taggart to help lift it."

Parnell's voice came back without delay. "10-4. Ten minutes."

After the mishap of staking Kenneth out at Three Pump, Parnell worried they couldn't be certain who else was listening to the police radio. Since scanners were in use all over town, they created coded references for nearly every part of Coldwater to be safe.

The code John used indicated he had Kenneth's location, but without personal confirmation. Other numbers represented different situations, all the way up to fifty-nine, which meant someone had personally spotted Kenneth, and the man was currently on fire.

The phrase "picnic table" referred to the warehouses, and Parnell's niece meant John was stationed at the north end.

John had memorized and linked everyday household objects to most of the major locations around town. Dining chair, sofa, curio cabinet, even rocking horse—language John could work into a common phrase over the radio, tied to a specific, tangible location.

Other family members were utilized for the directions: sister for south, wife for west, and aunt for east. John didn't dig deeper into why Parnell used a word starting with the letter *a* for "east," but it was a fun side of the sheriff to see. He hadn't figured Parnell for cyphers and hidden messages.

The old man still has some surprises left in him.

Not long after, a stealth caravan arrived with Parnell leading the way, followed by two deputy cruisers—lights and sirens off.

Parnell stepped out first, hat in hand as if attending a funeral. Clyde looked ready to chew nails. Even his kind eyes carried a slight hint of apprehension. Behind them, Dallas Taggart, twenty-six with bushy red hair and blue-green eyes flat as rifle barrels, nodded once.

Parnell spoke quietly. "So you all know, Foley's on administrative leave as of an hour ago. Won't get into details. The only thing

I'll say right now is that he accepted it without a challenge. So, take that as a sign of whatever you want."

"That almost scares me more," John said. "Innocent men usually don't take a beating without trying to defend themselves."

Clyde rested his thumbs inside his belt. "I don't know what you're planning, but I hope the four of us will be enough."

"We'll make it work with four," John said. He pivoted his head between the two grizzled veterans. "Do you agree?

John met the new deputy's eyes and asked, point-blank, "You got my back?"

Taggart nodded without hesitation. No purple shimmer. The lump in John's throat eased.

"Sheriff, what're our orders? What's a code-fifty-one? That wasn't in the book." Taggart asked as he surveyed the empty street around the metal-sheathed buildings. John and Parnell had kept the coded language just between them.

"This is Detective Chance's show. Let's hear it from him." Parnell nodded to John.

"A code fifty-one," John said confidently, "refers to the location of Kenneth Roy Atlee. I have it, and we're going to arrest him... right now."

Clyde smiled and patted John on the back. "Knew you'd find him."

"How good is your intel?" Taggart asked. "You sure he's here?"

"It's solid. I trust it. We're heading into Warehouse 7 over there," he said, pointing to a nearby building. "My info is fresh, just a few hours old. I checked the building from a distance... and it's the only thing around here showing recent activity."

Parnell squinted at the warehouse, then spun 360 degrees to assess their surroundings. "What kind of activity we talking about?"

"I saw a faint orange glow through a window. Didn't see him, but sure looked like someone left a furnace on in there."

Clyde chuckled. "Sounds like a familiar M.O."

"Agreed. Need to be ready for anything." John looked around at the team. "Which means I don't think we're wearing the right equipment, Sheriff."

Parnell put his hat back on. "You heard him, everyone. Gear up. Vests and weapons—anything and everything you think we'll need. You've got two minutes."

They moved together to their own trunks, digging out gear and strapping on ballistic vests. The sound of elastic bands being adjusted filled the air. When they reassembled, John's nerves kicked in. He had entered brand new territory.

His only action was to fish a belt holster and ballistic vest from the trunk of his Caprice, leaving the standard-issue Mossberg 500 pump-action shotgun in its case. He'd undergone weapons training since joining the squad, but ultimately felt most comfortable with only the semi-automatic pistol he kept in his shoulder holster. He switched to a belt holster and tightened his vest.

Looking around, an odd feeling washed over him. It was one of those rare moments when he realized he didn't quite belong, highlighting that he was genuinely a lawyer masquerading as a cop.

Each man in the group holstered their Smith & Wesson 5906, the model John had first shot at Parnell's personal shooting range.

Taggart, the ex-Marine MP, stood at attention in his bulletproof vest as if he were going to war. He wore the shotgun like a backpack, one-strapped across his chest. The barrel extended over his shoulder and mingled with his curly red hair, giving the impression of an Irish samurai with a sword sheathed on his back. He gripped a Ruger Mini-14 patrol rifle with both hands and menacingly clipped in its 20-round magazine. Two additional magazines hung from his belt.

John's eyes widened slightly as Taggart grabbed the charging handle, ripped it back—KA-CHANG!—and let the barrel droop toward the dirt. Taggart left no doubt he was ready for a fight.

Clyde stood more nonchalant but no less threatening. He

chose to carry his Mossberg, holding the grip in one hand while balancing the barrel on his shoulder.

Parnell, like Taggart, chose the Ruger and held the black rifle in his experienced hands.

"John, this is your show. How do you want to play this?"

"I'll surveil through the front window," John said. "Clyde, you're with me. Sheriff, Taggart—you two go around the far side and make entry at the loading dock. Once we're in place and with your permission, Sheriff—we breach on my command."

Parnell nodded, then looked at his two deputies. "I agree with the plan. Does anyone have an issue with our new detective calling the shots?"

"No, sir. Not a single one," Clyde quickly replied.

Taggart didn't hold back. "He's... a lawyer, right? Shouldn't you take the lead, sir?"

"He's a detective with my full support—and this is his catch," Parnell barked. "Any other issues you'd like to verbalize, Deputy?"

Taggart straightened more than John expected, as if he were back in boot camp. "Sir, no sir."

Parnell continued. "This is a capture mission, folks. Permission to go hot if you're aimed at, by a weapon... or anything else. He will not—I repeat, *will not*—break our containment. I do not want another *roundabout* situation."

Parnell swallowed hard, and John knew he was recalling the high-speed chase after they went to City Hall to arrange the arrest of former Mayor Cameron Raith. When Raith decided to run and sped away, he ultimately crashed, flipping his Blazer and dying in the process. Parnell did not wish the same fate for Kenneth.

Justice for him required bars, not the grave.

John pulled his 5906 from his holster and racked the slide.

"Let's move."

Once the clock ticked past six o'clock P.M, the industrial district resembled a graveyard of rusted conveyors and broken sodium lights. Warehouse 7, at the end of Dock Road, sat like a forgotten relic. Rust crawled up its corrugated iron walls, and half the windows looked as if they'd been punched out years ago.

As they approached, they could see the dull orange glow John had described earlier.

Back here, the trees blocked the setting sun, and in the shade, the late-September temperature grew quite cool. That is, until they moved closer and were within touching distance of the warehouse. Heat radiated off the building in sluggish waves.

"That heat's not electrical." Taggart's voice barely registered.

"No," John said. "It's not. No matter what you think is in there, you might not be ready for what you see. Eyes on a swivel."

"Don't worry, I can handle it," Taggart shot back.

"All right," Parnell said, voice low. "Everyone into position."

The four lawmen split up without saying a word. Parnell and Taggart moved quietly toward the loading dock. Clyde and John snuck up to the front entrance, where John ducked and crawled under the wide window by the door. Clyde inched to the window's edge, keeping watch.

Within moments, the radio crackled with Parnell's check-in. "In position. Ready on your signal."

"Hold—going to try and get eyes," John said, nodding silently to Clyde.

He leaned forward to peek through the grime on the window, not knowing what to expect. He figured, based on the recent trend of always being one step behind, that he'd be looking into an empty building.

But he'd have been wrong.

Within the shadows of his blurred peripheral vision, standing in the middle of an empty forty-foot bay, alone, arms hanging loosely at his sides, facing John's three o'clock, John saw him.

Kenneth Roy Atlee.

A perfect ring of fire burned on the concrete behind him. Its diameter spread across ten feet, with honed edges, as if cut with a torch.

"I see him," whispered John. "He's alone... standing there."

"What's the call? What do you want to do?" Clyde whispered back.

"Can't tell if he's alone. I think we—wait, he's moving."

John stayed glued to the window, peering at Kenneth when the brutish man's head twisted and looked directly at him. And smiled.

He knew they were coming.

"Shit!" John muttered, grabbing the radio. "He knows we're here! Breach! Breach!"

Clyde rose up and, with a fierce kick, broke through the rickety metal door. The thin latch exploded, and John hurried in, gun raised.

"Hands on your head!" John shouted.

Another set of footsteps approached from the loading dock door, the opposite end of the warehouse's wide-open floor plan. Parnell moved cautiously, weapon ready. Taggart's steps continued, then shifted to clangs against metal as he ascended a set of stairs to an overwatch position.

But Kenneth didn't run.

John and Clyde moved in, getting within about twenty feet of the fugitive.

"I said, hands up!" John repeated.

Kenneth raised both hands, sluggish, palms out. The temperature in the warehouse suddenly spiked, jumping twenty degrees. In an instant, it felt like a summer day in July. The air rippled around them, like a heat haze over asphalt.

"Enough!" Parnell pointed his Ruger and shouted from behind Kenneth, who lowered his hands. As he rested his arms at his side, the heat disappeared, vanishing like a light switch. The sudden chill raised goosebumps on John's arms.

Kenneth faced away, still turned away from the lawmen. He spoke to the darkness in a calm, low, and almost amused voice.

"Took you long enough to find me, John."

Taggart's voice echoed from above the open space, calm and

cold, where he had scrambled up the catwalk and gained higher ground. "Boss, I've got the headshot if he twitches."

Kenneth smiled at the empty air. "I'm not resisting tonight, Marine. In fact, I'll come quietly," Kenneth said casually. "On one condition."

John scoffed, pistol still aimed at Kenneth. "You don't get conditions."

"Of course I do. Whether you believe it or not, I have leverage. Because, if I don't get favorable conditions, this whole situation becomes much more... kinetic." Kenneth's broad shoulders finally shifted. His eyes caught the faint light and held it, reflecting red. "You want me in a cell. I want to stand trial. We both get what we want." He turned and placed his hands behind his back. "Your move, *Counselor*. You may cuff me now."

Clyde's shotgun lowered slightly. "This feels like a trap."

"Of course it's a trap," Kenneth said cheerfully. "But not one that springs tonight. And not the kind of trap you think."

John moved first. Stepping forward, his boots crunched on loose pieces of old concrete. The cuffs felt cold and heavy. As he got within arm's reach, Parnell stopped him.

"Hang on. Cuff him in front. When he's in the cruiser, we don't need his hands anywhere we can't see them."

"I'm hurt you don't trust me, Dane," Kenneth chided.

John glanced around, his focus settling on Clyde, who gave him an approving nod. "You heard the man," John said, inching closer to Kenneth. "Hands in front."

Kenneth obliged, watching John's approach like a man watching a slow-moving train he'd already decided to step in front of. Parnell angled in behind Kenneth, pressing the butt of his Ruger's stock into his shoulder, the barrel aimed at the back of Kenneth's head.

"Easy now, *Detective*," Parnell warned, correcting Kenneth's earlier taunt.

John eyed Kenneth as he approached. "If you light up... if I see one damn spark," he pointed up to the second-floor vantage point, "my buddy up there is going to end you before you can blink."

Kenneth's eyebrows lifted with a calming nod. "Oh, I've got every reason to believe that Mr. Taggart will do exactly as he's told."

John snapped the steel around one wrist, then the other. The metal warmed instantly, and John jerked his hands back.

Kenneth leaned in, breath hot against John's ear.

"Tell Annaleigh I'm looking forward to her cross-examination."

John rushed the brute, getting an inch within his face. "You don't get to say her name. Ever."

Kenneth didn't back down, only offering a closed-mouth grin.

John retreated a step, eyed his three backups, confirming their weapons were still trained, then shoved Kenneth toward the exit.

"Kenneth Roy Atlee, you're under arrest for arson, conspiracy, and any other damn thing I haven't thought of yet between now and the day you burn."

Kenneth chuckled softly, glancing at the sheriff. "They get younger every year, don't they? More arrogant, too. Not even going to read me my rights? That's fine. Consider them waived. Dane, you can scold him on that later, after his adrenaline has worn off. And, while you're at it, explain to the young lad that some fires... you can't put out." He took a step, then stopped, speaking with a low, smooth voice. "When the time is right, please remind the boy that he's the one who started this."

As Kenneth crossed the warehouse threshold, the burning circle behind them in the bay flared—one perfect ring of flame leaped waist-high, bright as magnesium, then vanished as if being pulled down into the concrete.

John looked back, wondering if it was a trick or if Kenneth really did have that kind of raw power. He'd seen Wesley Raith control the flames, but from contact with his hands.

Owning the fire... without touching it?

It had to have been a trick.

A really good trick.

Clyde loaded Kenneth into the back of Parnell's cruiser. The large man settled against the vinyl like an elder on a Sunday drive, watching through the partition as John slammed the door.

Parnell stared back into the warehouse, mesmerized by the ring of char still faintly glowing.

"He wanted us to find him tonight."

John frowned and crossed his arms. "Yeah, and I need to know why."

Kenneth tapped once on the glass from the inside and grinned with all his teeth. He shouted through the window, a half snarl, half growl that sounded like a supernatural incantation.

"*Potentia.*"

After everything John had experienced in the last three months, Kenneth's delivery of that word is what sent chills down his spine. He eyed Parnell, and as the two locked eyes, an unspoken concern floated between them.

Red and blue lights reflected off the rusted warehouse walls as the sheriff drove Kenneth Roy Atlee toward a cell John knew the man never intended to stay in.

9

BLOCKED BY JUSTICE

Dane Parnell had served twenty years as sheriff of Coldwater County without ever losing a prisoner. He had been shot at, spat on, cursed at in three languages, and even had a tractor run over him in '89. None of it had aged him as much as the time he spent supervising the custody of Kenneth Roy Atlee.

It had been almost twenty-four hours since the arrest of Kenneth Roy Atlee. To be fair, it was more of a rideshare than an arrest. Kenneth wanted to be caught, and Parnell's department had yet to figure out why.

Almost twenty-four hours of nothing of significance happening.

Only if you count loads of normal things happening… abnormally.

One hour after booking, the smoke alarm outside the cell in the corridor shrieked for a full ten seconds before quitting. No smoke. No heat. Just the alarm. Clyde had stormed down the hallway, red-faced, out of breath, and holding an extinguisher, looking ridiculous. He replaced it with a new one.

It wasn't the last strange thing to happen while Kenneth rented the holding cell.

Located in the back room of the station house, two of the holding cell's walls—the back and one side—were built from 6-inch-thick concrete brick. The front and other side featured floor-to-ceiling iron bars spaced four inches apart, specifically to allow for close observation of anyone inside.

Dallas Taggart, who had been assigned the first 8-hour watch shift, shrugged. "Wasn't him. Didn't see him move. He's been reading the whole time."

Parnell stood in the hallway, at the back room's throat, coffee gone cold in his hand. Kenneth sat on the lone metal bench in an orange jumpsuit, legs crossed, flipping through yesterday's Coldwater Cedar Creek Times like an old man waiting for a bus. Every few seconds, he'd smile at something in the paper, small and private.

Parnell hated that smile.

"Morning, Sheriff," Kenneth said without looking up. "You're looking a bit disheveled today. Rough night sleeping on the cot in your office?"

Parnell ignored it. "Alarm seems to have gone off again."

Kenneth neatly folded the paper and set it aside.

"Heard that. Damn noise woke me up. Fourth time, isn't it? You should have the wiring checked in this place."

"You wouldn't know anything about that, though, I presume?"

Kenneth met his eyes—steady, almost kind. "About the wiring? Naw, never did manage to break into that trade."

"Not the wiring. The alarms. You're telling me you have no idea why they keep chirping?"

"Dane, I've been sitting right here. Ask your deputy."

Taggart cleared his throat. "It's true, sir. He never left the bench."

Parnell studied the younger deputy a beat too long. Taggart didn't blink.

Overnight, the light bulb in the ceiling fixture burned out. It popped like a firecracker at 1:07 a.m. When Parnell climbed the ladder to check it, the filament inside had melted into a perfect silver bead.

Normal bulbs don't do that, especially in a sixty-eight-degree room with only one prisoner who never stood up.

Later, the coffee pot in the break room boiled dry and cracked —when Kenneth was asleep.

Nothing major. Nothing you'd be able to prove in court. But enough unusual circumstances to keep every man in the building on edge.

Parnell adjusted his glasses. "You're moving across the street today. County jail. Real cells. Real staff. You'll have four concrete walls and a steel door instead of my good nature."

Kenneth's smile broadened slightly. "You wound me, Sheriff. And here I thought we were friends." He stood, stretched, and walked to the bars. Placed his palms flat against the steel—careful, almost gentle.

"We used to be. But, that was before you and Cameron..."

"Before we, what, Sheriff? Before we refused to let you pin her leaving on us... what do you think happened? We killed her and buried her out in the woods?"

Parnell raised an eyebrow. "Is that what happened, Ken? Is that where she is?"

"Can't a man enjoy a good hyperbole every now and then? Not everything's a confession, Dane."

"I don't even know why I bother," Parnell muttered with a sigh. "Everything you say is a damn excuse."

A voice from behind the group called out. "Mind if I ask a few questions before our guest heads out?"

Parnell spun to see John lurking, eyeing the holding cell, with Clyde right behind.

"Of course, Detective, absolutely. Fire away," he sneered at Kenneth. "No pun intended, of course."

Kenneth offered no witty comeback. "Sure, Dane. Let the kid

have a shot at the man in the cage. What's the worst that could happen?"

John stepped up to the cage, displaying a confidence Parnell thought had vanished from the young lawyer-turned-detective after all the long nights. He held back a proud smile as John peered into the cell.

"Let's establish a baseline for your level of honesty," John said. "Tell me, Mr. Atlee, what's your full name?"

Kenneth smirked. "I ain't dignifying that question with a response. Serves no purpose. Hey, you found your dad yet?"

A confused expression flickered over John's face before he collected himself, glancing around at the other deputies.

"That cat came out of the box pretty quick, didn't it?" He turned back to Kenneth. "Let's stay on point, shall we?"

Another crooked smile graced Parnell's face. He'd seen John let his emotions influence his decisions before. The kid nearly twisted off the head of someone threatening Annaleigh at the community center, yet now, he acted calm and cool, as if he had the upper hand. Like nothing Kenneth said shook him.

"What about a yes or no question? You happy to be moving to a place with better beds?" He pointed at the narrow bench in the cell. "Can't imagine one can relax sleeping on that."

"A man can never truly relax until his work is finished."

John looked in at Kenneth, inspecting him. "Very enlightening indeed. What work would you say you're here to do?"

"You wouldn't understand, even if I drew it in crayons. But all valuable work needs a leader. All waitresses and no cook don't make for a successful diner."

"Again with the nonsense," John said, shaking his head. "Besides, this leader that you mention, everybody knows it was Raith. And he—your boss—died trying to jump across the roundabout. Not the smartest decision ever made by a mayor. Your... diner? There's no cook. No owner, no waitress, and no customers. All that's left is the bouncer, the dumb muscle. That's you, Kenneth. The only guy left to take the fall for everything."

Kenneth's breathing grew heavier, but he stayed still. Again, John leaned in, watching Kenneth closely, waiting for a response. He'd never seen John examine his suspects so carefully.

"I feel like I'm looking in a mirror, Counselor—er, Detective? Let's call you Johnny from now on, to make it easy? Arrogance must run in the family. Haven't seen so much since I last talked to your daddy. Want me to tell you who he is?"

Parnell flinched. He watched John's reaction and saw none. He looked at Clyde, who side-eyed the Sheriff in return. They both hoped that John would stay composed.

John's head tilted up as he looked at Kenneth down the bridge of his nose, a faint hint of a smile curling on his lips.

"Nah."

A look of disbelief crossed Kenneth's face. "Nah? What the hell does that mean?"

"It means I don't believe you."

Parnell and Clyde exchanged another look—one mixed with admiration and uncertainty about how John remained so calm. He had become a different detective compared to a week ago.

Maybe Foley's knock-out flipped a switch in the boy?

John kept on as Kenneth watched, his mouth partly open.

"Deflect all you want, Kenny," John said with added inflection. "Your bluffs are too predictable. For all the power you and the Raiths have wielded on this town—"

"You said it, *the Raiths*. Blame them. You don't have anything on me."

"Gotta practice those lies a bit more before we get you into court. Jury will never buy it."

"We'll see." Kenneth shrugged and winked. "Maybe the truth will set us all free."

"Nobody's going to set you free—that train left a long time ago. Tell me what happened with Evelyn Raith. Where did she, in your words, *run off* to?"

Kenneth's eyes hovered on Parnell, and he shrugged his shoulders. "Hard to say, young man. One day, she was here, and the next, she was gone. "

"And, you had no hand in that?"

"She was Cameron's wife, not mine."

"Never give anything straight, do you?"

"Only a fool expects answers from an enemy,"

"We're enemies?"

"You tell me. You're out there... and I'm in here."

"But I thought you were in there because you wanted to be? You're the one who said, *cuff me.* Right?"

"Finally." Kenneth smiled. "We agree on something."

Parnell stepped forward. "All right, I think that's enough for today, eh, Detective?" He looked at John, who nodded and stepped back. "Hands through the slot," Parnell said, raising his chin to Kenneth.

Kenneth complied. The cuffs clicked into place smoothly. As Parnell inspected the restraints again, Kenneth leaned in close so that only Parnell heard him.

"I saw it, Dane. Your reaction when I mentioned the kid's pop. When are you gonna tell him? If you don't... I will."

Clyde and Taggart led Kenneth outside and into a van for a short drive across the street into the county jail's more secure area. Parnell stayed in the cold morning air long after the taillights disappeared behind the gate, feeling the mustache twitch against his lip.

From this perspective, the county jail seemed solid. Modern. Safe. It wouldn't feel that way for long.

Kenneth Roy Atlee wasn't attempting to escape.

He wanted to be watched.

God help them if they look away.

* * *

John waited with Annaleigh in the small first-floor hallway outside the main courtroom. They had been summoned to Judge

Otto Chapel's chambers, and they weren't expecting it to be for tea and crumpets.

As if John would drink tea, anyway.

"How did he sound on the phone when he called?" John asked, watching Annaleigh.

"Sarah actually took the call," she said flatly, yanking the flaps of her suit coat. "I'm sure it's nothing. For trials of this level of importance, he probably wants to reinforce his code of conduct."

"Ex parte, though? No other lawyers here. Has Kenneth even asked for one yet?"

"Don't know. And this might be unusual, sure, but as long as we don't discuss evidence or specifics, it shouldn't be an issue."

"Seems like forever since I've been in court," John admitted.

"While we're in there, don't mention your detective title."

"What? You think he's still mad about that? Technically, Parnell bluffed Raith, not us."

"Parnell's the Sheriff. You're the Sheriff's detective. If the judge still has concerns about how we handled that little situation, you might want to throw together an apology... on Parnell's behalf."

Both heads snapped toward the door as it clicked open and swung wide. Judge Chapel stood in the doorway, wearing a scowl.

"Too late," Annaleigh whispered toward John. "Judge Chapel, we heard you wanted to see us. May we come in?"

Chapel grunted, then spun around to go back to his desk. "Shut the door behind you," he commanded without looking at them.

John and Annaleigh exchanged a worried glance, entered, and gently closed the door. They circled the two side chairs, planning to sit, but were stopped.

"Don't sit. This won't take long," Chapel said, sitting and placing his elbows on the desk, and lacing his fingers together. "It's come to my attention that the fugitive Kenneth Roy Atlee is now in police custody."

"Yes, Your Honor," Annaleigh said, chin held high. "He was

temporarily held at the Sheriff's Office during booking, then transferred to the County Jail."

"I see." Chapel paused, and an awkward silence hung in the air. He ran his tongue along his gums behind his cheeks. "Tell me more about his confinement during booking." He stared directly at John.

"Uneventful, I'd say." John felt relieved no one else saw the likely purple shimmer flashing around his own head. "We're stretched a little thin, Judge. We can't monitor the holding cell every hour of the day and protect the streets at the same time. It made sense to find him a better home until the trial."

Chapel nodded his head. "I heard mention of some... oddities occurring during his detainment?"

"Oddities?"

"You're telling me nothing out of the ordinary happened, young man?" Chapel asked with raised eyebrows. "I know you're not under oath in here, but I'd still appreciate an honest recounting."

"Your Honor, John has no reason to obscure the truth. I hope you're not implying—"

"Ms. Stanton, I am not implying anything. I am speaking facts. And one startling fact is that Mr. Atlee's arrest warrant was indeed used in a way that directly led to the death of this town's Mayor. There is clear evidence that members of the Sheriff's Office have concealed facts to get what they want."

"Your Honor, I'm here as a prosecutor, not as a detective. I don't speak for the department."

Chapel stood, leaning on the desk with his hands. "Counselor, I'm afraid there can be no such distinction. I can't bifurcate you like Solomon splitting the child. You may indeed wear two hats, but at the end of the day, you still only have one head to put them on."

John's mouth parted, but no words came out—the judge was right.

"I understand your position, Judge, but nothing of consequence happened. We held him overnight, I questioned him the next morning, and that's it. Uneventful, as I said."

"Deputy Taggart appeared to suggest otherwise."

"You spoke with him?"

"He mentioned some irregularities... that might challenge the understanding of a rational mind."

John scoffed. "Your Honor, if you're talking about the smoke alarm? Faulty wiring."

"And the light bulb?"

"Energy surge. It happens. Parnell said the filament melted."

"And... the coffee pot?"

"Your Honor, you've got to be kidding me. The stupid coffee pot broke. Clyde admitted he could have left the burner plate on, but he couldn't remember. It was in a completely separate room from where Mr. Atlee was being held."

"All the same, why did all those seemingly unrelated events only happen when Mr. Atlee was present?"

John met Annaleigh's eyes, sharing an unspoken concern.

"Judge Chapel," Annaleigh said softly. "Is there going to be an issue? Our intent is to bring Mr. Atlee to trial in this jurisdiction... in your courtroom. Are you—are you scared of this trial? Of... him?"

Chapel thumped his palm on the desk. "You are out of line, Counselor."

"Is she?" John stepped forward. "It seems like you're looking for an excuse to get us to change venues."

"Watch it, Counselor."

"Look," Annaleigh said, hands splayed. "John and I were there. We saw firsthand the kind of damage Wesley Raith was capable of." She gestured in a circular motion toward John. "God knows the result of what happened to Wesley was all over John's face. But, regardless of any unexplained elements of this situation, he and I are standing up to the only person left who can answer for those crimes. And that's Mr. Atlee."

"I agree," Chapel said calmly, sitting back down.

"Wh—what?" John's eyes widened. "Why are we here then?" After noticing his voice had increased, he quickly added, "Your Honor."

"I fully expect a trial, but only if we can ensure everyone's safety. Mr. Atlee, you two, the inevitable crowd, and, yes, of course, myself. Until you can prove to me that no harm can come to my courtroom, that man isn't setting foot in it."

10

COMPLICATED ARRIVALS

John and Annaleigh trudged upstairs and found Sarah busy filing folders. She turned when she heard John's voice and quickly dropped everything.

"I assume things didn't go so well with the judge."

Annaleigh shot a quick look. "No," she said sharply.

"Apparently," John explained, "he's still a little upset with the Sheriff, and he's taking it out on us."

"Oh, John. I'm so sorry." Sarah leaned against the desk next to John's, then playfully hopped up and sat on the edge, her feet dangling. "Anything I can do to help?"

Annaleigh, mid-stride toward her office door, spun upon hearing Sarah's offer. "That stack of files won't make its way into the cabinet all by itself. Maybe take care of that? And, let's have a little respect for centuries-old furniture, shall we?"

Sarah hopped down. "On it," she replied, giving John a side eye as if she'd been caught by a scolding parent. She leaned close to John, her smile bright. "I can stay late to review those briefs, John, if you need me." Her eyes flicked to Annaleigh, voice cooling. She straightened. "Unless you've got it covered, Annaleigh."

"*He's* got it covered."

"Actually, I wouldn't mind the help," he said. "If we do it

together, we'll finish in no time." He saw a small shudder ripple through Annaleigh's shoulders, but wondered why.

"John? Can I see you in my office, please?"

He leaned back in his chair and stood up. As he turned, he heard a whispered, playful tease.

"I hope getting called into the principal's office turns out better than the judge's chambers," Sarah whispered.

John gave Sarah a wide-eyed look and a thin smile, making her giggle and turn around to face the cabinet. When he fought back a laugh, it caught Annaleigh's attention. She stood in the doorway until he arrived, then stepped inside, gesturing him in. She swung the door shut behind them.

"Is this a boss or boyfriend conversation?" John plopped into a side chair.

"I hate it when you call me boss," she said, settling into the chair behind the desk. "Either way, you make it sound like I'm going to be mad at you for something."

"Didn't mean to imply anything. Hit me with whatever you want."

"First things first—do you have ideas on how we can schedule our trial? Is this something you can coordinate with Parnell or Clyde on?"

"Don't worry, I'll handle it. I saw what that power did—*from really close*—and I've already been brainstorming ideas... ways to neutralize it. I thought we'd only need it for sentencing and his eventual prison term."

"Well, we need to come up with something quickly. Kenneth will eventually get a lawyer, and I don't want us to encounter any Sixth Amendment issues."

John smiled and pointed at her. "Speedy trial. I know that one."

She stared back at him, her brows clenched. The tension in her shoulders eased as they lowered, and her lips curled into a smile.

"You're an idiot."

"But I'm *your* idiot. That probably says more about you."

"Are you?"

His head tilted. "What?"

"Are you mine?"

"Of course I am. Why—why would you think even think otherwise?"

"I... I don't know. Never mind. It's nothing."

The space around her head flickered with a violet glow that disappeared in a heartbeat. He rose and rounded the desk, leaning on it to her side.

"Penny for your thoughts, my dear?"

"Nope." She snapped her head up to him. "How about you? Anything you want to tell me?"

Wait... did she know?

A warmth spread over his shoulders and up his neck. "Quick deflection, there. No, of course not."

"Nothing at all? Maybe something new is happening?"

"I, uh—"

"I mean, you've been looking at me differently. Like... like you see something you don't like anymore."

He hadn't realized until now what he probably looked like as he inspected everyone's head for the appearance of the lilac shimmers. His neck craned in as he squinted without blinking, scanning the outlines of their heads. Strange indeed.

"It's nothing like that," he explained. "I just... can't take my eyes off you."

"Nice try. My point still stands. And, it's not only the weird way you've been looking at me. You've been doing a lot of things differently lately."

"What are you talking about?"

"How's the search for your dad going, John?" Slumped shoulders gave her his response. "Exactly. You and I used to talk about it all the time — about the people you've spoken to, the little clues you found. Then, it all stopped."

He walked over to the corner window, eyeing the horizon.

"My focus has been on catching Kenneth—"

"And, you did it," she said, leaning back in her chair. "It's time to restart all the other things you've dropped now. I'm willing to help."

He chuckled. "Just ask my mom, then. Maybe she'll tell *you*... seems determined to hide it from me."

"She's not hiding it, because I did ask her, by the way. She said that it's his choice—your father's choice. He has a family now, so he has to decide if... I mean, when to do it."

He spun away from the window and faced her. "He's... he's got a family? You actually talked to my mom about him?"

"Yeah," she said, squinting. "Was that okay?"

"Of course," John said, scratching his brow with a finger. "I've been thinking about changing my strategy. I have some different kinds of questions for her, and I have a feeling it'll jump-start the search."

"That's great, John. I'm serious, put me to work too... just tell me what you want me to—" A knock on the door interrupted the conversation. "Yes, Sarah," Annaleigh said, eyes rolling, hating the timing of the interruption. "What is it?"

The door creaked open, and the young lawyer peeked inside.

"Sorry, don't mean to bother anyone. Does anyone know when Genie is coming back?"

"Not for a while," Annaleigh replied. "She's taking some time off to see if she can get her bakery off the ground."

John perked up. "Really? She finally found a space?"

Annaleigh nodded. "Small building a few blocks away. I swore we wouldn't pop in unannounced, though, not while they're still trying to figure out all the recipes. I told her we'd wait to be invited for the taste tests."

His stomach rumbled at the thought of her cinnamon rolls, apple pie, or really, anything she made.

"Fine, I'll hold off on setting up a pastry raid. For now."

John and Annaleigh exchanged a grin, until Annaleigh's

vanished when she noticed Sarah's head still poking through the barely open door.

"Sooooo... she's not coming in today?" Sarah's eyes darted between John and Annaleigh.

"No, Sarah, she's not," Annaleigh muttered. "Something else you needed?"

"Um... there's a guy out here who says he needs to see you. Should I use Genie's calendar to make an appointment?"

Annaleigh stood up in a huff. "Why didn't you lead with that?" She adjusted her suit jacket. "It's fine. Send him in."

Sarah withdrew her head and spoke in a muffled voice. "Prosecutor Stanton will see you now, sir."

John leaned against the windowsill with his arms crossed, waiting for the man to come in. A soft knock, a series of creaks, and the door swung all the way open.

"It seems you've climbed a few more rungs on the ladder since we last saw each other."

Annaleigh's face went pale. Her lips parted, and her eyes widened. From her expression, she recognized the stranger standing in her office, though John did not—a man with slicked-back black hair, a clean-shaven face, thick eyebrows, and the posture of someone with a stick up his ass.

"Hoover." She snarled with a level of disdain across her face that John hadn't seen before. It was the kind of contempt you'd see on an executioner's face right before they drop the guillotine blade.

"The one and only." Hoover spread his arms wide, palms facing up, revealing a pair of extremely thin wrists poking out of his shiny suit. His pursed lips emphasized his arrogance. "When I heard it'd be you that I'd be going up against—"

"What in the hell are you talking about? What on earth are you doing here? Why are you in my office?" Her voice grew louder with each question.

"Thought I might drop by, maybe ask for a tour of this

charming little town. Oh, and to let you know, I also have a new client—Kenneth Roy Atlee."

At the mention of Kenneth's name, John's head jerked toward the man. He stepped forward and spoke with the inflated confidence of someone armed with a loaded weapon tucked under his arm.

"John Chance. Who the hell are you?"

Hoover sported a half-smile. "Ah, the boyfriend. Or, is it, Prosecutor? Wait, Detective? Sounds like you're a jack of all trades. You know what they also call that? Master of none." He chuckled to himself, arching his back. "Bradley Hoover, opposing counsel. It's your pleasure to meet me." He extended his hand, reaching for a shake, with his palm facing down.

John recognized the gesture instantly. A power move. A handshake masked in dominance. The same bullshit used by the former Coldwater mayor, Cameron Raith.

John despised the move.

He reached with his right hand and grabbed Hoover's, gripping it tightly. He jerked the man's hand and twisted it, flipping the alignment so that John's hand landed on top. He swung his left up and slapped it onto the back of Hoover's. It made a thwack sound that echoed throughout Annaleigh's office.

"But often better than a master of one, am I right... Chadley?"

"Bradley," he mumbled, before straightening up. "Most folks just call me Hoover."

John scratched his chin. "Hoover, you mean like the vacuum? The thing that sucks? That isn't bothered by eating dust and dirt, and at the end of the day, ends up in a bag of trash?" He nodded. "It makes all the sense in the world now, at least for the defense attorney that chooses Kenneth Roy Atlee."

Hoover shrugged. "Defendants who aren't viciously dismembered in fiery car crashes still need someone to defend their rights from overzealous, trigger-happy rookies, too."

John stared directly into Hoover's eyes, casually glancing up to his receding hairline. He said nothing but kept bouncing the attorney's hand. As he let go, Hoover inched backward, subtly running his fingers through his hair.

"So, *Hoover*," John said with a head tilt. "You seem to know a lot about me and this town. Where did you say you were from?"

"I didn't say, but this girl and I go way back. An old-fashioned Cobb County rivalry." He thumbed at Annaleigh. "Tilted one way, though. I did all the winning. Ran her right out of town, from the looks of it."

Annaleigh scoffed. "You've also become a master of embellishment since then."

"Truth hurts," Hoover replied.

"Add losing to us to your small list of accomplishments," John said, dripping with sarcasm.

"Once you see me in court," Hoover said, smirking, "you'll realize you should've taken that job in St. Louis."

"Sounds like fun," John teased. "But, I have to say, though, I've heard nothing about you. Like, zip. Zero. Gotta imagine you probably hear that a lot."

"Can't say I have."

"First time for everything, then. Here's your official welcome to Coldwater. May your stay be troubled and short."

Outside the door, Sarah suppressed a snicker. Hoover's attention returned to Annaleigh.

"Hope I didn't ruin your day, Leigh—"

"Don't call me that."

Hoover's smirk reappeared. "Whatever you say. See you in court, darling."

"God, you always make everything about you, don't you?" Annaleigh shook her head in disgust. "You're here on behalf of your client, but every word out of your mouth has revolved around yourself. If I didn't actually know who you were representing, I'd feel bad for them. But, in this case, it proves that the monster within requires another one to hold its hand. Get out of my office, Hoover."

John placed his hand on the attorney's shoulder and spun him back towards Annaleigh's office door.

"It's been fun. A sturdy but potentially dangerous set of tall stairs is right this way. I'll walk you out."

He pushed Hoover's back, jolting him away. Glancing back at Annaleigh's reddened face and blank stare, John immediately knew her day was, in fact, ruined.

John wasn't sure about her history with that jerk, but that man's presence on this case wasn't something she had expected. A complete and total curveball. Comforting her had to come later.

First, he needed to show Hoover the door. Fast.

At the stairs, John loosened his tight grip on the man's shoulder.

"Down you go."

Hoover wriggled free and quickly grabbed the handrail. His chin lifted as he flicked his eyebrows, his scrutiny returning to the direction of Annaleigh's office.

"Watch out for that one. She's a killer."

John bobbed his head condescendingly. "Oh, don't I know it. I've seen her in court." He leaned in. "You—and Kenneth—don't stand a chance."

Hoover mocked a small pout. "Oh, no, you don't understand. I'm really not joking. You... don't know? She didn't tell you?"

John's eyes narrowed. "Tell me what?"

"I'm not sure you're ready to find out."

"Like I'd ever get the truth from you."

"Oh, I've got nothing to hide. No agenda. No dog in the fight. *She* does, though. The last prosecutor she worked with back in Cobb County didn't end up faring so well."

"Oh, I've heard that story. I know all about—"

"No, no, I don't think you have. Otherwise, you wouldn't be her little white knight."

"That's enough—"

"If you knew what truly happened, you'd see her the way I do."

John shook his head. "I'm not entertaining... whatever this is... any longer. It's past time for you to go."

Hoover strode down a few steps, then paused and turned. "I heard about Doyal Gamble's unfortunate passing. My condolences."

"Passing? He got murdered, you jackass. In a criminal conspiracy with your client," John said, jamming his finger at the foot of the stairs. "Don't ever come up here again. If we need to talk, we'll do it in a room downstairs."

"I'm just saying... things seem really unlucky around her."

"Look, guy, just go."

"Two prosecutors dead... on her watch. As I said, watch out for that one."

Hoover's half-smile reappeared, and then he descended the stairs and disappeared.

Two?

He knew about the incident in Cobb County—she'd told of how her boss tried to take advantage of her and how he found out, the hard way, it was the wrong idea.

That guy is probably singing in a girl's choir now. Could... he have died from that? No way. She would have told me.

Was it possible that she hadn't told him the whole story? With his strange ability to detect lies, at least when he asked her about it, he had the means to discover the truth, whatever it might be.

11

CHAINS FOR FIRE

John cracked his knuckles and zoned out, staring at the linoleum floor. He leaned back at his detective's desk in the Sheriff's Office, eyes fluttering left and right, replaying the scenario in his mind.

After watching his new favorite defense attorney, Bradley Hoover, walk down the stairs and out of the courthouse, John returned to Annaleigh's office. He planned to use his new abilities to ask her about Cobb County and discover why she might have hidden the true story from him.

Curiously, no glow appeared around Hoover when he accused Annaleigh of being the cause of the deaths of two prosecutors. Except John knew the prosecutor in Cobb County hadn't died. The man had felt the wrath of a few knee thrusts and, as a result, apparently lived after that as a lesser man.

That John could tell when someone lied to him was certainly a useful skill in his line of work. Both his lines of work. And, maybe, in important conversations with Annaleigh, too.

His intentions flew out the vintage courthouse windows when he reentered Annaleigh's office and saw her wearing a scowl and scribbling furiously in a notepad.

Folders were scattered across her desktop. Papers were strewn about. An open box of pens with blue caps spilling out.

Her expression clearly showed she wasn't interested in discussing Bradley Hoover, Cobb County, or digging deeper into anything she wanted to forget. He had still tried, but got shot down immediately.

"Hey, hon, he's gone. I made sure of it. Are... you okay?"

"I don't want to talk about it."

"I get it. But, he said something... before he left. Maybe later we can—"

"Maybe it's best if you spend time on making Judge Chapel happy instead," she said, without even looking up at him. "I need to focus, John. Close the door on your way out, please."

Her tone remained pleasant, even though her true feelings were unmistakable. He had backed out of the opening and gently closed the door, its handle clicking and ending the conversation with finality.

When Deputy D. Clyde Brothers walked into the deputies' bullpen, it snapped John out of his daze.

"Hey there, Detective," Clyde drawled. "Didn't expect to see you here this morning."

"I didn't either," John replied, tapping the chair's armrests with his fingertips and not even bothering to correct Clyde. "We had a surprise guest come by the courthouse today. He riled everyone up a bit. Needed a change of scenery. Get this—Kenneth's found himself a lawyer."

Clyde's eyes widened at the notion, as Dallas Taggart, a rookie deputy, walked in behind him.

"That's curious," Clyde said. "When I talked to my buddy at the county jail yesterday, he told me Kenneth hasn't had visitors or phone calls either."

"Somehow he's managed to get representation, and it's not the public defender," John said, taking a deep breath. "Apparently, the lawyer even has some history with Annaleigh—some defense counsel douche from Cobb County. I've got a bad feeling about it."

"I'm sure it's nothing to worry about, young man."

"That's not the worst part, either. Judge Chapel has postponed the trial until I can show him the courtroom is safe with Kenneth in there."

Dallas chuckled. "He probably means himself. Seems like a scared old man. Wesley burned through steel—Kenneth's worse than that."

"Is that so?" John asked, giving him a surprised look. "I wasn't aware you'd actually seen any of it. You weren't around three months ago."

"Foley filled me in. Besides, I mean, the guy's bigger, right? It only makes sense."

"It's also odd because Chapel says you're the one who told him all about Kenneth's time in holding."

Taggart rummaged through a drawer at his desk, as if not paying attention. He kept his head down, choosing not to respond to John's accusation.

Clyde dragged a chair over next to John's desk and sat down.

"Let's figure something out then. Maybe we point a lot of big guns at him the whole time, for starters."

"I almost suggested that to him," John said, forcing a smile. "But Chapel's face didn't look like he was in the mood for jokes. There's no way he'd allow something like that."

"True, true," Clyde said, leaning back. "Otto's never been a fan of guns. Maybe we can set up something else as a deterrent."

"That's what I've been trying to do, but every idea feels stupid."

"Naw, I don't believe that for a second. You've got some of the best ideas I've heard in a long time, John." Clyde's kind eyes showed no hint of sarcasm.

John bobbed his head. "Maybe a little group brainstorming would actually help." He opened a notebook, flipped to a page in the middle, then slid it over for Clyde to see. "There's not much we can do to contain him if he chooses to flare up, but what you said is the angle I've been focusing on. Giving him a deterrent to prevent it."

Clyde leaned forward and squinted, looking over the drawings.

"This one," John began, "is something I thought of because of Wesley. If we get some bear traps and rig them to his hands, we could set them off if he gets crazy. I haven't figured out exactly how we would activate them."

"Bear traps?" Clyde's brows furrowed, then one lifted high.

"What about bear spray?" Dallas chimed in from across the bullpen. "Bet that would clear the courtroom, too. We could even accidentally set it off if the trial isn't going our way." He grabbed his midsection and erupted into a deep, belly laugh.

Clyde cleared his throat, regaining John's focus. "Tell me, young man, don't you think that idea is... a little barbaric?"

"Maybe, but it's the only way I know to absolutely stop him from burning everything," he dipped his head, biting at his cheek. "When I stopped Wesley..." a big swallow. "No, when Wesley stopped himself. I guess all I really did was stall long enough for him to lose control. But it worked, Clyde. I'm trying to repeat that here. Delay, stall, whatever. If he fires up, we only need a few seconds—long enough for each of us to put a bullet in him."

Clyde scratched his chin, clearly unimpressed with the plan.

"I guess I'm wondering why you plan to kill *him*, rather than kill the *fire*."

A pained expression crossed John's face. "I don't think you can separate the two. From what I've seen, that look in their eyes as the power takes hold... the man and the fire are one. It's like a disease. You catch it, and it changes you from the inside—and there's no turning back. An unholy union of emotion, pain, and complete destruction."

"Maybe so, but remember, proactive justice isn't justice. It's premeditation."

John leaned back, stretching his arms behind his head.

"Kill the fire," he muttered. "Kill the fire—"

As his shadowed eyes drifted upward, something on the ceiling caught his eye. He sat up straight, staring at the small metal protrusions descending from various ceiling tiles. "Are those new?"

Clyde looked up, nodding. "The sprinkler system? Not really. About a month ago. If we had it back in May, it might have saved us from some of the damage. Parnell pulled the trigger on the project not too long after that night."

"How did I not see them getting installed?"

"The guys only did work in the mornings. You're usually at the courthouse, so y'all didn't cross paths."

John bolted to his feet. "I've got an idea, but I need a second opinion... and I know just who to ask. Be back in a bit."

He sprinted outside, a big smile spread across his face.

* * *

EVEN THOUGH COLDWATER Fire Station No. 1 was the most modern building in town, the engine bay still smelled of ash and oil. Firefighters relaxed and played cards at a table in the back of the bay, but John's target happened to be the man shining the side of a bright red firetruck.

Toby Walsh, six feet tall and two hundred ten pounds of muscle, had become John's only friend in Coldwater after being a first responder at the intense scene at John's house back in May. After he became a detective, John ran into Toby while chasing a few leads, and a few beers later, they were swapping stories about law school and the fire academy.

Toby explained in great detail how he earned the scar that traced from his ear to his jaw, and John returned serve by sharing the gory details of how his cornea once popped out onto his cheek. It had been a few weeks since they last talked, but the underlying foundation of friendship between men is that the time in between doesn't matter.

"Missed a spot," John teased as he approached the fire truck.

Toby stopped, lifted his head, and scoffed. "Like you could even see it if I did, Square Law."

"God, if you're going to insult me, at least get it right. It's *Law Squared*, you know, as in twice the law."

Toby stood up and squared off with John. "Need I remind you that you came up with that nickname yourself... and again I'll tell you—it's totally lame."

"I was drunk. I cannot be held liable for my actions, Your Honor."

The serious expressions on both men's faces softened into smiles as they reached out for a hearty handshake.

"And what brings you to our neck of the woods, man? Been a while since we had a beer. It'd give you a chance to come up with a better nickname for yourself."

John raised his hands. "Guilty as charged. Been a little busy catching Coldwater's worst guy. Did you hear?" He leaned in, smirking. "I got him."

"Bullshit. I just saw him. He's roaming free, leaving behind a trail of destruction in his wake."

"What—?" John's mouth dropped, heart racing. "What are you talking about... he's escaped?"

"I don't know about escaped, but yeah, Coldwater's worst guy. Otis." Toby thumbed over his shoulder. "He's back in the bunks right now. Destroyed the head this morning, thought we needed to call in hazmat." He chuckled loudly, then went back to shining the truck.

"Not cool," John said, drawing a deep breath. "I won't lie, you had me for a second."

"All right, quit stalling. If it ain't that beer, what are ya doin' here?"

"I need your help, Toby. The judge won't start the trial until I show him that it will be safe. You and I both saw what Wesley Raith did to my house—I can't let it happen to that hundred-year-old courthouse, too."

"What do you want us to do? Drag a hose up to the stand and point it at him the whole time?"

"Nope, I've got a better idea. Maybe… I need your… dare I say, advice."

Toby tossed the rag on the floor and rubbed his palms together. He intended to clean the soot off, but it smudged it further. "You're in luck, then. I've got just the expertise you're after. Hand me the case file. I'll figure out your trial strategy in no time."

"No, that's not—"

"Oh," Toby continued. "My bad, then. Where's the evidence bag? I'll take a look and crack the case for you."

"Toby—"

"Can't help you, then, man. I mean, if you're not going to play to my strengths—"

"Shut the hell up!" John shouted, prompting an intense response from Toby. "I need fire expertise, dumbass."

A large frown spread across Toby's scarred jaw. "You know how to ruin a guy's fun, don't you?"

"Yeah, yeah, yeah. If it's any consolation, you can kind of wear both a fireman's hat and a detective's hat."

"They assigned you a special detective's hat? Let me see it…" Toby reached to rummage through John's pockets. John puffed out his cheeks and sputtered the air. "Say it," Toby pleaded.

"No."

"Say it, or I'm not doing nothing."

"That's a double negative," John said, rolling his eyes. "You just said you're going to do it—"

"Speak forth, Satan—"

"Jesus, Toby. What the hell? I'm not saying it. It's so stupid. Can we just—"

"Say it, *Square Detective*, or I'll conveniently forget everything I've ever learned, and you'll be S.O.L." John shook his head. "Saaaay it," Toby drawled, enunciating the syllable into one long tone.

"Fine. Fine!" John drew a breath. "You get to be... *Firecop.*"

"Yes!" Toby fist-pumped into the air. "Give me a gun, point me in the direction of a fire, and tell me who to shoot! Let's go!" His finger guns fired imaginary bullets into the ceiling.

"Dude, I'm not giving you a gun. Do you want to hear my plan or what?"

Toby tapped his fingertips together, dialing down his excitement.

"Lay it on me, boss."

"Finally," John said, exasperated. Most conversations with Toby went like this, although, to be fair, they were more fun when layered with alcohol. "I'm sure you've heard the specifics by now about Wesley Raith's power and how it works."

Toby nodded. "I've heard the rumors."

"I've seen it *this* close to my face, and trust me, the rumors are probably either completely bunk... or they don't do it enough justice."

"That doesn't sound cryptic at all. Come on, when do we get to the good part?"

John tongued his cheek. "Whatever you've heard, here's the truth. Kenneth can do it, too, believe it or not. Right now, he's in the county jail under armed, 24-hour supervision. But, once we get into the courtroom, we need to be more creative."

"Still waiting—"

"Alright... here's the truth. Kenneth can conjure and control fire with his hands." John paused, gauging the level of Toby's freak-out.

Toby's brows furrowed, as if confused. His chin jutted to the left, and his head tilted. "Wait... you're serious? I was waiting for the *just kidding.*"

"Dead serious. With Wesley, the flames ignited in his hands. Then a brilliant light, then wisps and flames, then there's this deafening sound... like a hum, or a pulse, or something. And then everything burns to the ground."

"Jesus."

"I know, it's crazy. One thing I realized is that his emotions drove the strength of his power. As he got angrier, the fire spread up his arms, past his elbows." John rubbed his forearm, miming flames. "Now, I haven't seen Kenneth use his, but Clyde did, at least from a distance. His power emits the same kind of light, though we haven't actually seen the flames. I have no choice but to assume that the power sets of all three are the same. I don't care about the light or the sound, which means just worrying about the fire and the heat."

"Crap, this whole conversation sounds nuts. But, whatever, fair enough assumption," Toby said. "What does all this have to do with me?"

"And back to the beginning we go," John said, splaying his hands. "I need to come up with something to keep Kenneth from burning the courtroom down, and I want you to help me build it. The foundation of my idea is detecting the heat that he'd produce with his hands. And, I think using those wicks you find in the sprinkler systems of buildings would work perfectly."

Toby rubbed his scar, eyes darting. "Interesting. We actually have some of those wicks here. I could grab a few, maybe integrate it into a fire extinguisher—"

"Nope, those don't work. Annaleigh sprayed Wesley at my house. All it did was make it look like my living room got covered in cocaine."

"Likely excuse, and your drug secret is safe with me. *It was from the fire extinguisher, Officer. I swear.*" Toby scanned the equipment floor, talking to himself. "No hoses, no extinguishers. Don't want to flood the place. Can't coat it with drugs. Let me see..." He wandered over to a set of shelves and rummaged through some boxes. After a few minutes, he snapped and pointed at John. "You know what, come over here, take a look at this."

John approached him near a stack of brown cardboard boxes on a pallet by the far wall. Each box had a white label and the letters "FM-200" in bright red ink.

"We recently received these," Toby explained. "They're experimental canisters of a gas called FM-200."

"Just like the label—I can read, man. What is it?"

"It's the new drop-in for Halon–you know, the stuff they pump into those computer rooms and bank vaults. Same knockdown power for fires, but it doesn't tear a hole in the ozone layer. Plus, this new stuff won't choke you out if you happen to be in the room when it releases."

"Not killing everyone in the courtroom is definitely a good start. Do you think this is something we can borrow for my little project?"

"*Our* little project. I'll talk to my captain about it, but I'm sure it won't be a problem. We're supposed to try it out, anyway... no better way to test it than dousing the supernatural flames of some maniac, eh?"

"I'm sold," John said, clapping his hands. "Got some time to throw together a prototype? I'd love to demo it to the judge and get our trial back on track."

"You bet." Toby gestured to another fireman sitting at a nearby table. "Hey, Hayes, come over for a second."

The man, who appeared to be in his forties, had a jet black beard without a mustache. A distinctive look, and the kind of dark black that often looks like it came from a box. Toby introduced him.

"Shep Hayes, this is John Chance. John here has a fun little proposition for us, and I know how much you like cobbling together impossible projects around here."

John's brows lifted. "Shep? Is that a nickname, or did your parents really name you that?"

"Short for Shepherd, and yeah, gotta blame the parents," Shep said gruffly. "Not sure they thought it all the way through. Gonna play with the new stuff, Walsh?"

"Yeah. We might've finally found a good use for the FM-200. Grab that box over there. I'll get the tubing and Kevlar."

"Kevlar?" John asked. "You guys have Kevlar here?"

"Oh, yeah," Toby said. "Wait and see how we'll use it. You're gonna love it."

* * *

John stood on a small concrete patio on the courthouse's north side, shifting his feet. He and Sarah had waited outside while Annaleigh went inside on a mission to coax Judge Otto Chapel outside. When she returned without the judge but gave him a thumbs-up, his knees shook.

How well this demonstration went would determine the fate of the entire trial.

"No need to be nervous," Sarah said, spotting the contraption in front of them. "I know I couldn't explain it, but I've heard you practice. You're gonna kill it."

"Thanks for the vote of confidence. Because I'm not sure what we'll do if Chapel doesn't like it."

"Then you'll just come up with something else. Do you know why?" She approached him, straightened his suit jacket, and playfully punched him on the arm. "Because you're brilliant and I know you can do whatever you put your mind to." She lingered on him, only interrupted by a throat clear by Annaleigh. John's freshly straightened collar masked a warmth welling underneath it.

Annaleigh's eyes flicked between them, but her face stayed expressionless. "Judge Chapel will be out in a minute." Annaleigh raised her eyebrows at John. "You sure we're ready?"

He looked around, as if expecting someone. After a few seconds, he nodded. "Sure. I can do this." It's possible he was saying it to himself, rather than to her.

"I'm here! I'm here!" An out-of-breath Toby Walsh bolted around the corner of the building. His yellow firefighter coat hung loosely and clanged with each step. He stopped a few feet away and slow-walked over to Sarah, his chest heaving up and down as he caught his breath. "Just had to get one last thing from the car."

John's knees settled.

"Now we're *really* ready," John said, holding back a smirk.

Judge Chapel ambled around the courthouse corner, eyes wide.

Next to a bucket of sand and a length of rebar, four silver canisters, each about the size of a thermos, were placed on the ground. A clear tube extended from each canister's neck, with the rest of the tube coiled on the ground. On the other end of one of the tubes lay a fireman's glove.

Chapel visually examined each piece, then looked at John silently.

Time to shine.

"Your Honor, I understand how this might look, but this restraint isn't a makeshift device based on science fiction—it's built on proven fire department technology that we've adapted for courtroom safety. We've taken standard firefighter gloves and fitted them with small canisters of a substance called FM-200. It's a relatively new, clean-agent gas that the department is testing as a Halon replacement. It's safe, leaves no mess, and extinguishes fires without causing harm to anyone nearby."

John bent down, picked up the glove from the ground, straightened the tube, and held it up for the judge to see.

"Here's how it works, Judge. These canisters will be strapped to Mr. Atlee's arms every minute he's in the courtroom. Each one is sealed at the neck with a thin diaphragm. Running along the wrists and into the palms are heat-sensitive links—similar to the wicks in overhead sprinkler systems that melt to release water in case of a fire. These links are made of a special material that gives way once the environment reaches 135 degrees Fahrenheit. Usually, 165 degrees is when flames become dangerous, but these are even more sensitive fuses." He paused. "Clear so far?"

Chapel's eyes narrowed, but he gave a barely perceptible nod.

John continued. "If the defendant tries to use his abilities and generates fire from his hands, the heat hits those links first. They'll melt, releasing a compressed spring attached to a piercing pin. That pin jabs right into the canister seal, and the FM-200 gas rushes out under pressure, flooding the gloves through built-in tubes. It absorbs the heat and starves the flames of energy, putting them out before they can do damage. I know it sounds like a lot of dominoes falling in sequence, but these actions happen almost instantly once the wick melts. We'll strap a canister on each arm with heat-resistant Kevlar straps and have backups sitting on the ground by each foot. Even if one fails, the others will kick in."

More silence from Judge Chapel as he scanned the setup. His eyes lingered on the canisters and traced the tubing until they reached the gloves.

"May I?" he asked, reaching for it. John obliged. Chapel inspected the outside and observed how John and Toby connected the tubing. He pulled the flaps open and looked inside before inching his hand in. "I expected the tubing to feel uncomfortable, maybe even jab my hand. But I can barely feel it. Dare I say, almost agreeable."

"Yes, Your Honor," John replied. "Asking the defendant to put on these gloves will definitely be unusual. We weren't trying to be cruel, too."

Toby chuckled, making Sarah spin around and hide her own laugh.

Chapel slipped the glove off and handed it back to John. He pointed at the metal canisters on the ground. "And those? Those are what you plan to strap onto his arms?"

"Not all of them, Your Honor," John said, reaching for one. "Each canister only weighs about five pounds. Only need one of those on each arm. We agree it might be cumbersome to wear a combined twenty pounds on your arms every day of the trial. Two would get wrapped and set on the ground at his feet, but still tubed into the gloves as backup. He wouldn't have to bear the weight of all four, just two."

John pointed at Toby. "Firefighter Walsh is here, Judge. He's here to give you an active demonstration with real fire. That's why we asked you to meet outside instead of in your chambers."

Chapel rolled a canister between his hands, switching it from one to the other as he nodded, lips out.

"Let's see it then, Counselor," he said, handing it back to John. "Fire away, as it were."

Toby stepped forward, reached into the pocket of his turnout coat, and pulled out a handful of thin cedar shims, the kind carpenters use for leveling doors. He fanned them like playing cards.

Chapel raised an eyebrow. "Son, if your plan is to light those and stuff them in the glove, how do I know the glove itself isn't starving the fire of air? I need irrefutable proof that the gas is the one doing the work."

Toby grinned. "Exactly what I figured you'd say, Your Honor. All part of the plan." He tossed the shims onto the ground and reached deeper into the same pocket, producing a small plastic squeeze bottle. The label had long since worn off, but everyone on the sidewalk recognized the sharp smell the instant Toby cracked the cap.

Methanol. Clean, hot, and unforgiving.

"Little trick we use when the gear reps swear their new Nomex won't burn," Toby said. He turned the test glove inside out, gave the palm and fingers three long, deliberate squirts until the lining glistened and a few drops pattered onto the concrete.

Then, he turned it right-side out and gave it a shake so the fuel coated every inch of the interior.

He nodded to John, who grabbed the rebar from the ground and pushed it into the bucket of sand, twisting it until it settled to the bottom. Toby clipped the glove's cuff to the rebar and stepped back.

From his other pocket, he pulled out a torch—a full-size Bernzomatic with a dull brass trigger. He thumbed the striker, and the flame roared to life, blue at the core and yellow at the edges, and loud enough that everyone else retreated a step or two backward.

He opened the glove wide, like a catcher waiting for a fastball, and slid the torch head deep into the palm. Flames licked up the fingers, hungry and consuming. His head bounced as he counted —one second, two, three—then pulled the torch free.

Judge Chapel leapt back as the inside of the glove erupted into a swirling orange ball. Tall flames burst from the wrist opening in a steady column, bright enough to light up everyone's faces.

In an instant, John's face flushed with heat. The air shimmered with heat and crackled with the scent of burning fuel.

The wick melted with a quick pop, triggering the spring that pushed the pin into the canister.

Then came the hiss—a stinging sound, almost angry.

A thick white cloud shot from the cuff and the vents sewn along the knuckles, swallowing the flame so quickly it looked like someone had slammed a lid on the sun.

The fire vanished. No remnants. No afterglow.

And, no smoke, only the faint smell of warm rebar and the sight of a glove hanging steaming on its wire, palm still dripping unburned methanol onto the sidewalk.

Toby turned off the torch and let the silence settle, smiling at John.

"FM-200, Your Honor," John said calmly. "About two and a half seconds from ignition to extinction. The only wet object in the room is the inside of that glove. Enough to extinguish the danger without the water damage from traditional hoses."

And give the deputies time to fire their weapons, but that part can be left unsaid.

Judge Chapel stared at the dripping Nomex gloves for a long moment, then gave a grudging nod of his head.

"I'm convinced. This trial shall proceed."

12

ECHOES OF THE COURT

"I want to throw my hat in the ring, Annaleigh. I caught him. I want to see it through."

John paced in his living room, practicing the speech he planned to give to Annaleigh for the upcoming trial.

He'd caught Kenneth.

He'd been the one to fashion a restraint system to keep everyone safe.

The only fair conclusion? That he take the first chair and be the one to finally put Kenneth away.

"Now, I know what you're going to say... that it's too early, that I don't have enough experience—"

He stopped mid-step, realizing the truth. He *didn't* have enough experience, not for a trial of this magnitude. Technically, he had no experience at all. He'd only been at the prosecutor's table in court to answer boilerplate questions from Judge Chapel about plea deals and other minor details. Hell, Sarah had more courtroom experience than he did, whether in a 'muni' court or not.

No—they needed to slam the door on Kenneth's prison cell so hard that he'd hear it ringing for years.

He sat at the end of the sofa and puffed out his cheeks. He patted the middle cushion, then slid over onto it.

My spot is her spot, too.

He closed his eyes, recalling his first day as a prosecutor—the first time he saw Annaleigh in court. He might currently have the ability to tell when someone is lying, but she had the power to enchant an entire courtroom.

* * *

John entered the courtroom quietly, surveying the proceedings at the front. He tried unsuccessfully to muffle his footsteps against the creaky wooden floorboards of the Coldwater County courtroom as he gently closed the large doors behind him.

As the defense attorney reclaimed his seat, Prosecutor Annaleigh Stanton rose gracefully and glided toward the jury box. Her motions, like a seasoned performer stepping into the spotlight, commanded the courtroom's attention, and he couldn't help but admire her poise and focus. He stood there in the doorway, realizing she was about to deliver the closing argument.

"Your Honor, ladies and gentlemen of the jury," she began. "Don't let the defense's smoke and mirrors cloud your judgment. The truth is as clear as day—the defendant is guilty beyond a reasonable doubt. And, when I'm done explaining all you've seen here, you'll undoubtedly agree."

John scanned the room, searching for a discreet spot to sit. This caught the eye of the tall, lanky bailiff standing to the right of the door. His bright white button-up shirt highlighted the badge above his left breast pocket and a crooked plastic name tag on his right. An embossed Dymo label reading "Harlan" stuck precariously to the tag.

Harlan saw John standing in the aisle and waved his hand downward as a subtle hint for him to take a seat.

John looked to his left and saw the entire bench empty and

available. He pointed at the pew to Harlan and raised his eyebrows, silently asking for permission. Harlan pointed back, and John immediately turned to enter the row, completely missing Harlan's additional gesture of shaking his head side to side.

John sidestepped into the pew and sat down, unaware that the bench had been carefully balancing itself on uneven legs after years of use. The added weight from John sitting caused it to rock backward, then slam forward. A loud thud echoed through the hallowed courthouse walls.

"The defense has attempted to distract you—"

The noise made Annaleigh stop talking and turn her head to look at the back of the courtroom. Everyone in the room followed her, curious to find out what caused the sound. All eyes focused on John.

Feeling his internal temperature rise, he raised both hands in a surrendering gesture, mouthing the words "sorry" multiple times to anyone watching him. The silence in the room lingered far too long for John's taste. Seconds felt like hours. A single squeak of a floorboard broke the silence as Harlan uncomfortably shifted his stance.

"—with irrelevant details... and... technicalities," Annaleigh continued, still looking at John. She tilted her head slightly as a look of recognition washed over her face, causing her eyes to widen.

On John's first day on the job, she seemed to already know him. She cleared her throat and gathered herself, still maintaining direct eye contact with him.

"I want to welcome you..."

His breath caught. Not only did she recognize him, but she also addressed him. In the middle of her closing?

"...to the truth," she said, turning back to the jury with a dramatic spin. "As for defense counsel's story? I say, 'Don't fall for it.' Keep your eyes on the big picture. Now, let's review all the evidence that points to a guilty verdict."

Embarrassed and acutely aware of the unwanted attention, John's cheeks flushed a deep crimson as he met Harlan's eyes. The man's disapproving head shake only worsened his mortification, emphasizing that his loud entrance had not only disrupted the courtroom proceedings but also had thrown off the prosecutor's rhythm, even if for a moment.

John quickly averted his eyes and shook his head, silently cursing himself for drawing such undesirable scrutiny. As regret faded, John's attention returned to Annaleigh, having effortlessly regained control of the courtroom.

With confidence, she carefully presented each piece of incriminating evidence, weaving a compelling story that kept the jury hanging on her every word.

Where she walked, the jury's eyes followed.

Their heads nodded up and down as she gestured in the air, emphasizing each point. She had perfected her craft, capturing the courtroom's focus through her confident delivery and compelling storytelling.

"Assistant Prosecuting Attorney Stanton is one of the best attorneys ever to come through this office, myself included," Prosecutor Doyal Gamble had told him earlier that morning. "My protégé, some say, although, honestly, it seems like I haven't taught her as much as she's learned on her own. She's uniquely talented, believe me. Young man, if you want to advance in this business and be a prosecutor like me one day... learn all you can from her." He had leaned in, cheeks tight. "By the way, she hates being called by her first name. Feels it's unprofessional." He swallowed. "You'd best call her Ms. Stanton to get on her good side."

John's nervousness caused him to miss the slight curve in Doyal Gamble's lips.

The prosecutor also explained that Annaleigh never shied away from trying a case in court. She explicitly requested to take cases most likely to come before the judge. He said she loved it, and it showed.

She had a way of working her magic on jurors.

A microcosm of this small town, this jury united in its intense focus on her persuasion. A young man in his mid-twenties, wide-eyed and eager with a hint of fawning, scrawled notes as if the prosecutor's words were gospel. An elderly man, face lined with wisdom and experience, leaned forward, listening closely to each word. A middle-aged woman listened as if she were a trusted confidante sharing secrets over a glass of wine.

Even the hardened gentleman at the jury box's end, whom John guessed probably worked in construction of some kind, sat with his callused hands folded and hung on Annaleigh's every syllable.

Her magnetic presence had cast a spell over the diverse jury, making them hang on her every word like a lifeline. It wasn't only the jurors under her spell, but many other members of the courtroom as well.

The second bailiff, Baz, a name John would later learn was short for Sebastian, stood motionless between the judge and the jury, fixed on her. His intuitive eyes examined every word and gesture she made, as if searching for signs of weakness or flaw in her presentation. John could tell Baz's focus wasn't driven by skepticism or doubt but by a keen understanding, having watched hundreds of trials during his career as the judge's protector.

Noticing Judge Chapel's engagement with her argument, John couldn't help but see the man's subconscious nod of agreement. Almost immediately, the judge regained his composure and resumed his typical stoic expression, adjusting his steepled hands.

John wondered if the defense had seen this fleeting display of partiality, and sure enough, a look at the defense lawyer confirmed it—a subtle shrug showing they, too, had noticed the brief lapse and understood the case as a lost cause.

Even the court reporter, diligently focused on transcribing each word with practiced precision, couldn't help but look at her with admiration and appreciation.

As Annaleigh's closing argument reached its crescendo, the defendant sat hunched in his seat, his head buried in his hands.

After a quick, subtle elbow from his attorney, he sat upright again, though his head still drooped. With each eloquent point she made, John knew the man felt his hopes of acquittal slip away, like sand through his fingers.

"The evidence speaks for itself," she said. "Piece by piece, witness by witness, we've built an airtight case that points to one, and only one conclusion. The defendant did, in fact, commit this heinous crime."

John's fascination with her went past her words, too. He couldn't help but notice her flawless courtroom attire. A sleek jacket hugged her figure, perfectly tailored to emphasize her slender frame without losing a professional look. Paired with a pencil skirt that further highlighted her silhouette, the outfit radiated confidence and elegance. Her shoulder-length brown hair bounced in a lively, natural style, carefully balanced between the seriousness of the courtroom and a friendly, relatable touch of natural wave.

She's easily the best-dressed woman I've ever seen. Except... for Genie, of course. That woman wins every competition with a style of her own.

He quietly smiled at the thought, then his mouth watered thinking about cinnamon rolls.

With each purposeful stride, Annaleigh's short heels punctuated her closing argument with a series of soft clicks and clacks. To John's attentive ears, this rhythmic soundscape evoked images of a grand ballroom, where couples swayed in elegant unison. The sounds were a metronome, further mesmerizing anyone listening to pay full attention.

He studied her, captivated by the unwavering intensity in her eyes. Each carefully enunciated word resonated with deliberate rhythm. The precision of her arguments had been expertly crafted to emphasize her point. It became clear to John that Doyal Gamble's assessment was spot on.

"The defendant's actions reveal his guilt. You all saw it in his own testimony. His lies, evasiveness, and inconsistencies—all indicate someone hiding the truth." She paused for emphasis, stopping her movements, then rested her hands on the short wall in front of the seated jury. Leaning in, she created an intimate connection with the panel, the atmosphere tense with anticipation as everyone waited for her next words.

"Justice demands," she said in a softer tone, "that we hold the defendant accountable for his actions. Returning a guilty verdict is the only way to ensure that justice is served here and that the victim's memory is honored. When you retire to the jury room and discuss this trial, I want you to remember three things—the evidence, the defendant's testimony... and that this man no longer deserves to walk the streets of Coldwater as a free man. We ask that you find him guilty."

Her final statement echoed through the antique air, resonating within the historic walls of the hundred-year-old courtroom. John half-expected applause to break out. She glided gracefully back to her seat and cast a quick glance toward the back pew, her eyes instantly locking onto John's. In the silence, a wordless exchange occurred. She radiated pride. He filled with awe.

Judge Chapel finished the proceedings and sent the jury out to deliberate. The courtroom felt heavy with anticipation, even though everyone secretly knew the eventual verdict.

She gathered her materials and walked toward John. He stood up from the bench, causing it to rock and thud as it settled. With the courtroom in recess, the thumps blended in with the footsteps of others leaving the gallery. He pushed his leg behind him to steady the bench while glancing at Harlan near the door. The rotund bailiff gave another disapproving shake of his head.

With a polite yet confident demeanor, Annaleigh extended her hand for a firm handshake as she introduced herself.

"Hello, John. As I said before, welcome back to Coldwater."

His hand met hers. "Ms. Stanton... I appreciate the warm welcome, though I must admit I'm at a bit of a disadvantage here. I'm sorry, but have we met before?"

He offered a sheepish half-smile, with a hint of curiosity and amusement in his voice. As they grasped hands, they both squeezed lightly without actually shaking. John found it odd, but when their eyes met, this handshake felt... different.

He liked it.

Perhaps too much, considering this was their first introduction.

"Oh, we haven't met. It's a small town, and I have my sources." A playful wink from her shifted John slightly off balance. She gradually pulled back her hand, letting her fingertips brush lightly against his. John's hand instantly felt clammy. He hoped she hadn't noticed. "Oh, and it's Annaleigh, not *Ms. Stanton.* Did Gamble put you up to that? God... makes me sound so old. Plus, he knows I hate it. Between you and me, I only let a select few use it. When I get upstairs, I'm smashing that *Best Boss Ever* mug on his desk."

"Impressive closing," John said, changing the subject. "Gamble assigned you as my supervisor. What are the chances you can teach me how to control a jury like that?"

"Call me a mentor instead, okay? You'll still report to him, and I'd prefer him to yell at you when you staple a case file the wrong way."

"Seriously? This place is that strict?"

"A thousand percent. Your predecessor once put trial docs in a folder upside down. It was his first—and only—strike. He didn't make it through the day before Gamble threw him out on the sidewalk. The man is lean, but deceptively strong. For your sake, John, I hope your staple game is up to par."

John stared at her with wide eyes, swallowing hard. His eyes whizzed around—taking in Annaleigh, the noisy bench, and Harlan—what in the world had he gotten himself into?

Annaleigh burst out laughing, quickly joined by Harlan.

"Do you see his face, Ms. Stanton?" Harlan joked. "He might pass out right here and now."

"Pale as a ghost, the poor guy." She pouted her lips. "I'm teasing, John. This room is serious enough. Every now and then, a joke is warranted." She gestured toward the exit. "Manners are optional, though appreciated."

John sprang into action and opened the door, gesturing for her to go out. Annaleigh stepped through the threshold and paused briefly to look back over her shoulder.

"You coming or what?" She winked at him again and whisked herself away.

John stood still, pondering whether he really saw a wink or if she maybe had something in her eye. He stepped aside from the pew and looked at Harlan one last time. This time, the man returned a sly smile.

"You saw what you saw," Harlan said. "If I were you, I'd hustle on after her."

John gave a subtle nod and quickly left, taking long strides to catch up with her as she glided toward the stairs leading to the upstairs office.

* * *

JOHN OPENED HIS EYES, and that afternoon from months ago still felt as fresh in his mind as his last breath. Playing second fiddle to the best violin in the orchestra was still a pretty good position to be in.

13

LIES IN THE LIGHT

Time protracted as Annaleigh entered the main first-floor conference room and locked eyes with Kenneth Roy Atlee's defense lawyer, Bradley Hoover.

A nuisance from her past who had suddenly appeared in her present, he served as a reminder that she wasn't ready to face the truth of what really happened back then in Cobb County.

If she told John the truth, the glint in his surgically repaired eyes might fade when he looked at her.

John and Sarah entered the conference room behind her, and, although it was unplanned, they all sat down in sync on one side of the long, ornate wooden table. She looked across the table and saw Bradley still staring at her and smirking.

"Ready to get this show started?" he asked.

She shook her head and shot him a disapproving look. "Just like you to think a trial like this is a show, Hoover. It's a deposition. You never did take anything seriously."

"And yet... I recall winning against you. A lot."

She sensed John tense up, as if about to jump in and speak. She grabbed his leg under the table without acknowledging Hoover's taunt. She craned her neck toward Judge Chapel's court reporter, sitting at the end of the table.

"Let's just begin, shall we? Would you please swear in the witness?"

The older woman stood and raised her right hand, signaling the man sitting next to Hoover to do the same.

"Please raise your right hand." She paused until the man obeyed. "Do you solemnly swear or affirm that the testimony you are about to give in this matter will be the truth, the whole truth, and nothing but the truth?"

"I do."

"Thank you. Please take a seat."

The wiry man leaned back into his seat and lowered his hand, using it to smooth his graying beard with long strokes. The reporter sat down gracefully, gently placed her fingers on the keyboard, and nodded.

Annaleigh focused on the witness. "State your full name and occupation for the record."

"Broden Taylor Reed. I tend the bar down at Three Pump."

"Did you have conversations with Mr. Hoover, or anyone else, to prepare for your testimony today?"

"I object," Hoover said loudly. "Any potential privileged information is off-limits, Annaleigh. You should know that."

"In this setting, Mr. Hoover, let's maintain some decorum. It's Ms. Stanton. And, asking about the content of those communications would absolutely be privileged. Asking if those communications occurred... is not." She angled back to Reed. "You may answer the question."

The witness gave Hoover a sidelong glance, and he simply offered a subtle nod, signaling permission to answer the question. "He came to the bar yesterday. We talked."

Annaleigh wrote something on the legal pad in front of her. "How long have you worked at Hank's Three Pump?"

"It's Three Pump. Hank's long gone."

"My apologies, Mr. Reed. How long have you tended bar at Three Pump?"

"Prolly eight or ten years."

"Mr. Reed, please be as specific as you can. Not just with this question, but with all of them."

"Now, now, Ms. Stanton," Hoover said smoothly. "Let's not pick on the poor man, shall we? He's a bartender, not developing a process for nuclear fusion."

She sighed. "Is that an objection?"

"No, I was—"

"Then, unless you're objecting, there shouldn't be words coming out of your mouth."

Out of the corner of her eye, she saw John sketching something on his legal pad. Without moving her head, she flicked her eyes over and saw a large 'T' with her name scrawled above the top left, and Hoover's name at the top right. John quickly drew a tick mark underneath her column, then he shot daggers at Hoover with his eyes. She tried her best to hide a faint smile as she kept going.

"Mr. Reed, please describe your typical duties—do you interact much with patrons?"

"Objection, compound."

"I'll simplify. Mr. Reed, could you explain what you do during a typical shift?" she asked, shooting a shrewd glance at Hoover.

"I don't know, I hand 'em drinks, I take their money, and clean up when they make a mess."

"And, tell me, in what manner do you interact with your patrons?"

"I chat if they want to."

"Are you familiar with regular customers?"

"Familiar?"

"Repeat customers. Those who visit either frequently or multiple times. Do you have patrons that fit that description?"

"Yeah, sure."

"How do you recognize them?"

"Uh, by their faces?"

"Objection."

Her focus snapped to Hoover. "What exactly are you objecting to? You can't just say—"

"It was a stupid question. We all know it. I thought I should call it out—"

"That's not even a valid objection. Why do you feel the need to turn this into a—"

"Into a what? A referendum on which law school you attended?"

The court reporter cleared her throat louder than expected for such a small, elderly woman. Both attorneys immediately stopped talking.

"I need you to speak one at a time. For the record, please."

Silence settled over the conference. Annaleigh tugged at her suit coat, adjusting it. "Apologies, ma'am."

Hoover stayed silent, refused to apologize, and instead looked pleased. Annaleigh resumed her questions.

"Do you recall seeing Kenneth Roy Atlee at Hank's... er, Three Pump?"

"Sure, I've seen the guy."

"How often would he come in?"

Reed shrugged. "A few times, maybe."

Annaleigh felt a tap on her foot from John. She ignored it and kept going. "Can you describe a typical visit—what time of day, what he ordered, how he paid?"

"Objection, compound... again."

She inhaled deeply, steadying herself despite her rising temperature. These questions were basic, meant to assess the witness's cooperation and gather essential facts in case he tried to change his story at trial. Hoover had no reason to object so aggressively—unless getting under her skin was his objective.

Even though she had figured out his strategy... it still worked.

"Hoover, this isn't court—"

"Mr. Hoover..." he muttered.

"—so we don't need to match the formality of it."

"Compound questions can be confusing for the witness."

"Fine, for the sake of *the witness,* I'll rephrase—what time of day did Mr. Atlee usually visit?"

"I don't know... at night?"

More foot taps from John.

"He never frequented the bar at any other time?"

"No."

Tap. Tap. TAP.

"Are you sure?"

"Objection, asked and answered. Come on, Annaleigh. This is Lawyer 101, ain't it?"

She ignored his verbal jabs. "What did Mr. Atlee typically order?"

"Objection, relevance."

She curled her fist into a ball, pinching the pen into her palm. "When Mr. Atlee ordered a drink, how did he pay?"

"Before he left."

She wanted to roll her eyes. This idiot knew exactly what she meant. But he'd been coached by Bradley Hoover... to be an asshole.

"No, Mr. Reed. Not when did he pay—how? Cash? Credit card? Traveller's check? Bag of coins?" The more options she listed, the more sarcastic she unintentionally sounded.

"Cash."

"When was the last time he came in?"

Reed jabbed at John. "Ask that guy? He was stalking my place that night. You tore through my lot, spitting rocks everywhere. I've got ruts everywhere—"

"Give me a break, like that hole in the wall had a flat parking to begin wi—"

Annaleigh spoke so quickly that John had no chance to finish, delivering a solid kick under the table to shut him up.

"Please state the date, Mr. Reed. When was the last time you saw Kenneth Roy Atlee enter your bar?"

"I don't know... Friday. The 24th. I think."

"Of September?"

"It certainly wasn't *this* month, was it? Since that hasn't happened yet. Duh, lady. It was September."

"At that time, were you aware that Kenneth was wanted by the authorities?"

"No."

As soon as the word left Reed's mouth, John tugged on Annaleigh's elbow. She leaned in closer to him as he closed the gap. "Stop tapping and grabbing me," she whispered out of the side of her mouth, barely audible.

"He's lying. He knew."

She pulled back slightly to look at him through her brows. "*I know.* May I continue?" She turned back. "Mr. Reed, did Mr. Atlee's behavior change in the last three months?"

"Objection, vague," Hoover said with a smirk.

"I can restate. Did you notice anything different about Mr. Atlee's behavior on Friday, September 24th, that was different from his most recent visit?"

"No."

"Nothing at all?"

"Objection, asked and answered."

"Did he ever mention where he was staying or who he was with?"

"Lots of people come in. I don't ask where they live."

"Would you consider Mr. Atlee a close friend?"

"No."

"So, your testimony is that you would treat him like a typical customer?"

"Yeah, sure."

Annaleigh pulled a sheet of paper out of a folder. She held it up for him to see, but did not hand it to him. "I have your statement here, given to Deputy D. Clyde Brothers on the night of the 24th. At that time, you said you allowed Mr. Atlee to use Three Pump's rear exit—the employee exit. Can you explain that?"

"I was busy. Prolly pouring some beers. He asked to take out the trash. So, I let him."

Tap.

"Do you permit all your usual customers into the employee-only, restricted kitchen to access the rear exit?"

"No, I—"

"But you let Mr. Atlee?"

"Yes, but—"

"Are you still sticking with your classification of Mr. Atlee as a typical customer, then?"

"Objection, badgering."

"Did Kenneth ever come in with others?"

"No."

"Never? Not even once?"

"I don't remember."

Tap.

"Your testimony is that Kenneth Roy Atlee drank alone on every visit to your bar?"

"He could have. I don't babysit. I serve the drinks, lady."

"Let's assume he never arrived with anyone. Did you overhear conversations he might have had with anyone that he met there?"

"Nope."

Tap. Tap. Tap.

"You can't remember if you saw him come in with anyone, but you're positive that you never heard conversations?"

"Objection, badgering."

"Pointing out the inconsistencies in testimony is *not* badgering, Hoover."

"It's Mr. Hoover, remember? I thought this situation called for decorum, no? And, yes, it's badgering if you use *that* emotional tone with him."

"What? Are you serious?" She smacked the table with her palm. "This is ridiculous—"

"Mr. Reed," John interrupted, placing a hand on Annaleigh's arm, "think carefully. Did you ever hear Mr. Atlee mention the word Potentia?"

"I've never heard that word before in my life."

Annaleigh shot a glance at John—a mixture of confusion and surprise. She didn't need his help. Yet, at the same time, Reed had just answered a question with the most coherent sentence of the entire session.

Maybe John asked an oddball question to throw him off?

John pressed against the table, glaring all around Reed's head for a few seconds. She opened her mouth to continue her questioning, but John kept talking.

"Fair enough, Mr. Reed. Did you perhaps hear Mr. Atlee mention other words that you hadn't heard before?"

"No, not really. We didn't talk that much."

John looked in, then smiled. "Mr. Reed, we have depositions lined up with many other patrons of your bar. Any idea if they'll tell us you had conversations with Mr. Atlee?"

"Objection, speculation."

"Hoover," John said firmly. "Your interruptions are appreciated but unnecessary. There's no judge here and no audience for your little performance. Also, Mr. Reed is not your client, so unless there are actual privilege issues with the man you do represent, we'd appreciate it if you sit there and shut up." Hoover's lips parted, but John interrupted. "No—watch and listen. Your only tasks. Sound good?"

Silence fell over the room again. Annaleigh's cheeks reddened as she wished she had been the one to say it.

"Fine," Hoover said, sinking into his chair. "But I'll reserve a motion to strike this entire line of questioning for the trial record."

"More power to you. Now, Mr. Reed, if we ask your other patrons whether you've ever had conversations with Mr. Atlee, will they give us a different answer?"

"Whatever, man. They probably will."

She side-eyed John, frowning. She had assumed Broden was lying... John, however, acted as if he knew. His questions were too confident—almost unnatural. On the other side of John, Sarah's eyes smiled at him and lingered, like a needle in Annaleigh's side.

Was she losing this case to him—or losing him to her?

"Would you like to change your testimony, then?" John asked, maintaining the pressure.

"Uh... fine, we would talk. But he didn't say anything I didn't understand. I'm not stupid."

"Understood," John continued. "Tell us about some of the words he said to you that you did understand, then."

"Forest," Reed muttered.

"Please speak up so everyone can hear you. Did you say 'forest'? What does that mean?"

"I don't know, he would say that sometimes. Like, instead of saying goodbye, he and this guy would say they'd meet *at the forest*? I don't know why."

John studied Reed's face, then offered a head tilt.

"*At* the forest? Not *in* the forest? That's what he said? Those exact words?"

"Did I stutter?"

"Have you ever been to the forest? The place Mr. Atlee would talk about?"

"No."

John's head jutted back, as if he heard something unexpected.

"So, this guy, the one who met with Mr. Atlee, would you recognize him if you saw him again?"

"Sure."

John pulled a folder from under his legal pad, opened it, and then pulled out a sheet of paper. He rotated it and slid it across the table to Reed. "I'm showing you a photo lineup. There are eight pictures there. Take your time and look at each one—do any look familiar as to the man Mr. Atlee interacted with at Three Pump?"

Annaleigh examined the upside-down lineup. She saw photos of a variety of men, from their thirties to their fifties, some rugged and weathered, others neat and well-groomed.

Criminals, probably.

On the bottom row, however... one headshot looked different

— a younger man with a familiar face. She shot John a wide-eyed look. He shook his head silently, pleading with a look she understood as one to let things unfold.

Reed tapped the sheet, his fingertip smashing onto the younger man's picture. "This guy."

A confused expression crossed John's face. "Let's address each issue one by one. You're sure this is the man you saw talking to Mr. Atlee at your bar?"

"Yeah."

"Let the record reflect the witness identified photo number six from the array. And, Mr. Reed, you saw them talking on more than one occasion?"

"A few times."

John squinted. "Mr. Reed, how many times would you say is a few? Please remember our other scheduled depositions with your patrons, and we'll ask them the same question."

Reed shrugged. "A few times a week for at least a year. Maybe more. Like I said, I serve drinks, and they don't tip if I'm spying on them."

"Do you know the name of this man?"

"No."

"This man has frequented your bar a few times a week for at least a year, and you've never spoken with him? Never got his name?"

"I told you, no. He's a little dipshit kid. Looks full of himself. Rarely orders drinks, too. Which means he don't tip, neither."

"Have you ever been arrested, Mr. Reed?"

"Once."

"And when was that?"

"Prolly twenty years ago, man. I don't have the exact date for you, if you're gonna ask. Did shots with this crazy chick right before closing, then wrapped my pickup around a tree. If you want more, go ask the damn Sheriff. He's the one who got me."

"Excellent, thank you so much. I appreciate your honesty and your patience throughout the constant interruptions." His eyes flicked to Hoover, who glared back. "Annaleigh? Do we have anything else for this witness?"

"No, I think we're done here," she said, splaying her palms. She thanked the court reporter and stood, causing John and Sarah to follow her.

The report quickly packed her equipment and left, with Reed following behind.

Hoover walked to the door, then spun around. "I don't know what kind of law you practice here in Coldwater, Annaleigh—but you'd be glad we're not back in Cobb. My judges would throw out this entire depo."

Annaleigh scoffed. "Your judges? Maybe that's why you won, then? You can't stack the deck here, Hoover. Prepare yourself for an unbiased judge, for once. And then we'll see how things go."

Hoover tongued his gums and shot back with a sly grin. "Until then." He slid out the doorway and out of sight.

Sarah, who had been quietly observing at the end of the table, smacked John on the shoulders and then tightly gripped his forearm, shaking it. "Oh my God, that was awesome! You totally had his number! It's like, you knew exactly when he was holding back and when he was lying. Phenomenal!"

"What can I say?" John said, squirming a little and looking at Annaleigh. "He... uh, had a tell. I picked up on it."

"You'll have to teach me that one. I need to learn this new superpower of yours."

Annaleigh shot Sarah a sidelong look. "Superpower?"

"Yeah," she said, eyes wide. "Remind me not to play poker with this guy."

Annaleigh gathered her things. "Sarah, would you mind heading upstairs? I want to have a quick word with John."

"Sure, see you both in a bit!"

After Sarah hurried away, Annaleigh moved over to the door and shut it.

"Can we talk about what happened?"

"With Sarah? I think she was excited, I promise you, there is nothing going on—"

"No, it's about you jumping in during the deposition."

"Oh, about that. Look, I had a hunch he was lying and—"

"Is that why you kept kicking me? Between that and Hoover's objections, it was pretty distracting."

"I'm sorry. I saw you get a little upset, and I thought approaching Reed from a different angle might help."

"It worked," she said, shrugging. "I trust your gut, John, I do. I just wish we had talked about it beforehand."

"I know, but I didn't realize I was going to do it until it happened. I'm sorry, you have to believe me."

"You prepared a lineup, John. That's a detective move, not a lawyer one. It's clear you had some idea of it beforehand."

"I had an idea, but only planned to use it as a last resort. I wasn't trying to steal your thunder."

"I know I don't cuss that often, but what the *fuck*, John? You put a deputy's picture in the photo array? Let me say that again... you put Cason Foley—a Coldwater deputy—in the photo array? When Parnell finds out, he's gonna be furious."

"I know, but I'll handle that later. But, still... Reed chose him. Can you believe it? *Reed picked him out.* Foley's been suspicious from the start. I knew it."

"No, you were jealous of him from the start, thinking he and I had history. But, still, if he's hanging out with Kenneth, then he's at least shady."

"And suspended."

"You still need to tell the Sheriff. He needs to know."

"I will, but not quite yet. I need to approach this carefully. Right now, we know something that Foley—and Kenneth—don't. Maybe we can turn this info into something more useful for the trial."

"I'll admit, you were pretty good. He was pissed at first, but you cracked him. You're also going to make me agree with Sarah, too. You knew which buttons to push. God, John, you always find new ways to impress me. By the way, I saw you were keeping score on your notepad." She reached out, playfully grabbing his forearm. "Let me see the final tally."

"Nope, no," he said, hiding the legal pad behind his back. "Look, I, uh, stopped keeping track—"

"After Hoover got to me?"

"Those little hashmarks don't matter. And impressing you is a good result, but I'd be happy to see Kenneth burn for everything he's done."

"Maybe you can do more than that, John. Not only do I want to see Kenneth put away, but I also wouldn't mind hanging a big fat loss around the neck of Bradly *fricking* Hoover. So, why don't we split duties? I'll open and close, but... you take the crosses. See if that new superpower of yours works on everyone."

14

FACING THE TRAITOR

John's boots stomped across dewy grass, lungs burning.

Backyards blurred past in the darkness of night—chain-link fences, plastic kiddie pools, forgotten tricycles tipped on their sides. Kenneth somehow stayed ten yards ahead, coat flapping, never quite close enough to catch.

John vaulted another fence and landed hard. He felt the jolt start in his knees and reverberate up his spine.

Get going! Move! You can't stop now!

Up ahead, Kenneth rounded the corner of a brick ranch house. John pushed harder, breath ragged, his peripheral vision narrowing onto the dark shape ahead.

He slid around the same corner.

Annaleigh stood there.

Alone.

His head moved left and right, desperately searching for Kenneth. If he's still here, she's in danger. Calm dominated the area. No other sounds except his labored breathing.

Moonlight illuminated her face. She opened her mouth to speak, but no sound emerged. Instead, flames ignited from her throat—slowly at first, then surging outward in a blazing white wave. Her eyes became beams of light as the fire burned within her. It radiated and spread, consuming her hair, crawling down her arms and legs.

She didn't scream. She couldn't.

She stood there and burned.

John reached out—fingers clawing at the air—but the heat pushed him back. Annaleigh's knees buckled as if her bones had turned to melting wax. She didn't lower herself, but dissolved downward, collapsing to the ground in a confused heap.

She reached out to him, silently pleading for help. He surged through the heat and grasped for her, only to have his hand go right through her. He'd impaled her liquefying body with his fist.

His whole world turned orange, then black.

He bolted upright in bed, his chest heaving and hands soaked with sweat. The room was dark except for the clock's faint glow.

3:14 a.m.

He twisted, craning his neck to see past his shadowed peripheral vision. He lay in Annaleigh's bedroom. He smelled her lavender shampoo and the cedar candle she'd lit earlier. His body felt like he'd fallen asleep minutes ago, even though he distinctly remembered sliding into bed next to her shortly after midnight.

No rest for the wicked.

His heart still hammered as if he'd been running for miles. Annaleigh stirred beside him, her voice thick with sleep.

"John?"

He didn't respond immediately. He sat there, zoning out at the wall, waiting for the flames to stop flickering in his mind. She sat up, her hand finding his back. Her fingers moved in gentle circles between his shoulder blades—soft and patient.

"You're shaking," she murmured.

John forced out a laugh that sounded more like a cough. "Just... tired."

Annaleigh moved closer, her cheek resting against his shoulder. "You're the only man I know who's so tired he keeps waking himself up in the middle of the night."

"Perks of the job." He rubbed his face with both hands.

"It wouldn't have anything to do with deciding to do two full-time jobs at once, would it? Both of which require eons of extra work to *really* be good at."

"Is that your way of saying I'm dogshit... times two?"

She didn't laugh and kept rubbing his back. "I know you thought it would be easy," she said quietly. "After the mess Mumber left, you assumed you could step in, clean house, prove Parnell right—that you'd be a good detective from the moment he pinned the badge on you."

John exhaled through his nose. "Something like that."

"It's more than just solving puzzles—"

"I know, it's also sitting in a car for five hours every night, watching things not move."

Annaleigh pulled back slightly to look at him. Her serious expression contained no trace of teasing.

"You can make light of it if you want, but most people can truly only be great at one thing, John. Really great. If they split that focus, maybe a few can be half-good at both. Or maybe they're dogshit at both—your words, not mine. But, honey, it's almost impossible to be exceptional at both."

He met her eyes. She didn't blink.

"You can be a great lawyer, John," she said. "Maybe one of the best. Not better than me, but I know you have the potential to come pretty dang close." She pinched her fingers together, teasing for a brief moment. "But, you have to trust yourself enough to jump in with both feet. Maybe stop trying to carry everything at once."

John looked down at his hands—they felt warm, still from the dream, maybe. He flexed his fingers, half expecting fire to spark. Annaleigh reached over and covered his hand with hers.

"Hey, look at me. You don't have to prove anything to anyone," she said. "Not Parnell. Not Clyde. Not even me. But, you might be happier if you just... choose. And then go all in." She leaned in, kissed his temple, then his cheek. "Now try to sleep. We've got to get up in a few hours."

John eased back down. Annaleigh curled against him, her head on his chest. He stared at the ceiling, listening to her even breaths.

He didn't sleep.

But for the first time in weeks, the weight on his chest felt a little less like guilt.

And a little more like choice.

* * *

JOHN SAT on a park bench in the grassy area north of the courthouse, arms crossed, patiently waiting for Cason Foley.

Foley shocked John by actually agreeing to meet, especially since John had not revealed the conversation's purpose. The deputy only had two conditions—a public place and a neutral party in attendance.

"For your protection," Foley had boasted.

John checked his watch. Noon. He scanned the area and saw two men approaching from the east side of the square.

Cason Foley led the duo across the street, skipping the well-worn path and walking on the grass toward John's location. He stopped about eight feet from the bench.

"You ready to apologize for getting me suspended?" Foley barked.

"If that's what you expected from this, you're going to be disappointed," John said, standing. He looked at the other person. "Didn't expect you to be Foley's protector."

Dallas Taggart held up his hands, bushy red hair waving back and forth in the wind as he shook his head. "Hey, man, I'm just a third party here. I'm on nobody's side."

"Says the guy who arrived with one of the sides."

"Read into that if you want," Dallas explained. "But, so what if I wanted to stay in touch with him until he got off suspension? It's a free world."

"Can we get this over with?" Foley asked, annoyed. "If you're not here to apologize, then there's no reason to stay." He turned to leave.

"I had an interesting deposition yesterday," John said. "Broden Reed. You know him?"

Foley stopped, turning back slowly. "Sure. I've arrested him a couple times."

"Really," John said, crossing his arms. "That's how?"

"Scout's honor." Foley held up his middle finger. "I remember making fun of his name during booking. He defended himself, saying that when he was born, his mother wrote his name down wrong on his birth certificate. Twenty hours of labor and sleep-deprived, or something. So, that's why he's Broden, instead of Braden."

John's mouth dropped open. "That's the more carefully crafted lie I've ever heard. Somebody's protesting a bit too hard, you think? I know it's not from arresting him."

"Is that so?"

"He's under oath, saying he saw you at Three Pump. As a patron. A lot."

"He's as good a liar as his mom was at spelling. He's wrong."

The lie slipped out, and the air around Foley's ears shimmered with a brief plum haze, then vanished instantly.

"So, you're saying I should charge him with perjury? Got proof to back that up?"

"You want me to prove I *wasn't* somewhere?"

John jabbed at Foley through the air. "I think the simpler answer is... *you're* lying."

"Whoa, now," Dallas interjected. "Let's take this down a notch. It's one guy's word against the other, isn't it?"

"No... it's really not," John stammered. "You don't know what I know."

Foley advanced. "So, you have more than the word of a bartender?"

John's lips curled into a smile as his cheeks lifted. "I never said he was a bartender, Cason."

"I… uh, knew because… he mentioned it during booking."

John saw it again. A translucent purple flare, formless, radiating outward then collapsing inward, gone. "Wow, you guys sure talked a lot, then. You two got pretty close over fingerprints and mugshots? I'm sure his arrest record will have your name on it, if I checked?"

Foley's brow furrowed. "So, this is why you wanted to meet? To accuse me of knowing some idiot?"

"Not exactly." John deliberated how to present his next accusation. "It's not that you know Broden, it's who Broden said you met with at Three Pump."

Foley's eyes widened. His lips pressed together. He cracked his knuckles. His weight shifted onto the balls of his feet, fists clenched. Monotonous words filtered through gritted teeth.

"What… did that asshole… say?"

Dallas stepped forward, acting as a buffer.

"Well," John said, "he told us you met with someone that, until very recently, we didn't know where he was."

A swallow dripped down Foley's throat.

"A three-month manhunt, completely wasted." John's voice rose. "Working day and night, busting my ass… when all I had to do was ask you."

"I don't know what you're talking about," Foley said, dipping his head.

"Of course you do, Cason. You're not a stupid man—well, maybe."

Foley lunged. "Shut your—"

Dallas stretched out an arm and caught him. "Cason? What is he saying? Who were you talking to?"

"Tell him," John taunted. "Tell him who you've been sneaking around with, in the dark, over whiskey. See if he switches sides."

"You motherf—"

"It's Atlee!" John yelled, causing everyone to halt suddenly.

Dallas panned to Foley. Foley stood still, huffing.

John continued. "That's right, Kenneth Roy Atlee. You've been meeting him, planning God knows what. Under all our noses!"

Dallas lowered his arms as Foley drew back. "Is that true, Cason? You've been meeting with Kenneth... er, Mr. Atlee, at Three Pump?"

"This is bullshit," Foley muttered. He paced back and forth. "Pure bullshit."

"Then deny it, man," John said. "Because all I've heard so far is deflections."

"Fine—I deny it."

The lie sparked a fleeting lilac halo, shapeless and trembling, then disappeared. It caused John to grin, which only made Foley angrier.

"Quit smiling, dickhead." He held out his wrists. "You wanna cuff me? Go ahead and try it. See what happens."

John shook his head. "I can't arrest you for talking to someone, as fun as that would be. But, once the Sheriff finds out, that whole *administrative review* on your deputy's career might not turn out in your favor."

Foley offered a wry smile. "Do it."

"Wait... you want me to do it?"

"Go ahead. Run to Parnell and tell on me. It'll be the end of everything."

"Is that a threat?"

"No, it's a fact that you'd know if you ever spent time at the station. Parnell's on thin ice with the state after what happened. Losing a deputy and a detective in a breakout doesn't look so good."

"You're the one who let Wesley out, so whatever trouble Parnell's in is on you."

"If he loses another deputy, they'll shut down the whole department, and the State Troopers will step in and take control. You can kiss your little detective job goodbye."

"You can't bluff your way out of this, Foley—I'll gather

enough proof to put you in a cell next to Kenneth, and you both can fry—"

Foley lunged at John again, catching Dallas flat-footed. John expected it, though.

He spun to avoid Foley's fist and yanked on his upper arm. Foley lost his balance and wobbled. John charged forward and tackled Foley face-first to the grass. John knelt on Foley's back, pushing on the back of his head while Taggart tried to knock him off.

The wail of a siren permeated the air as Sheriff Parnell's black police cruiser skidded to a stop. He jolted out and yelled with a booming voice.

"Hey! That's enough!"

John rose to his knees, and Foley rolled and sat up, scowling. They both gave each other one last shove before getting to their feet. Foley rubbed at his face, knocking off blades of broken grass and bits of dirt.

Parnell strode over to the group and stood in judgment, hands on hips. "What in the world is going on here? Foley? What are you doing here?"

Foley dusted himself off. "I was just leaving." He glared at John and walked off, heading back east.

"Taggart? How'd you get involved in this mess?"

"Sorry, Sheriff, I've been checking in on Cason while he's out... to make sure he's okay. Thought I could be a middleman."

Parnell removed his hat and looked at Taggart through narrowed eyes. "I appreciate that, son, but I can't have my active deputies communicating with suspended ones. That stops today, you understand?"

"Yessir."

"Good, now head on out. I need a word with Detective Chance."

Dallas nodded and looked at John before heading south, past the courthouse. Parnell waited until Dallas walked completely out of earshot before moving closer to John.

"Ms Stanton called. She thought your little conversation might turn sour. Looks like I got here right on time."

John twisted at the waist, glaring at the upstairs courthouse windows. He knew she meant well, but he didn't need backup.

"I had it handled, sir," John explained. "I heard some damning information in a deposition yesterday... and..."

"And what, young man? You ask questions and argue for a living, so I know you're not tongue-tied."

"It's... I needed to confirm..." Foley's crack about Parnell already being under increased scrutiny from the state made John pause. Maybe he needed to keep the secret for now. "It's nothing, Sheriff. My apologies for dragging you out here. I've got a few leads I'm still following for the trial. We're good."

Parnell adjusted his glasses, looking John over carefully. "You sure, son?"

"Positive."

The Sheriff gave John one last disapproving look, then spun around and headed back to his cruiser. He killed the lights and drove north, toward the station.

John half-regretted not arresting Foley, but perhaps it was better to gather more evidence before charging a fellow member of Parnell's department.

After all, with John's new superpower, he'd be able to extract the truth from anyone, anytime.

15

THE NAME SHE WON'T SAY

John eased himself through his front door, closing it behind him with a deliberate click.

He didn't often come home during the day, but he knew he'd find his mother on the phone, selling yet another property in Coldwater. He strolled through the living room and smelled the lemon polish his mother used in large amounts whenever she was anxious.

It meant one thing—an in-progress deal... and it wasn't going well.

He peeked around the corner and saw her sitting at the kitchen table, her palm resting on her cheek as she stared. MLS printouts littered the surface, and a red pen in her other hand had circled various details of multiple properties.

"Mom... who is he?" he asked, leaning against the doorframe.

Bonnie's shoulders tensed, but she didn't look up. "I thought I heard you come in. Hi, honey."

"Who's my father, Mom?"

"Not even a hello? Sweetheart, we've been over this already. I made a promise a long time ago, and you'll need to respect that."

"Twenty-four years is a long time, Mom. I should rank first, not him."

She finally met his eyes. "It's more complicated than that."

He studied her head. Nothing.

No mist, no shimmer. No colors. Only wisps of her hair, silhouetted in the morning sun that shone through the windows.

Where's the complication? It's a name, not some national secret. Unless it went deeper than that. Maybe she got involved with someone horrible, like Kenneth? Or Mayor Raith?

Oh, God, it's not one of those two, is it?

"What is so complicated about him? Is he dangerous? Did he hurt someone? Is that why he's hiding? Is that why you're protecting him?"

"No, no—he's a good man." Bonnie's shoulders slumped. "Better than most around here."

"So... a good man? That has nothing to do with his son?"

Her voice cracked as she kept speaking. "It's not like that. You've already talked to him. He's someone you've seen a lot since you've been home. He's involved in your life, just in a different way than you'd like."

No glow.

His stomach dropped. "Then, why has he not said anything?" He threw up his hands and shook his head. Almost instinctively, he narrowed his eyes and looked upward. "There's Parnell, Clyde, Baz, Harlan, Gamble, Amos..." He stopped himself, barely noticing a slight shift in her posture. "No," he said to himself, "they're both dead. Maybe it's Mumber?"

He glanced at her after he spoke, observing the space around her head. She put her pen down.

"Annaleigh says you've been staring at people strangely after you ask questions. Like you're waiting for something to happen. You're doing it now... what exactly are you up to?"

He didn't like being called out.

Bonnie lowered her voice. "Whatever you think you're seeing, you won't use it on me like I'm some witness on the stand." She reached across the table for a sheet, and her sleeve caught on something, knocking a short stack of MLS listings to the floor. He bent down, picked them up, and set them back on the table. Her hand grabbed his. "Honey, some secrets aren't mine to tell, and some marriages are still worth protecting."

Oh, shit.

"You two... were married?"

She frowned sympathetically. "No. *He* was."

Double shit.

"I only exist because some asshole cheated on his wife?"

"As I was saying," Bonnie explained softly and evenly, "it's more complicated than that. We had history, but then we grew apart, and he married someone else. Then, later, it went a little too far—"

"Feel free not to bless me with the details of my conception."

She smiled. "Wouldn't dream of it. But know that what he and I did may have been a mistake, but you... you, John Deacon Chance, are not."

John's voice dropped. "He was married." He sank into the seat, desperately trying to process the new information. "All this time, I thought he didn't want me. Turns out you didn't want to blow up someone else's life. Just mine."

Bonnie reached for him, but John shot to his feet.

"He kept choosing that life over me, again and again, for twenty-four years." He spun around to leave. "And left you alone to deal with... the fallout. With me."

"Oh, John, that's not at all—"

"When the trial's over," John interrupted, "this promise ends. If you don't tell me by then, I won't go around asking quietly. I'll start asking loudly—and he won't like what happens then. I'm done waiting."

He left her at the table and thought he heard a soft "John" from her, but it didn't stop him from slamming the front door on his way out. He slid into the seat of his ugly brown detective's car and gripped the door handle, pulling it shut with a loud thud. He smacked the upper ring of the steering wheel with his palm. A loud thump echoed through the car, then a dull pain set in.

He checked the steering wheel—and his palm—for damage. The wheel was fine, but his hand throbbed. He drew a deep breath, exhaling to dull the pain.

Outside his window sat a familiar friend, in a shade of pale green. His Dart didn't get many miles these days. Hearing that twenty-year-old engine turn over comforted John. That car had carried him through a lot—college, law school, and the whole mess that happened when he first came back to Coldwater a few months ago.

Those cold, vinyl seats hugged him, like sitting in your favorite recliner after a long day's work. The detective's cruiser felt... different. After all, he sat in Hollis Mumber's car. That man sat in this car for so long that he got rewarded with early retirement.

He made quite an impression, mostly in driver's side seat cushion. And Mumber's backside was quite a bit bigger than John's.

Nothing felt right.

Not the car, nor that his dad—no, his biological father—chose to stay silent his entire life rather than tell the truth. The affair ended over twenty years ago. A one-time fling that left him sitting in someone else's ugly brown Caprice.

John's middle name, given to him as a reminder of the man who chose someone else.

Deacon.

A stain. A jagged shard that cut deep.

Time to find a way to call out the coward.

16

STARTS, STOPS, AND DISTRACTIONS

"You may call your first witness."

Annaleigh's blood boiled. Her ears rang. She subtly tongued her cheek as Judge Otto Chapel's instructions went unheard.

She silently fumed after hearing Bradley Hoover, defense counsel, speak. He said nothing true in his opening statement. All spin, directed at her, John, and Sheriff Parnell, blaming them for what happened in May.

The events that were entirely the fault of former Mayor Cameron Raith and his son, Wesley.

They were the monsters.

Not her.

Not John.

Yet, Hoover's spin-filled monologue was tempting for the jury to believe. Especially since the rumors of the mayor's supernatural powers had never been confirmed publicly. The town only knew bits and pieces, retellings of snippets from those who saw the mayor fleeing the police.

Additionally, first responders who helped put out the flames at John's house only knew the outcome, not the cause, of Wesley's rampage. They weren't inside to see him proudly display his powers. They arrived too late to witness him conjure flames from his hands and control them at will, at least until his mind spiraled out of control and caused his hands to explode.

The paramedics tended to a kid who, for all they knew, might as well have blown his hands off in a freak fireworks accident that set fire to the Chance's living room.

She knew the truth. She witnessed it.

Bradley Hoover didn't have the slightest idea.

But, judging by the faces staring back at him in the jury box, his attempt to twist reality and depict Kenneth as an innocent bystander caught in a web of retribution had traction with them.

It had already been a battle during pre-trial motions as Hoover requested a mistrial over the contraption the court forced Kenneth to wear on his hands and arms. Judge Chapel disagreed and dismissed the claims of prejudice. Annaleigh knew that those gloves, the tubes, and the miracle FM-200 gas, which extinguished flames as quickly as they ignited, came at the request of the judge himself.

There was no way this trial was going to happen without that mess strapped to the defendant's arms. Nevertheless, Hoover threatened to appeal. Chapel didn't back down. But Hoover's trap had been set. A preview, based on the nonsense coming from Hoover's mouth during his opening, that he intended on turning the trial into a minute-by-minute fight.

Her unnatural hatred of that man was truly going to be her downfall. She felt it in her bones.

She also felt a quick, firm nudge on her arm from John's elbow, snapping her back. She side-eyed him, her brows knitting in confusion. He responded with wide eyes and nodded toward the judge's bench. Her eyes moved upward and met Chapel's.

"Ms. Stanton... your witness?"

She swallowed and tried to mentally estimate how long she had been drifting. She blinked, completely exiting her daze, and focused on Judge Chapel looking down the bridge of his nose at her.

"Annaleigh?" John whispered softly in her ear.

She quickly stood up and adjusted her suit jacket. "Apologies, Your Honor. The prosecution calls Sheriff Dane Parnell to the stand."

As Sheriff Parnell rose from his seat in the gallery and headed toward the witness stand, John grabbed her hand.

"You okay?"

"Yes, I'm fine," she replied in a low tone, leaning in towards him.

While Parnell sat to be sworn in by Baz, John tried to get her attention again. "Babe—"

"I'm fine, John," she whispered back, pulling her hand away. "I've got this."

I hate lying to him. But now's not the time. Time to focus.

She slid out from behind their attorney's table and walked to the witness chair. "Please state your name and occupation for the court," she said, calmly.

"Dane Parnell, Sheriff of Coldwater County."

"Sheriff, when did you first meet the defendant, Kenneth Roy Atlee?"

"Don't have a specific date for that, but we were kids. At this point, it's been well over forty years, I think."

Annaleigh moved toward the jury box, settling at the end. Her position made Parnell turn in his chair, facing the jurors directly, a common tactic she used when she wanted an examination to feel more like a conversation.

"Were there other children in your friend group, Sheriff?"

As Bradley Hoover stood, he scooted his chair back with a screech. "Objection, Your Honor. What's the relevance here? Ancient history has no bearing on my client's current charges." He paused, then flicked a glance at her. "I'll ignore the leading question, by the way."

"Foundation, Judge," Annaleigh explained to Chapel. "Because of the witness's prior experience with the defendant, he has a four-decade skill in describing state of mind and motive."

Chapel moved his chin up and down, then pointed to the defense table. "Overruled." As Hoover sat down, Chapel's focus shifted back to Annaleigh. "But, let's not dwell too long covering the mid-century, understood?"

"Yes, Your Honor."

"You may answer the question, Sheriff," Chapel said.

"I'm sure it's well known, but we had a third member in our group, former Mayor Cameron Raith."

"And," Annaleigh continued, "what is the current state of Mayor Raith?"

"He's deceased, ma'am. Three months ago. Single car accident after fleeing from—"

"Objection." Hoover rose again, stopping Parnell's testimony mid-sentence. "Both on relevance and that this line of questioning assumes facts not in evidence. Cameron Raith was never charged with a crime, and even if he had been before his *convenient* death, his actions are irrelevant to these proceedings."

Annaleigh drew a deep breath.

Of course, this is his strategy. Rattle me. Interrupt me. Just like the deposition. Need to stay on point. I don't need John to save me this time. I can handle Hoover. I can handle Hoover. I can handle Hoover.

Chapel bit his lip, looking upward. "I understand your intent, Counselor. But, usually, in my court, I give some leeway to a witness's initial testimony before I start closing doors. If something prejudicial comes up, I'll reconsider. Overruled, for now. I promise to provide you the same leeway, as able."

"Understood, Your Honor," Hoover said.

"Ms. Stanton, you may continue, but let's be cautious about diving into that particular end of the pool."

"Of course, Judge," she said. "Sheriff, describe the nature of the prior relationship between Mr. Atlee, Mr. Raith, and yourself."

"Sure," Parnell drawled and glanced in Kenneth's direction. "Back then, we were inseparable. We used to ride our bikes everywhere—that's what helped me learn every nook and cranny of this town. But, even then, Kenneth tended to gravitate more toward Cameron than me. Don't know why. It's not something I can put my finger on, but even so, the three of us stayed close through high school, then we all enlisted and got deployed. First time we really were separated."

"Can you describe Kenneth's role in your childhood group?"

"From a young age, Kenneth was naturally bigger than most kids in town. He often played the enforcer role, keeping everyone in line, not just me and Cam. Big and quiet. He'd throw out a fancy word every now and then, like he just read it in a book and wanted to show off. I was the rule-follower. Kenneth, the muscle. Cameron, the brains. Always scheming plans."

Annaleigh chuckled. "You make it sound like you kids were out robbing banks." She flashed her smile to the jurors, locking eyes with them for a moment. They returned her smile.

"No, no," Parnell said, waving a hand. "Nothing like that. Just our personalities back then."

"Does that description still fit the defendant today?"

"Objection," Hoover shouted, not even bothering to stand up from his chair. "Speculation."

"The Sheriff of this town can absolutely have an opinion about members of his community, Your Honor," Annaleigh huffed, fighting to contain her glare toward her nemesis. "Especially since he has a basis from which to make an apt comparison."

"Overruled."

"Sheriff?" Annaleigh asked. "Does that description still fit?"

"It sure does. Kenneth always knew how to make things happen without saying a lot. Most of us are not too far from where we started back then."

"Describe your relationship with the defendant today."

"Distant. Been that way for years. Especially since... Evelyn."

"For the court record, who is this Evelyn you are referring to?"

"Evelyn Raith, Cameron's wife."

"And, what about her caused this distance?"

"It's the worst-kept secret in all of Coldwater, and it centers around her disappearance. Cameron—and Kenneth—insist she left town suddenly and abandoned her family. Others aren't so sure."

"Did you suspect foul play?"

"Objection. She's leading her own witness, Your Honor."

Before Chapel ruled, Annaleigh spoke. "I'll rephrase, Judge. Based on your investigation, what conclusions did you draw?"

Chapel nodded, allowing it.

"It wasn't a complete investigation," Parnell explained, "but with what I was able to do, I suspected foul play. I couldn't find anyone who saw her pack. No one saw her drive away. I couldn't find a single person to confirm their side of the story. After additional research, I found no financial transactions in her name since we last saw her. No home purchases, rent applications, or credit cards. Nothing. I even checked using her maiden name—Mallet. But, no results."

Hoover lumbered again to his feet. "Your Honor, how long are we going to entertain this completely irrelevant line of questioning?"

Annaleigh's hands splayed outward. "Not an actual objection, is it, defense counsel?" She spun towards the judge. "I'm almost done, Your Honor. I assure you, it's leading to a point. It's hard to make that point when I'm interrupted every other question."

"Go ahead, Ms. Stanton. I'm sure you'll conclude it and move on momentarily, won't you?"

"Absolutely, Your Honor. Sheriff, why would your investigation into Evelyn Raith's disappearance affect your relationship with the defendant?"

"Because he—and Cameron—disagreed with my... take on the situation. They didn't think an investigation was necessary. Told me not-so-politely to stop digging around. Officially, the case is still open, but cold. Unofficially..."—he made eye contact with Kenneth—"I've never stopped looking for her."

"Thank you, Sheriff. After Cameron Raith's death in May of this year, did you know the defendant's whereabouts?"

"Initially, he was at his cabin on the Raith property. As we had an arrest warrant for him, I sent two of my deputies to bring him in. He evaded them and escaped. He was then on the run until his capture and arrest."

"Can you elaborate on how he evaded, to use your term?"

"He blinded my deputy with a bright light, then ran into the woods."

"What type of light?"

Parnell shifted in his seat and swallowed. "Bright as the sun, but it didn't come from a flashlight. It came from his hands—"

Hoover leapt to his feet. "Sidebar!"

Her shoulders drooped as she narrowed her eyes at him. Both attorneys approached the bench and leaned in towards Chapel.

"I move—again—for a mistrial," Hoover argued softly. "The prosecution's questions are both highly irregular and completely prejudicial. Now she's got her witness spouting statements tantamount to magic spells. I mean, at the very least, it's hearsay. Regardless, combined with the ridiculous gear my client is forced to wear, this entire trial seems to be rigged in her favor."

Chapel's eyes shifted to Annaleigh and waited silently for her reply.

"Your Honor, what's irregular is the ongoing disruptions from the defense. You haven't sustained a single objection yet. He's performing for the jury, like in his opening statement."

Chapel pursed his lips and squinted. "First off," he said softly, "request for mistrial is denied. Take caution in your accusations, Counsel. Saying it's rigged in the prosecution's favor means I am the one doing the rigging." He flashed a scold in Hoover's direction. "I assure you, the playing field is level—as it always is and will be in my courtroom. As I have said before, I will issue jury instructions to address your concerns regarding the equipment. Second, whether I sustain or overrule any objection is my judgment, Ms. Stanton. Not yours. Lastly, if you have problems with his opening, I suggest you disprove his statements by proving your own case. Now, can we get back to it?"

Dual "Yes, Your Honor" whispers exited from both counsels as they turned to return to their table. Within a few steps, Hoover veered into her path, lightly brushing her shoulder with his.

"Still can't play fair? Whining to the judge about my opening? You're not still that emotional little girl you were in Cobb, are you? Step it up if you want to beat me."

She froze as he pivoted away, leaving her alone in the well. A surge of adrenaline coursed through her. By her side, she squeezed her fists to prevent her fingers from trembling.

Damn him—turning everything into a battlefield.

She glanced at John and Sarah and received supportive looks. "You got this," John mouthed. With a quick tilt of her head, she turned to face Sheriff Parnell.

"Sheriff, to clarify, you said light emitted from his hands. That's pretty hard to believe, isn't it? Can you explain that to the court, please?"

"I'm not sure I can, ma'am. I'm not sure I have the words. All I know is that without anything in his hands, he almost blinded my deputy, then used that distraction to escape arrest."

Hoover stood. "Your Honor, I renew my objection to hearsay. You didn't actually rule on that during our sidebar. He's only relaying what his deputy saw. If she wants that on the record, she can call him to the stand."

Judge Chapel looked at Annaleigh, speaking deliberately. "Sustained."

"We'll move on, Sheriff. Speaking of his evasion, during his three months on the run, did Kenneth show signs of having a support network?"

"It wasn't long before tips dried up quickly, almost like he had eyes everywhere. We had heard he was hiding in plain sight, frequenting spots like the bar, Three Pump. That's where we initially found him, but he dodged arrest there as well. If someone was tipping him off, well, I don't put too much stock in that.

Kenneth? He's not the type to build alliances. That's Cameron's old playbook. Ken probably just intimidates folks into silence. The only respect he ever got was because of his size, not 'cuz he earned it, but he still complained. I don't think too many others agreed."

"Objection," Hoover said dramatically. "Hearsay. Again. The witness can't speak for my client."

"Your Honor, this is an out-of-court statement, offered for truth."

Chapel thought briefly before ruling. "Overruled, but narrowly. Since it's a party admission, and that party is the defendant, I'll allow it. I'm sure defense can address it via cross or when counsel presents its defense."

A thin smile curled on Annaleigh's lips before she wiped it away. Hoover mumbled, "Of course, Judge," then sat back down.

"Sheriff, let's focus on the defendant's eventual arrest. Please explain what led up to that event."

"Our detective received a tip. We tracked it down and found the defendant hiding in a warehouse, next to a ring of flames. We were able to make the arrest without incident."

"Did you observe anything about the defendant's physical state during the arrest?"

"I had my detectives cuff him in front, and as he did, I happened to notice scars on both of his wrists."

"Can you describe these scars in more detail?"

"From my experience, they were burn scars. I was pretty familiar with them, based on the autopsy of Cameron Raith and the arrest of Wesley Raith. Both of those two individuals had the same marks."

"Were you able to determine the cause of Mr. Atlee's scars?"

"They didn't appear to be recent, but usually those scars come from playing with fire—and having it strike back."

"You mentioned Wesley Raith had the same scars. Please tell us more about that."

"Sure, the young Raith boy also had scars around his wrists. In fact, they went all the way up his arms."

"During your investigation, were you able to identify the source of Wesley's scars?"

"We believe most of them came from the activity at the Chance household, when he took Bonnie Chance hostage and displayed some... unusual behavior."

"What kind of behavior?"

"Our official report states that the boy was able to, um, conjure fire around his hands and control it."

Gasps echoed through the courtroom. A random laugh started, then stopped abruptly. Judge Chapel pounded his gavel and called for silence. After a few moments, he nodded for Annaleigh to continue.

"Was there anything similar to the events your deputy witnessed?"

"Young Mr. Raith's hands glowed and shined like flashlights when it happened. We saw that same light inside the Mayor's Blazer while he was fleeing. And, at the defendant's cabin, while executing the arrest warrant. I don't know how to explain it, but when they do the fire thing with their hands, the light seems to be a side effect."

"Objection," Hoover said, overenunciating the word. "The witness is drawing a conclusion—a conclusion I fear might require experts in physics, flames, and even reality to refute. I can't provide an adequate defense if I'm expected to prove or disprove the existence of magic, Your Honor."

"Judge," Annaleigh explained, "the witness is testifying to events he either witnessed or that are documented in official county records. He's drawing no conclusions that aren't already publicly available."

Judge Chapel leaned back in his chair, steepling his hands. He turned to Hoover. "I'm inclined to allow it if he's describing observed behavior. Unless you have legal objections to that?"

"Never mind, objection withdrawn. Let her dig this hole. I can tear it apart in cross, anyway."

"Your Honor!" Annaleigh's hands flared out.

"Now, now," Chapel said, gaveling again. "Let's keep everything civil. That means both of you. Now, Ms. Stanton, please continue."

She clenched her teeth. This was going swimmingly. She'd had defense attorneys before that tried to get under her skin. None of them had succeeded. Hoover wouldn't be the first.

"Sheriff, can you describe—what you saw—in the defendant's demeanor at the time of his arrest?" She side-eyed Hoover halfway through the question, expecting a trivial objection. None came.

"He was calm, almost grinning... like he'd won something. One of the most unusual arrests in my career."

"Did the defendant make any utterances after being read his rights?"

"That's part of what made the whole situation unusual. The defendant waived his rights. You don't see that every day. Then, he muttered something strange after we got him into the squad car."

"What did he say?"

"A single word—*potentia*. He shouted it through the closed window of a patrol cruiser with an eerie smile. At the time, I didn't know what it meant, but I knew it wasn't English. Still, the way he said it, I saw it as threatening."

"Objection, Your Honor. What's the relevance here? Speaking in a different language is not a threatening act."

"Judge," Annaleigh explained, "it's a statement made by the defendant after waiving his right to remain silent, regardless of the language. Seems pretty textbook to me."

Chapel nodded. "I agree. Overruled. Continue, Ms. Stanton."

"In your investigation, did you find a meaning to that word?"

"Took me a while and a visit up to Mineral Area College to talk to an English professor. Apparently, it's Latin."

"And, in that research, did you determine what it translates to?"

"It means *power*."

"What do you think he meant by that?"

"Objection," Hoover interrupted. "The witness can't possibly know what was in my client's mind during any utterance."

"This one I'll sustain," Chapel said, much too quickly for Annaleigh to refute. "Ms. Stanton, please rephrase or move on."

"Of course, Your Honor. Sheriff, what do you understand that word to mean, in the context of the arrest?"

"I'm not sure. The word power can mean many things, but it is something the defendant had previously said he wanted. Why he said it in Latin, I don't know. He's a fighter, sure. Maybe it means physical power, like strength. But when I think of power... now that was more Cameron's style. Like him or not, he might have run the ship onto the shore, but he had no trouble steering. The defendant was more of an order-follower than a leader. Honestly, I think it was meant to sound intimidating. Maybe he didn't even know what it meant and saw it somewhere. I wasn't too worried about what he said, though. He got arrested for what he did."

"Thank you, Sheriff." She shifted her attention to Judge Chapel. "No more questions."

Chapel turned toward the defense table. "Mr. Hoover, are you ready for your cross-examination?"

"Absolutely." He rose and strode into the well as Annaleigh sat. Her heart rate felt elevated, and she hid her hands under the table after rubbing her mouth.

She didn't dare lose focus, though. She withstood Hoover's interruptions during her questioning. He was about to find out she could dish it, too. She ignored John's tap and light squeeze on her leg. She itched to object to anything questionable in Hoover's exam—a wrong word, a mistimed stutter, or even the wrong kind of inflection.

Let's see how he likes his own strategy used on him.

Hoover stayed close to his table, prompting Parnell to answer his questions while facing away from the jury.

"So, Sheriff Parnell, it's your testimony that you never saw Kenneth as capable of leading?"

"It's not what I saw," Parnell said, shrugging. "It's how he was."

"Makes you wonder why we're here today, then, doesn't it? My client is charged with a whole list of things, but according to your own testimony, he's not capable?"

Parnell tongued the inside of his cheek, thinking deeply before answering. "You don't need to know how a car works to drive it. But when you turn the key, you're the one who started it. Being capable of leading is different from being capable of doing. That's why your client is here — because he did the doing."

"Sheriff, I would advise you to answer the question concisely and not elaborate beyond what I ask."

Annaleigh shot up from her seat. "Objection—he's badgering my witness. If the defense doesn't like the answer, he's free to ask more tailored questions."

Hoover waved a hand in the air. "Withdrawn, Your Honor. Sheriff, you testify that you were once childhood friends with the defendant, but you're not now. Is it common for you to arrest anyone you believe has wronged you in the past?"

"I wouldn't characterize it like that—"

"Yes or no, please."

"That's not really a yes or no question. I arrest people who have committed—"

"I'll move on. These so-called lights you mentioned. You weren't there to see them?"

"My deputy was there—"

"But you yourself were not?"

"No."

"And, these scars you say you saw on my client's wrist. There are many different ways someone could obtain scars like that, wouldn't you say?"

"In theory, but in this case—"

"Would you say it's infinite? An infinite number of possibilities?"

"I don't know about infinite, Counselor—"

"It might as well be infinite. Unless you can prove how he got them?"

"Let's get him up here and ask him, shall we?"

"Your Honor," Hoover said, "the witness is being unresponsive."

Chapel held back a grin. "You asked the question. Move on."

"Fine. The primary charge against my client is arson. Yet, you haven't presented evidence of that today, have you?"

Parnell looked at Annaleigh. "It's my understanding that Ms. Stanton will—"

"But apparently not today, eh? And not with the top law enforcement officer in the county? Let me get this straight. You used to know the defendant, but don't anymore. You weren't present when he allegedly shone a flashlight at your deputy. Big crime there. You saw some scars on his wrist that may or may not match someone else's, but you don't know how he got them. You've placed a lot of importance on a single, irrelevant word. And you've brought no evidence to support your charges. I'm afraid you may have wasted the court's time today, Sheriff." Annaleigh leapt out of her seat, but Hoover cut off her objection. "Withdrawn, Your Honor. Nothing more for this witness."

"Redirect, Judge?" Annaleigh asked, already heading into the well. Chapel waved her on.

"Sheriff, defense is suggesting the scars on the defendant's hands are completely unrelated to the same marks on the wrists and arms of both Raiths. Based on your arrest observations, how did they match the descriptions in former Mayor Raith's autopsy?"

"Identical patterns. Puffy scars, organic edges. Layered in the same way as Wesley Raith, and shaped exactly like the ones found on Cameron Raith."

"So, you'd say those marks indicate they all came from the same source?"

"Objection. Leading! She's testifying now, Your Honor."

"Sustained."

Her cheeks flushed, a rare sight in a courtroom. Hoover smirked and muttered to himself as he sat down, loud enough for her to hear. "Still forcing square pegs."

She glared at him with her eyes, as if drilling holes into him. She caught John's attention, who hovered his hands over the desk and pressed, signaling for her to try to calm down. She drew in a deep breath, desperate to slow her racing heartbeat, searching for a solution.

"Sheriff," she said, voice cracking, "let's discuss defense's claim that we've presented no evidence. Can you refute that?"

"Isn't that your job?" Hoover asked quietly.

"Absolutely," Parnell said. "The scars I mentioned, we have photos that can prove they are related and caused by similar sources. As to the top charge, we have preserved evidence of tire tracks—"

"Whoa, now!" Hoover exclaimed as he hurried to his feet, which made Annaleigh furious.

"Objection!" she snapped. "Wait, no, I meant—"

The damage was done.

Hoover belly laughed as he bellowed, "Your Honor, even the prosecution objects to their own witness! Sanity's finally been restored to your courtroom!"

Laughter echoed through the crowd, causing Chapel to repeatedly pound his gavel.

"Order! There will be order in my court!" he shouted. Once under control, his focus returned to Annaleigh.

"Ms. Stanton... you may continue."

She didn't answer immediately. Instead, her eyes carved deep ruts into the wooden floor as she bit down on her lower lip. Her nostrils flared. Her cheeks reddened. She could feel her heartbeat in her throat.

"No further questions."

She returned to her chair and slumped into it. John stood up at the same time, as if her seat cushion had somehow launched him into the air.

"Your Honor, the prosecution would like to request a fifteen-minute recess."

Chapel's sympathetic brows raised as he said, "Granted. The court is in recess for fifteen minutes."

Annaleigh's elbow jerked as he banged his gavel.

17

MURDEROUS WHISPERS

Annaleigh watched the jury rise and meander out. Their faces showed a mix of unwanted expressions. Some looked confused, unsure of what they had seen. A few joked with each other, laughing before quickly covering their mouths.

They're laughing at me.

Baz and Clyde escorted Kenneth to a nearby holding cell, with Baz carrying the pair of backup FM-200 canisters, careful not to snag the tubing on the way out. Members of the gallery went outside to stretch, chat, and even light up a cigarette.

Soon, the entire courtroom had cleared out.

Annaleigh, John, and Sarah were sitting silently at the prosecution's table. Sarah spoke first.

"I'm sure a lot is running through your mind right now, Annaleigh. But we made some good points today. It was a solid start with our first witness."

Annaleigh stayed quiet, fumbling her fingers in her lap.

John placed a hand on her shoulder. "I agree with Sarah, this isn't as bad as you might think."

Agreeing? With her? She's babying me.

"I objected to myself, John," she said in monotone. "I lost it. That never happens to me."

"Don't worry," John said, rubbing her shoulder blades. "This trial has miles to go and loads of time for us to—"

"To what?" she snapped. "Fix my screw-up?" John stopped rubbing. "Sorry, I'm not trying to blame you. It's on me."

"No," he replied, soothingly. "Time to prove our case and put him away. Ridding this town of him... for good."

She rose to her feet, then leaned on the table, pointing. "Did you see the jury? Did you see their faces? In one instant, I became a joke. I might have already lost us this case."

"Not at all, Annaleigh," Sarah said. "I watched them the entire time. Sure, there were a few... um... hiccups, but I could tell they were getting tired of Hoover's antics too. At least until the end. Then... yeah, sorry. Honestly, it could go either way at this point."

Annaleigh already felt bad about her performance—she didn't need Sarah's pity on top of everything. She paced back and forth in the well, coming up with a plan.

"Okay," she said, softly stomping her foot. "Here's what we're going to do. We're calling our next witness, as planned. But, John, you're running it."

His brows shot up. "Me? The direct? I thought we agreed I would only cross."

"As much as I hate to admit it, Hoover got under my skin. I don't want it to impact anything else, and I don't think he'll treat you the same way. Like when he sat back in the deposition when you... took over."

"He's unpredictable, but it's worth a try. He doesn't have a history with me, so he can throw whatever he wants. I can handle it." He froze. "Wait, that came out wrong. I didn't mean you can't handle—"

"I know what you meant, John," Annaleigh replied. "I dug this hole for us, but it will take all of us to get out of it and put *him*"—she pointed toward the empty defendant's table—"in it." She moved to the opposite side of the prosecution table, looking both John and Sarah both in the eye. "If anyone has concerns with our approach, speak up now."

"None here," John said simply. "I'm with you."

All eyes turned to Sarah, whose tongue fiddled with her bottom lip. She looked up and gave a quick elbow to John's upper arm. "You're going to kill it, John. Never had a doubt. Let's go win this thing."

Annaleigh spun around before anyone noticed her eyes rolling upward.

* * *

As John stood up, his knees trembled inside his slacks. In his first high-profile court case, he was about to lead the direct examination of his first witness.

Annaleigh's opening had been spectacular—the kind of dominance he remembered from the first time he saw her. She engaged the jury, the gallery, and once again, he even noticed Judge Chapel slightly bobbing his head to her speaking rhythm.

The direct examination of Sheriff Parnell could have gone better. Annaleigh couldn't be blamed for that. Defense counsel—an evil nemesis from her past—bore sole responsibility. Now that John knew where the potholes were in the courtroom, he could swerve to avoid them.

"Please state your name for the record."

"Issabel Camp. That's I-S-S-A-B-E-L," she said, looking around the courtroom with wide eyes. "Uh, hi everyone." She waved a friendly hand toward John. "I know it's different with the has two esses in it, but I blame the hospital for what they wrote down. Been explaining it since Sunday School. Wow, I ain't seen the view from this chair before."

John smiled gently and moved toward the end of the jury box, right next to the witness stand. "That's perfect, Ms. Camp," he said. "Can you state your occupation, please?"

"Of course. I'm the secretary at St. Michael's the Archangel, diagonal from City Hall on West Main—you know, people always confuse us with Saint Michael Parish on East Main, but I always think of it as God doesn't care which one you go to, as long as you're there."

"My mother would agree, Ms. Camp. Can you describe the view from your office window?"

"Oh, sure. Looks straight out onto West Main. I mean, once I look past the big oak tree in the churchyard. Been watching it grow up for the past fifteen years or so now."

"Besides the traffic, what else can you see from your window?"

"I think I already mentioned it, but City Hall is right across the street. We're kind of caddy-corner from it, so I can see both the front and side doors. Usually it's just deliveries on the side there, 'cept for... well, that one time."

"Yes, I do, ma'am, but could you please clarify for the court as to what you're referring?"

Issabel shifted slightly in her seat, visibly uncomfortable.

"One day, around lunch, I heard some yelling coming from over there. I saw a scuffle, then tires screeching, followed by a lot of police cars. It was the day the mayor died." She sniffled as she spoke.

"Ms. Camp, do you need a minute?"

"No, young man, but thank you. I get sad sometimes when I think about it. I didn't know the man well, but after he died... you know, it's just sad when someone loses both parents."

"You're a very empathetic woman, ma'am. It's admirable. Do you participate in regular evening activities at the church?"

"Yes, sir. Bible study most nights from seven to eight-thirty. Sometimes we have cookies afterward, and then I lock up, so I'm not out of there until about nine-thirty."

"During any of those evening activities, or while working late, have you ever noticed the defendant, Kenneth Atlee, at or around City Hall?"

Issabel looked down at her lap, avoiding eye contact with the defendant's table.

"Oh, plenty of times. He'd slip in and out at all hours—nine, ten at night, sometimes past midnight. Front door, side door, didn't matter. Looked like he owned the place, comin' and goin' like that."

"If your Bible studies usually end at nine-thirty, how can you be sure he was entering the building at those times?"

"Most places don't run without hard-working secretaries, dear. The church is no different. I get calls at all hours of the night to go up there, turn off lights, close doors—everything and anything. I'm glad I don't live too far away."

"How often would you say this happened?"

"Couple of times a week, easy. For months, maybe years now. Sort of lost track since it's been going on so long, ever since the old mayor—God rest him—first got elected. But not so much lately. Every time I saw it, made me wonder what kind of business couldn't wait till morning."

Hoover rose calmly, grinding his chair backward.

"Objection, Your Honor—speculation. The witness isn't privy to City Hall schedules."

"Overruled," Chapel said, leaning back. "I heard only a question, not a conclusion. The jury can weigh it."

Hoover sank back into his seat, muttering, "Small-town eyes see every little damn..."

Chapel cleared his throat toward Hoover, causing Hoover to raise his hands to act as if he had coughed, rather than dropped insults.

"Ms. Camp, can you remember a particular moment when you stayed late at the church at night that is memorable to you?"

"Yes, about two months ago. Bible study finished up, but I got a call from Mrs. Hargrove saying the lights were still on upstairs. Second time that week, if I remember right. So I drove back around eleven-thirty or so to turn 'em off—no need to waste God's electricity."

"What, if anything, did you observe at that time?"

"I glanced out the window, and there was Kenneth with a young man—the mayor's son, I think—standing by the side door of City Hall. They were facing each other, and these bright lights flashed off their hands, like they were playing some kind of game, seeing who could shine brighter. Kinda like kids with flashlights, but... brighter, almost unnatural. Most flashlights I've seen have this yellow glow. These lights were bright white, whiter than anything I'd ever seen. Gave me the chills, to tell the truth. Don't know why. But it did."

"Ms. Camp, have you ever observed the defendant interact with anyone else?"

"No, not that I recall..."

John parted his lips to ask a follow-up question, but Issabel kept speaking.

"Well, maybe," she said, gently patting her lips. "I mentioned the mayor's son losing his parents earlier. It makes me think about one night, years ago, in the fall. I saw him arguing with someone by the side door. The leaves had already fallen, so I could see pretty good through that old oak. It was late, but the parking lot lights lit up everything. I saw Evelyn."

John's head snapped toward Annaleigh. He kept a stoic expression, but the unspoken message to Annaleigh was clear. Issabel never mentioned the mayor's missing wife in her deposition. They were expecting her to testify about seeing business owners entering City Hall at random hours of the night, each time carrying identical thick white envelopes, then leaving empty-handed.

Hoover leaned forward but stayed quiet. John sensed he was itching to object at any moment.

"Eveylyn, who? Ms. Camp, do you know the woman's last name?"

"Evelyn Raith, of course."

"Are you sure you saw Evelyn Raith, the wife of the late mayor, Cameron Raith? How could you tell?"

"Saw her as plainly as I see you. She was wearing that nice-looking, flowered blouse she wore to church many times. Her necklace even sparkled in the streetlights. It was so beautiful. I could tell they were arguing, though I couldn't hear what about. I saw that man raise a hand and hit her—she cried out, heard it even with the window closed. Not too long after, I hear everyone's saying she *left town*. I don't buy it. She fell down in that parking lot after he smacked her, then he threw her in a station wagon and drove off. I don't know anybody who can leave town on their own if they aren't walking. From what I saw, I think he hurt her... bad."

More gasps spread through the courtroom gallery. Hoover shot up out of his chair.

"Objection! Relevance! Speculation! This is pure hearsay and gossip about unrelated events." He tilted his head and shot a look at John. "Prosecution digging up old rumors now?" Then he turned to Annaleigh. "How desperate do you have to be?"

Chapel gavelled the room back into silence.

"Order in my court, everyone! Order!" He cast scolding looks around the room. "Defense's objection is sustained, but I won't be striking anything from the record. Ms. Camp, please limit your answers to what you saw and avoid drawing conclusions. Do you understand?"

She nodded meekly. "Yes, sir, Judge Chapel. My apologies."

John continued after a nod from the bench.

"Let's dig a little deeper on this. This observation about Evelyn Raith—did you mention it at all during your deposition?"

"No, sir. It slipped my mind until now. I think seeing him over there in court must have jogged my memory. But, I did tell someone about it."

John leaned in. "Who exactly did you tell?"

"I told Hollis... er, Detective Mumber, first off—he came by the church the next day for some different reason, but I told him everything I saw. Later on, that poor deputy stopped by for no reason in particular—the one who died back in May. Deputy

Hinkle, I think. Told him, too. Far as I know, nothing ever came of it. They both said they'd look into it. Guess not."

Hoover vaulted to his feet again. "I have to object once more, Judge. Witness is calling for hearsay about what others did or didn't do."

Issabel put her hands to her lips. "Oh, did I do something wrong again?"

John shook his head. "Ms. Camp, you're fine. Judge, no one is trying to slander the dead or the recently retired. Since Mrs. Raith actually disappeared shortly after this encounter, the witness's statement is factually accurate."

Chapel waved his hands in the air. "I spoke personally with Hollis Mumber a few weeks ago, so I know firsthand what condition he is in now. Since he and the deceased, Amos Hinkle, can't testify on their own behalf, I'll accept her statement as it's relevant to the report."

"Your Honor", John said, his chest held high. "No further questions."

As he sat, he leaned into Annaleigh. "This changes everything—on top of everything else, if we can tie him to Evelyn's disappearance, there's no way the jury won't see it our way," he whispered.

"And plus, Hoover has nothing to fight back with. Issabel with two 'esses'? Church secretary? Polite? She's untouchable. Great job, John."

Sarah squeezed her head in, gripping John with both shoulders. "Oh my God," she said quietly, "that was awesome! You were unstoppable. I can't believe you got that on record. What a great first time!"

Annaleigh shot her a stern, scolding look. "Let's all focus on the cross. This isn't done yet." Sarah retreated into her chair, head bowed.

John struggled to hide a smile forming on his lips. The trial now had a new purpose. Not only would Kenneth get what he deserved, but they might even crack open another cold case. One Parnell was never able to.

The best part? Something he hadn't even realized during his questioning? Not once did he see a shimmer evaporating around Issabel Camp's head. No violet hues, no purple wisps.

Nothing.

She had spoken the truth. Every word.

If he was this skilled in a direct exam, he could only imagine the fun of cross-examinations.

18

RISING AND FALLING SATURATIONS

John navigated the quiet halls of Coldwater Memorial during an extended lunch break granted by Judge Chapel. Passing by the nurse's station, he locked eyes with Tammy. She spun in her chair and hurried off in the other direction.

Still embarrassed from their last encounter, perhaps.

"That double date offer is still on the table," John said as she rounded a corner and disappeared from view. "I mean, if you and Dallas are still together," he mumbled to himself.

He approached Dr. Abigail Jensen's office door feeling hopeful yet cautious. She'd completed her analysis, which hopefully meant hearing results, rather than giving blood.

She knows about seeing colors, but not when it occurs—or why. Remember to keep those details unsaid. If you tell her you can see lies, she might keep you for seventy-two hours on an involuntary psych hold.

Ironically, some of the worst news he imagined was that the weed killer in his blood had disappeared. That Issabel Camp's testimony contained only unvarnished truth was indeed a convenient explanation. But what if, instead, his power had just... gone?

What a strange expectation—to hope that you still have herbicide in your blood.

"You wanted to see me, doc?"

He poked his head through Dr. Abigail Jensen's cracked door and saw her deep in concentration, gazing at the scattered papers on her desk. Hearing his voice, she greeted him with a warm smile.

"Thanks for coming in again, John. Please sit... I know you've been through a lot since May—mainly my fault with all the tests."

"No blame comes your way, doc. Your hands didn't explode in my face."

"True. I finished all the analysis, and I thought you'd want to know what I found. The results are... revealing."

"Does this mean I won't need to give any more blood? Because you were wrong—it doesn't get easier each time."

Jensen pinched a strand of jet black hair from her cheek and tucked it into her messy bun. She offered a half-smile.

"That's what we say to make sure you come to your next appointment. Otherwise, people would run for the hills. Trust me, nobody *likes* needles."

John sat with his left ankle resting on his right knee, leaning back and interlacing his fingers. He squinted.

"How bad is it? Lay it on me."

"It's not only about your results. I'm sorry, I should have made that clear. I've finished analyzing all the samples—yours, Mr. Atlee's, and Wesley Raith's."

John lowered his foot to the ground and sat up straight.

"Oh—I didn't realize that's what you meant. If this is something that might make it into your testimony, we should probably include Annaleigh in this conversation."

"It's your call, John. There's a gray area here, between your personal results and the ones you might want to use in court."

"As much as I want to include Annaleigh, let's get this over with. My blood, my mess. I'll loop her in later."

"Let's get to it, then," Jensen said, leaning into a drawer and pulling out a folder labeled "Comparative Analysis: Picloram Exposure." She balanced it on its spine and let both edges fall to the desk. "Once we were able to identify the Picloram in your blood, I performed multiple sets of analyses. One was on your multiple blood samples to see if the levels were degrading as I expected. I also compared your blood to that of Kenneth Roy Atlee, based on the samples we received after his arrest, as well as from the autopsy of Cameron Raith and the hospitalization of Wesley Raith. Some of this was ethically tricky, but with the trial approaching, my testimony pending, and, more importantly, your health at stake, patterns began to emerge that couldn't be ignored."

"Whoa, you've been busy."

"Never a dull moment. As I've learned more, Picloram is, at its base, a toxin—but it has also altered your cellular structures in ways I don't fully understand. The exposures among all of you vary, but the concentrations tell us the story."

"Is there any risk that this won't be admissible? We have a guy who objects to almost everything, so I assume he'd throw the kitchen sink at something like this."

"It might sound crazy, but it's just science, John. I'll explain it to you, and then it's up to us both to convince him that my work is neutral and without bias. But, realize this is a bit outside the testimony I typically give."

Jensen pulled out a bar chart, with each series of tightly packed rectangles shown in a different color.

"Your first test showed moderate exposure, right after the incident in May. With each draw, the concentration steadily decreased. Good news for your health. I expect it to be completely filtered out of your blood in a few more weeks, plus or minus."

John's eyes drifted up as he calculated in his mind. Would he be the same kind of lawyer that Annaleigh expected if his blood cleared and the wisps never returned?

"As for Wesley Raith, his exposure level is what I'm calling mid-range. It's higher than yours, over twice the concentration. Unless you're showing the same symptoms, I'm assuming his levels are within the minimal range that can cause his... uh, manifestations."

John remembered his dream of Annaleigh burning and melting, then recalled waking up with hands that felt like they were on fire. It was probably nothing. It was a dream, after all. He shook his head and wiggled his white-tipped fingers in the air.

"As cold as can be, considering the temperature inside this place."

"Interestingly enough," she continued, "the other two, Mr. Atlee and Mayor Raith, reached peak saturation. Identical levels, with minor fluctuations in Mr. Atlee."

"Identical? The day the mayor died, the... manifestations he had, as you call them, caught him off guard. Almost like it was the first time it had happened. I don't get that same impression with Mr. Atlee." Addressing Kenneth formally felt strange.

"After I saw your results, Sheriff Parnell and the infirmary at the County Jail assisted with multiple additional draws of Mr. Atlee for me to test."

"And he consented? I would have thought he'd fight tooth and nail."

Dr. Jensen shook her head, causing a few more strands of hair to fall. She quickly tucked them away.

"He had no issues, other than disliking the needle pricks."

"I hope they had a hard time finding a vein. If anybody deserves a few extra pricks, it's that guy."

Her eyes widened slightly, but she stayed professional.

"The fluctuations I mentioned—in between draws, his saturation levels rise and fall unpredictably. It's almost like something is controlling it."

John's gut thumped. "You think he can control what's in his blood?"

"In my opinion, something is there. But, I don't think I can scientifically explain that he's doing it intentionally."

"You said that Wesley was mid-range, double mine. What about Kenneth?"

Jensen flipped the paper back towards her, running her finger over the graph until it stopped on a small box of numbers.

"Three times Wesley's sample, so... roughly six times the level you have in your blood. That's the upper range, if I had to label it. It's astonishing, really, but, to be honest, I have no idea what the actual limits are. If you weren't sitting right in front of me now, even your level of minimal exposure should have been deadly."

"Never been called a zombie before, doc," he said, chuckling. "But, if I'm hearing you right, if Wesley was a parlor trick, Kenneth might be a firework? But, probably not a nuke?"

Through pursed lips, Dr. Jensen looked back.

"Not sure if I agree with your metaphor, but I certainly hope not. This case has really challenged some of the boundaries of what I thought were pretty rigid scientific definitions." She set the paper aside. "Tell me—are you still seeing the colors? How has your head been feeling since you fell?"

John shrugged. "Now and then. There really isn't a pattern I've been able to detect with them."

"But, not as often? If I recall, it was happening pretty frequently a few weeks ago."

"Actually, I haven't seen them in a few days." His shoulders drooped.

"That's great news, John. Glad to hear it. As I expected, it's probably the aftereffects of your concussion—and they're fading as you heal. There are many other side effects of concussions that you haven't experienced, so make sure you come back and tell me if anything changes."

"You bet."

As John closed the squeaky door of his ugly brown Caprice, he couldn't wait to tell Annaleigh the details he'd found out. Whoever ran the direct on Dr. Jensen was going to have a blast.

Getting her qualified as an expert wouldn't be hard—a well-known and highly trusted medical professional within the Coldwater community would sail past Judge Chapel's qualifications.

Passing this so-called science through the objection gauntlet of Bradley Hoover? A different fight altogether.

Dr. Jensen's words echoed in his mind—six times higher.

Fluctuations. Upper range.

John's edge dulled. Kenneth's tests didn't indicate the same possibility.

And if Kenneth's levels moved to his tune… what kind of dance could they expect if he took the stand?

19

HUNTING FOR TRUTH

Bonnie Chance crept her car into the parking lot, searching for two specific vehicles. If she spotted either one, it might not be safe to go inside.

The kind of conversation she needed would be best kept private.

And if an ugly brown Caprice or pale green Dart were parked nearby, it probably meant John was inside. This chat was supposed to be *about* John. Not with him.

No sign of either vehicle.

A shiver ran up her spine as she slid into an empty spot near the door. She heaved a deep breath and stepped inside.

As she pushed open the door to the Sheriff's Office, she looked left and right. Nothing but empty desks—no deputies in sight. She focused on the only law enforcement officer present and strode into Sheriff Dane Parnell's office, stopping on the opposite side of his desk.

"We need to talk, Dane. John needs answers, and I'm afraid I can't keep it from him anymore."

Parnell paused his writing and gently set his pen down as he looked up at her.

"Some context might help here, Bonnie."

"He knows his father is here in Coldwater. I had to tell him that so he wouldn't run off to St. Louis. But—"

"But now he's even more determined to find out who it is? You really didn't think it would light a new fire under him?"

Bonnie slumped into a metal side chair and crossed her arms.

"I'm... not sure I thought it through completely. He was home, Dane. I... I didn't want him to leave again. I couldn't let him go because of a lie."

"Why not tell him, then?" Parnell said, shifting his weight in his seat. "I mean, what's the harm now? It's been long enough, hasn't it, Bonnie?"

"Because I promised not to sabotage someone else's marriage, that's why. I wouldn't do it then, I sure as heck won't now. At least... not without giving a little warning."

"And, you showing up today... this is the warning?"

She pursed her lips, weighing her words. "Yes. I think it's time."

Parnell tongued his cheek, then adjusted his short mustache with his fingers.

"Message received. I'll have a talk with him."

* * *

John pulled Annaleigh aside during a short recess of the afternoon court session. He shared a summary of Dr. Jensen's analysis, not expecting a wave of shock to sweep over her face. Her first reaction resulted in a left jab thrown into his shoulder.

"You have herbicide... in your blood? Why am I just now hearing about this? How long have you known?"

John hadn't quite experienced being yelled at in such a soft voice before.

"It's nothing, really. Doc says I'm going to be fine."

"That's not the point, John."

"Hey, if you want to blame someone, blame the guy living the prison life without hands."

"He's lucky he's behind bars, if you ask me. I could kill him for what he did to all of us."

"Oh, don't I know it... look, slight change of subject here, if you can stop hitting me for a second. I can't get Issabel's testimony out of my head, Annaleigh. Our witnesses for the rest of today are more City Hall employees, right?"

"Stipulation—the change of subject permission lasts only for five minutes. You and I are going to have a long talk about you and your blood. Got it? Witnesses... uh, yes... Raith's secretary and the County Clerk. Why? What kind of plan are you concocting?"

"Can you handle those directs?"

"Can I? Of course I can, John," she said, indignant. "Hoover's strategy was a one-time occurrence. Now I know just how low he can go. Piece of cake. Why? You tired of being in court already?"

"No, it's not that. I want to follow up on what Issabel said. If I can find Evelyn, it changes everything about this trial."

"I agree, but what exactly did she say that makes you think it's a viable lead? That Kenneth threw her in a car? Anything could have happened after that."

"True, but it made me think about something Kenneth joked about when we had him in our holding cell. He made a crack about killing Evelyn and burying her in the woods. Now, with Issabel's testimony, what's the only place Parnell couldn't fully search? The Raith property. Lots of woods there... and the mayor never allowed Parnell to look. I'm willing to bet there's a good reason for that. She could still be there."

She leaned forward and kissed him on the cheek. "I'll take care of court. You get to it—and be careful."

* * *

The Raith family home sat nestled inside a sprawling fifty-acre estate tucked away at the edge of dense forests on the south-eastern outskirts of the county. The fifteen-minute drive from the courthouse wound through hairpin turns, narrow roads, and rolling hills that John had forgotten Coldwater had.

Exiting beneath a sparse fall canopy of trees, he turned onto a long driveway and eased onto the brakes. A familiar all-black police cruiser parked at the entrance of a gaudy iron arch labeled "RAITH". Sheriff Dane Parnell waved from his rolled-down window, motioned for John to follow, then continued up a gentle hill, eventually parking in front of a two-story log cabin at the top of the property. John parked beside him and surveyed the scene.

Thick, red tape bearing "Do Not Cross" sealed the house's door. Yellow crime-scene tape cordoned off the four-sided porch, clearly indicating that the house was off-limits to anyone with banal or curious interests.

To the right, a worn dirt path with tire tracks led to a smaller guest cabin. It matched the description in Clyde's written report about his failed capture a few months ago.

"That's Kenneth's cabin," Parnell said. He pointed to the left, behind the main house. "A few outbuildings are that way. A newer sheet metal outbuilding, like a garage. He tore down some old stables and put up that monstrosity a while back. Beyond that, an old wooden barn, barely inside the tree line."

"You seem to know an awful lot about this property, Sheriff."

Parnell's cheeks flushed. "Visited Cameron a time or two. Only official business, I swear."

The setting sun backlit Parnell. A ripple might have shimmered around him—though it could've been the sun's rays.

"Before or after Evelyn disappeared?"

"Mostly after," he stated casually. "I already checked that crawlspace under the house. Nothing but cobwebs and mouse droppings. Didn't find squat. At least expected to run into a snake. I didn't have much time, so I wasn't as thorough as I'd have liked."

John sensed something off with Parnell's search details. Maintaining a neutral tone, he observed the Sheriff's expressions closely.

"You came here without a warrant?"

Parnell kicked a rock, eyes darting. When the sheriff shuffled his feet to the side, John reoriented himself to put the sun at their side. After a beat, Parnell shrugged.

"Didn't need one. I was doing a welfare check—heard Evelyn hadn't been seen in a few days, so I came to see if she was okay. Walked the open areas and found the barn doors open. Might have taken a peek or two. No lines crossed. All above board, young man."

A faint violet haze bloomed around Parnell's head for a heartbeat. John clocked it clearly.

Still got it.

"Really?" John pressed. "No warrant? No formal consent? You walked onto private property and went under the house? I didn't realize the crawlspace was considered an open area." He hardly contained his smirk.

"Well... alright, maybe I stretched it a little. I knew Cameron and Kenneth were both gone that day—something about a City Hall meeting. I knew the place was empty, so I drove up and checked the open spots. Barn doors were standing open, and the crawl space hatch wasn't locked. Figured if Evie was hurt... or maybe hiding... I couldn't sit on my hands. But, technically, no, I did *not* have permission that day." Parnell stared at John as silence grew between them. "I can see those wheels turning in your head there, Detective. The welfare check allowed me on the property, but I only bent the rules. I don't break 'em."

No ripple, no shimmer.

"If it was to locate a missing person, I can't really fault you there," he said, nodding. John raised both hands. "I promise I'll keep the rule-bending to a minimum."

"Make sure you do. Today's different. The whole property is a point of interest, so we go wherever we need to. A few hours of daylight left, where do you want to start?"

John spun in place, scoping out the landscape.

"I suggest we walk the entire property and look for anomalies. Start at the main house and radiate outward?"

"I agree," Parnell said, his lips shifting to one side. "Really been doing your homework, haven't you? Might I suggest this—six feet apart, six feet focus left and right. Means we can cover an 18-foot swath as we go. We walk in tandem. Ready?"

They set out together, eyes scanning the ground for sunken spots, disturbed earth, or overgrown patches. The property's entire front half yielded no clues. Nothing irregular, only scattered oaks shading overgrown grass.

As the sun dipped below the treetops, the grid search brought them near Kenneth's cabin. Ground that tilted differently than anywhere else on the property.

It sloped downward and led to a small lake off in the distance. Here and there, the ground leveled out, but as it got closer to the woods, scars remained where water runoff had eroded the earth.

Each step became more cautious, confirming solid footing before shifting weight from their back feet. They had cleared everything back to the guest cabin when Parnell broke the hour-long silence.

"Right here is where Clyde lost Kenneth back in May," he admitted. "Sometimes I wonder if we'd all have been better off if Clyde had ended this whole situation with a few bullets. Think of the time, money, and trouble it would have saved."

John wasn't quite sure how to respond. He'd be lying if he hadn't had the same thoughts. It wouldn't have changed anything for the Raiths—or would it?

If Clyde shot and killed Kenneth, he still might have radioed in, but that could've been before they were tucked away in the tight City Hall hallway. Mayor Raith wouldn't have heard about the escape. Maybe he wouldn't have run at all. He wouldn't have died jumping the roundabout, and in turn, Wesley wouldn't have felt the need to break out of custody and horrifically murder a cop.

Deputy Hinkle would still be alive, and Detective Mumber still lounging at his desk, snacking on something or nodding off.

And John would have spent the past three months improving his skills as a lawyer.

But if he hadn't fought Wesley, he would never have learned about their incredible ability to control flames with their fingers. Wesley's hands wouldn't have exploded in his face.

And he wouldn't be able to see lies.

Coldwater would have been a drastically different place indeed.

John's mind raced with possibilities as he casually examined the property's edge where it transitioned into "the woods."

An organic boundary of dirt and grass traced a wavy line where the tree's canopy shaded the ground from the sun. Fresh, brown leaves had been falling for a few weeks now, piling up on top of last year's shed that had yet to decompose. Nature's beautiful division, contrasted against the green grass, in living color.

Something unusual caught John's eye. Surrounded by five feet of dirt, the grass in this area grew in relatively straight lines, outlining a rough rectangle on the ground.

"Sheriff," John said, pointing. "See that?"

Parnell leaned in, frowning. "Seen this before—sometimes it's pets that have been buried, and the decomp supercharges the grass. I've also seen cases where it's someone burying garbage they didn't want to burn." He turned back to John. "Could be nothing... or not."

Excitement and terror swirl inside John. His pulse quickened. "It's the *not* that worries me..."

"I've got a couple of shovels in my trunk. Let's find out."

They walked up the hill back to their cruisers, then drove down the slope, positioning their cars at the site. Both turned on their headlights and directed their mounted spotlights at the patch. The fading daylight still filtered through the large tree trunks, but darkness steadily approached.

"I know you've dug holes before, John, but not as a cop. We dig smart, not frantic. Judging by this grass, whatever's underneath has been here for a while. This isn't a rescue mission—remember, it's recovery. We'll get there when we get there, and we don't kill ourselves on the way."

John pressed his lips together and bobbed his chin as their shovels pierced the ground.

Working on opposite sides of the grassy patch, they pushed the blade into the ground with their foot and outlined the target. Each time the spade-shaped metal entered, it exited, throwing a chunk of dirt into separate piles.

"So," Parnell said, breath heavy, "your mama came by the station. Said you're asking questions again... about your daddy."

John jabbed his shovel into the ground, wiped sweat from his brow, and looked up at Parnell.

She went to Parnell? Why him?

"Looking for your roots is good, son. But, sometimes the past stays buried for a reason—it protects folks."

"So, in the same vein, you're telling me that if Evelyn Raith is buried in this hole, we should leave her there. To *protect folks*?"

Parnell removed his Sheriff's hat and tossed it like a Frisbee onto the hood of his cruiser.

"Now, son, that's not what I meant."

John arched another chunk of dirt onto his pile, ignoring the gentle scolding. He shoved the blade in again and pushed on it with his foot, then rested both hands on the handle and leaned his chin on them.

"Sheriff... if you were in my shoes, would you really do anything differently? I assume you knew your father?"

"I did." Parnell smiled, as if recalling a memory. "Believe it or not, I wasn't born in Coldwater. I was born in 'the big city.' My father was a cab driver in St. Louis. My mother, though, was born and raised here. She and her family would travel up to the city now and then. They met when he picked her up as a fare, fell in love, and he moved here with her before I started school." The smile on his face lingered. "I see your point."

John's fingers trembled as the words formed in his mouth.

"Is... is it you?"

Parnell threw another chunk of dirt onto his pile. He looked at John's eyes.

"No, son. I wish, John. You're a right fine young man. But, no."

No purple shimmer. No haze. No glow, or shine, or ripple. Nothing but the truth swirling around Parnell's mind. John expelled an audible breath. He swallowed.

"But, you know who?"

Parnell sighed. "I do. Look, it's complicated—old promises, old hurts. Some things need to come out on their own. Never forget your mama's carrying a heavy load."

John craned his neck, rolling it around his shoulders. The Sheriff's admission hurt but didn't surprise him. Another door cracked but failed to open.

"I don't understand why everyone here is carrying this stupid secret." He gripped the wooden handle and squeezed, his volume rising. "I mean, is it me? Am I a disappointment? He doesn't want to be associated with who I am? I don't get it—"

As his tirade turned into shouts, he raised the shovel into the air and drove it deep into the ground, letting out a frustrated yell. When his shovel struck something unexpected, he composed himself.

"Did you hear that?" A dull thud echoed, replacing his shout. John used the shovel's point to sweep away dirt and revealed a long, slender piece of light gray material. "Tree root?"

Parnell knelt, squinting. He grabbed his flashlight from his utility belt and shone it on the object. He shook his head.

"Nope. Bone."

His heart pounded in his chest—had they found her? Should he feel happy? Or sad that this woman's life had been confirmed to be extinguished?

With deliberate movements, they each dug around the object, exposing a thick, dirty bone. John didn't know what to think. He tilted his head to the side.

Wait... were human bones... that big?

Parnell backed up and jabbed his shovel into virgin ground.

"Not Evelyn."

"What?" John asked, confused.

"Bone's too big—maybe Kenneth's leg is that size, but it's probably something else. Cow. Horse. Farm animal—the Raiths had a mare and a filly some years back. See the size? The joint? Definitely not human." The weathered bone's diameter matched the width of John's forearm and lacked both skin and muscle tissue. "Doesn't mean she's not here somewhere," Parnell said, comforting John. "Just not in this spot."

Both men filled the hole with loose dirt to preserve the site for further inspection, if necessary.

"There's a lot of the property left to search. I'll keep at it—I'll grid the rest and call Wayne County in the morning... see if I can borrow their cadaver dogs. Might take a few days for them to spare the time, maybe a week, but I'll keep asking. It would definitely speed up the search. You, though—you should be in court. Get justice where it counts. Kenneth's trial. A guilty verdict is how we honor the missing."

It hurt John to admit it, but Parnell had a point. Finding Evelyn would be the icing on the cake, sealing the already slam-dunk verdict. But, ensuring that decision with their existing evidence needed to be John's top priority.

Driving back into town in the dark and silence, a flood of thoughts clouded his mind.

Blood tests indicate his powers were fading, but at least they still worked—for now.

His father was still a shadow, a secret kept for reasons John couldn't understand.

And Evelyn Raith remained a ghost.

Nevertheless, Parnell's words before John left echoed.

"If she's out there, we'll find her."

20

FRACTURED TRUST

John pushed through the full-panel glass door of Froggin's Diner, and his senses instantly flooded with familiar sounds and smells.

The welcome jingle announcing his arrival brought back fond memories of his time here with his mother. The smell of the grill and frying oil stirred a few rumbles in his stomach. He'd worked up quite an appetite digging in a field with Sheriff Parnell.

His disheveled appearance had escaped him until he glanced down. His pant cuffs were mud-caked, despite his best efforts to shake them off before leaving the Raith farm. Faint dirt smudges stained his sleeves, and the combined effort from the wind and digging had mussed his hair, sending it in all directions. The complete opposite impression he typically presented in court, but he was too tired to care.

"Let me guess, the dirt pile won?" A familiar voice called out from the counter. He turned and saw Sarah Sinclair sitting alone on a swivel chair, strawberry milkshake in hand.

"Something like that," he responded. "If only I had backup, things might've turned out differently."

"All I do is wait by the phone, man, but you never call." She slurped the straw, forcing a piece of strawberry stuck in the middle to shoot into the back of her throat. She fell forward, coughing, her blonde hair, no longer tied into a tight bun, draping over the front of her shoulders.

"Easy there, if you die, I'll have to rope off this whole area and create a crime scene. And I'm starving. Don't make me shut everything down."

She swallowed, eyes watering as she caught her breath.

"She's over there, by the way," she said, pointing at Annaleigh in the corner booth, her back to the door. "I'm assuming you're not here for me."

"Maybe I come back later, but first I gotta fill her in on a few things. Speaking of which, why are you sitting here alone? I would have thought you'd be in that booth with her."

"Nah, she came in after me with some folders and sat down. Don't think she even noticed me... and I don't get the impression she'd want my company."

"Nah... I'm sure she's still warming up to you. "

"Doubt it," Sarah said, shaking her head. "She's always got her guard up around me. Not sure why. But, it's all good—this is my new favorite spot. I come here a lot and always sit alone. It's fine."

John gently placed a comforting hand on her shoulder. "Next time, give me a shout. Milkshakes will be on me."

She giggled. "You mean, like the dirt's on you? I don't think they'll appreciate having to clean the floor up after you."

"Oh, shut it. Next time, you. Me. Strawberry milkshakes. Got it?"

"Sure, but maybe just chocolate next time. Annaleigh can't have both of us choke to death."

John strode down the aisle toward the far corner booth, the old linoleum squeaking beneath his dirty boots. Annaleigh had multiple folders open and an untouched legal pad in front of her. Her expression shifted from relief to concern when she noticed his condition.

"My God, John—you haven't actually been grave-digging, have you?"

"Close enough," he said, sliding into the booth opposite her. "Parnell and I walked everywhere, looking for spots where Evelyn's body might have been buried."

"Assuming she didn't actually leave town," Annaleigh added, her tone tinged with suspicion.

John's brows furrowed, surprised by her response.

"Sure, but my gut is telling me she didn't. So does Parnell's."

He reached across the table to take her hand, squeezing it. She pulled back, grabbing a pen.

"What did you find? Anything actionable?"

"Found a square patch of grass beyond Kenneth's cabin that looked like something had been buried there. As you can tell, we dug there. Found bones."

Her eyes lifted. "Really?"

"Yes, but Parnell thinks it was an animal bone. So, no... not actionable."

"Oh." She jotted down a few words—then her pen drifted, drawing small shapes.

"But, we'll keep looking. There's more property. Parnell even says we might be able to get some cadaver dogs down there."

"Good."

"And, next to the bone, we found a few bars of gold. There's probably more there... just gotta dig them up. Then, we'll be rich."

"Nice," she replied, staring at the pen in her hand.

"Annaleigh," John said briskly.

"What?"

"You're not even listening. I told you we found a stash of gold, and it didn't even register."

"What? Oh... okay." Her response totally ignored his concern.

John pulled the pen from her fingers and clasped her hand.

"Is everything okay, Annaleigh? You're kinda spacing out here."

"Our witnesses didn't really strengthen our case today."

"Oh, no—I'm sorry. What happened?"

She pulled her hand back again, dropped it into her lap, and leaned back against the bench seatback.

"The City Hall witnesses got demolished on cross. Hoover shredded half of my evidence—on technicalities. Chain-of-custody and relevance. Then, once it came out that the records room door stayed unlocked most of the time, everything derailed. We got the consulting projects and Kenneth's shell company into the record. But Judge Chapel limited how far we could push it. Our case got thin today, John. Really thin."

She glanced around, lowering her voice.

"And, no Evelyn body means no smoking gun for the violence angle. Even the tire tracks from your driveway don't definitively link him to the arson. Jury might see him as a thug and ask about lesser-included charges. Or, worse, they might find him not guilty."

"We've got him dead to rights with the medical evidence, though. We can connect the Picloram to both of the Raiths, and what they've done is on record. We've got the same scars on all their wrists, Issabel's testimony—"

"Speaking of Picloram... why didn't you tell me immediately when Dr. Jensen found it in your blood? You've been getting tested for weeks, John. You continually made it seem like it was only a vision issue."

He leaned forward, resting his chin on his interlaced fingers.

"It's nothing, really. The vision issues were concussion side effects—"

"Stupid Foley," she muttered.

"—and she said my levels were dropping, anyway. Like I said, no big deal."

"No big deal?" Her volume rose too high before she caught herself. She looked around, cheeks flushing, then leaned in. "You've been hiding medical results... whatever's been happening with you. You didn't think I needed to know?"

"It's not like that," he said, staring at the table. "I really didn't think it was important."

"I… I thought… you would have wanted to confide in me."

Sensing a stalemate and feeling guilty, John chose his words carefully. "I'm sorry. I promise I'll tell you everyth…" He realized mid-sentence that he was still holding back, still hiding things from her. Even when he thought about explaining it out loud, the words felt pointless. Impossible.

How do you explain that because some jackass thunked you in the head, you see colors every time someone lies?

"I promise, anything doc tells me from now on, you'll be the first to hear about it."

She nodded, trying to force a smile.

"Now, about this trial," he said, shifting the subject. "I've been thinking of a plan. It's unconventional, but it might work."

"After today, I'll be all ears."

"We push Kenneth, like we did with Wesley. Provoke him on the stand—make him lose control, flash his lights, show the flames, all in open court. Parnell will be there with multiple deputies, too. We'll be armed… and everywhere. But everyone in that room will see what he's attempting to do. Case closed."

"Are you insane?" she asked, with wide eyes. "First off, if Judge Chapel figures out what we're trying to do, he'll shut everything down. Second, the gloves, John. The FM-200, your design. He'll be wearing them. They stop him from being able to do his… fire… or whatever. The judge will never agree to let him take those off."

John waved his hand in the air. "Even the attempt—him trying and failing, getting angry—it shifts momentum. Chapel might yell, but he won't want a mistrial and to start over. And the jury will remember the outburst."

"That's reckless. Borderline unethical," she said, shaking her head wildly. "I'm not sure what's going on with you, but lately you've been making a lot of questionable choices."

"Huh?" John looked confused. "Like what?"

"Like keeping your bloodwork from me, for one. Like this new crazy plan… risking everyone's safety in that courtroom.

And... the way you are around... her." She glanced at the counter, where Sarah still sat. "I'm not blind, John."

"Now, who sounds crazy?" He chuckled. "You think there's something going on between Sarah and me?"

"Like I said, I'm not blind."

"I still don't understand what you're talking about, but fine. Let's bring everything to light. Starting with something Hoover told me."

"Hoover? When have you ever talked to him?"

"The first day he showed up. You remember when I kicked him out of our office? He told me something. That the guy, your boss, you *defended yourself* from? He didn't walk away. He died."

Annaleigh drew in a quick breath. The color drained from her face. "He told you... what?"

"He said the guy died, Annaleigh. I'd think that would rank higher than me sharing some stupid blood test."

"Oh my God." Annaleigh covered her face with her hands. She sat quietly for a few seconds, and when she removed her hands, her eyes were moist and reddened. John's stomach ached. He knew he'd gone too far.

"Hoover's twisting it," she said quietly. "Everything I told you was true. He attacked me. I defended myself. He had surgery after... after what happened. I found out weeks later that an infection set in or something. It wasn't my fault. The guy didn't go back to get it checked out. He tried to tough it out. Once he finally did, there was nothing they could do. It was like sepsis or something. I never hid that he was hurt—like you, I didn't think the rest mattered. But, this time, it's because it didn't. He made those choices. And he dealt with the consequences."

John watched her intently, eyes flicking around her head—her left, her right, above.

"STOP. DOING. THAT." Annaleigh yelled in a whisper again. "Every time we talk lately, you stare at my head like you're searching for something. What the hell is going on, John?"

He exhaled, his shoulders dropping as the diner's ambient

noise—clinking silverware and distant laughter—faded into the background. It all dulled away. He couldn't hide it anymore.

"I need to come clean about something," he said, his voice subdued. "Something I've been carrying alone. But, you're right. I should trust you. I *do* trust you. And I should *always* trust you. You should know this."

She leaned forward, her once defensive posture shifting. She reached for his hands, holding them both.

"Then say it. Right now. Before you stop yourself."

John opened his mouth but hesitated. He wet his lips with his tongue, then squinted one eye as he looked at her.

"I… I can tell when people lie."

21

TRUST REBUILT

"What the hell does that even mean?" Annaleigh asked in a stunned whisper.

John shrugged apologetically. "Exactly what it sounds like. I see something whenever somebody tells a lie."

"That's not... humanly possible."

"Neither is controlling fire with your hands or having your hands explode because you got too angry."

"Touché. But... how?"

He shook his head. "No idea. At first, I thought it was a weird side-effect from the concussion. But those got better. This, though... it stayed."

Her eyes narrowed. "What is it, exactly, that you see?"

"A shimmer. Or a ripple. Sometimes it's like a mist, too. Maybe it varies depending on how big a lie is, but I haven't figured that out yet. All I know is that something blooms around people's heads. And... it's always purple."

"Because of the Picloram?"

"I honestly can't tell you, but it makes sense. It's the common link to all our blood. I don't know why it shows up differently with me, though."

She leaned in even closer. "So... no fire?" The whisper was

almost inaudible.

"No. Thankfully."

She sat up straight, rested an elbow on the table, and balanced her chin on her palm.

"It still sounds crazy... prove it."

He paused, rubbing his lips with his fingers.

"Ever played two truths and a lie? Tell me three things about yourself, in any order. But make up one of them. I'll tell you which one is fake."

"You're serious? Fine," she said, tapping her fingernails. "I hate olives. I've never been to New York. I was a cheerleader back in high—"

"Cheerleader." He didn't even need to let her finish as the lavender pulse revealed her lie.

"Damn," she muttered.

"I kinda wish that one was true, though. Thinking about your long legs in a short skirt makes my mind go to fun places."

"John!" Her cheeks flushed as a waitress appeared from around the booth's corner to refill her coffee. She mouthed the word "stop" to John and tried to hide a smile.

"You want somethin', hon?" the waitress asked John.

He hovered his hand over the table. "Famished, but give us a few minutes, please?"

Plopping her menu pad back into the front pocket of her apron, she offered a meek smile. "You bet. Yell when you're ready," she said to them over her shoulder as she walked away.

"Keep it in your pants, mister," Annaleigh playfully scolded. "We're in public. Anyway, I might have already told you about my high school days, or you could have guessed. Let's go again."

"It's your dime," he joked.

"I was adopted. I've always wanted to learn how to ice skate. I love public displays of affection."

As he listened, two distinct ripples appeared around her head, separated by a brief delay.

She's trying to trick me.

"First off," he said, "I'll take you ice skating when it gets colder. I promise. No, you weren't adopted. And, you have to stop caring about other people. Kissing you in public is kind of like a badge of honor. I mean, look at you! I've got the most gorgeous girl in town." He winked at her, confident he'd passed the second test.

Her face turned sour, a small frown crossing her lips.

"Not the time for flattery. You're making a joke of this, but you've... been reading people this whole time? And... me?" Her eyes danced around, as if recalling every moment with him over the past few weeks. "Oh my God, Broden Reed's deposition? That's how you knew how to press him."

He nodded.

"John, you've been playing me this whole time. God, I feel like a fool. Like an idiot." She sat back, twisting in the booth until her back rested against the side wall. "You had this... ability, and you didn't tell me. We're supposed to be partners—in the case, in... everything."

Without warning, her eyes widened, and she leaned in, drastically lowering her voice as she glanced around at the nearby tables.

"And you used it on witnesses. In court! And on *me* sometimes. I don't even know if that's legal! And... and it's definitely not fair. I can't tell if you've lied about anything."

"No, no, Annaleigh," he said, reaching for her. "I've always done my best to be truthful with you—"

"And faithful, too?"

"What—?" John's head snapped back, caught completely off-guard. "Of course!"

She nodded toward Sarah at the counter.

"You've been awfully friendly with her lately. Close, even. Since day one. Working together at the office, her little compliments to you. She's flirting with you! And it sure looks like you flirt right back. As I said earlier, I'm not blind."

His lips curled into an innocent smile.

"Trust me, it's nothing. She's like a little sister to me, I promise. I think you've misread this."

She peered into his eyes, scrutinizing him.

"Fine. Let's test it. *Your* way. Wait here... and pay attention."

Annaleigh scooted out, stood up, and straightened her pants. John watched with tense muscles as she strode over to the counter and sat on the opposite side of Sarah, so that John could see Annaleigh's face but only the back of Sarah's head. Eyes sparkling with mischief, she smiled at Sarah and started talking.

John strained to hear, but the noise from other patrons and the jukebox playing old '60s tunes made it impossible. The chat lasted barely a minute, with John squirming in his seat, thinking about what was being said.

What is she asking her? Is she telling Sarah my secret? What in the world is Sarah saying back?

Annaleigh forced a smile, laughed lightly, then returned to the booth. "Okay, hotshot. I asked her three questions. Which one was the lie?"

"That's not quite how it works if I don't know when you asked each question. But, if it makes you feel any better. I didn't see any flashes at all. I think everything she said was the truth."

"Interesting," Annaleigh said, smirking. "The first two questions were about the trial—boring stuff about files and evidence. Then, I said to her, 'John's had the hots for you since you started working with us.'"

"You—what?" John asked, eyes bulging, clearing his throat.

He glanced at Sarah, grimacing.

She wasn't looking. Thank goodness.

Annaleigh sat back, crossing her arms. "Would you like to know what her exact words were? 'Eww, gross—he's like my brother.' Then she asked me to try to keep you in line. You *really* didn't see anything? No shimmer, no purple at all?"

John exhaled, shaking his head. "Nothing."

They both burst into quiet laughter—shoulders shaking,

hands over each of their mouths, trying to keep it in. Whatever tension had built up broke loose.

"God, I've been so dumb," Annaleigh said, wiping her eyes.

"We both have. Me, more, I think."

"God's honest truth, that statement right there," she said, taking a sip.

"I wasn't kidding earlier. The tests indicate that my blood levels are dropping, so if that's what's causing this... thing, then it's likely to be gone soon."

"Good for you... but maybe bad timing for us."

John's brows furrowed. "Bad timing? Are you saying you want me to keep doing it... in court?"

"I still think your plan is extremely risky, but if it means winning this trial... let's use every tool we have." She reached across and squeezed his hand. "John Chance, *you* are that tool."

"Ouch," he said, smiling. "Guess I deserved that."

"Damn straight," she said, pointing. "And, I'm only going to say this one more time. No. More. Secrets. Don't make me tell your mother on you."

John surrendered with his hands. "I promise... now, where did that waitress go? I really am starving." He waved in the air to catch the waitress's attention, not realizing the gesture also caught Sarah's eye, sitting directly in between.

Sarah meekly waved back, chin raised, brows clenched.

"Oh, yeah, this won't be awkward at all," he said.

Annaleigh's shoulders bobbed as she smiled. "You created this mess, buddy. Have fun cleaning it up."

22

REVELATIONS ON THE STAND

Early morning sunlight filtered through the windows of the first-floor courtroom. Motes floated around, dancing in the beams of light, seeming to settle on the prosecution table in front of John's chair.

The music has to stop eventually. Hopefully, today is Kenneth's day.

Judge Chapel rapped the gavel, and echoes echoed off the wall-to-wall hardwood. Annaleigh rose gracefully.

"The prosecution rests, Your Honor."

After the disappointing testimony from the ladies at City Hall, Annaleigh had no choice but to close on a low note. She hoped to use cross-examination of defense witnesses as additional leverage to bolster their case.

John still had the ability to spot lies—their secret weapon. And, based on defense attorney Hoover's past actions, the Cobb County fraud would have an assembly line of people willing not only to bend the truth, but shatter it if it meant helping Kenneth avoid accountability.

Judge Chapel nodded to Annaleigh. "Very well. Mr. Hoover, are you ready to present your defense?"

Hoover pushed his chair back and stood. As his lips parted,

Kenneth's shackled hands reached up and pressed down on his elbow.

"One second, Your Honor," he said, in what appeared to be a rehearsed interruption. An intense, whispered argument followed. Hoover gestured emphatically, while Kenneth shook his head stubbornly.

A silent performance art piece unfolded in the courtroom. Between head shakes and inaudible whispers, Hoover cast glances at the prosecution table, smirking at Annaleigh, then refocused on Kenneth, flapping his hands to ensure everyone in the gallery understood a major disagreement was underway.

"Mr. Hoover?" Judge Chapel had clearly grown tired of the antics. "Do you have a witness or not? We're not here for theater."

A deep sigh escaped Hoover's mouth as he patted the air in front of Kenneth. He stood up.

"Your Honor, the defense was about to rest their case, seeing that the prosecution hasn't proved anything. But, against my strong advice, the defendant wishes to testify on his own behalf."

A chorus of gasps echoed through the gallery, prompting a series of gavel strikes from Chapel. "Easy now, folks. Easy now." He gestured to the bailiff. "Baz, please escort Mr. Atlee to the stand."

Baz stepped into the well, nervously tugging at the same crisp white dress shirt and dark slacks he'd worn every day of the trial. He shuffled along the floor, never taking his eye off the defendant, even when he bent down to lift the backup canisters of FM-200 off the floor.

Kenneth stood, fully exposing the customized restraints John had built for all to see. Until now, the jury's view had been mostly blocked by the defense table as Kenneth had kept his hands beneath it throughout the trial. As the jurors both entered after and exited before Kenneth at the start and end of each day, they had no opportunity to get a good look.

The firefighter gloves, which were large when John first tried them during testing, fit snugly on Kenneth's large hands. He kept his fingers pinched tight, making the gloves resemble bulky oven mitts. With tubes poking out, it looked as though he were preparing for a deep-sea dive, but only his hands needed to breathe.

John watched the faces of the jury members. A mix of astonishment, curiosity, and disgust washed over each one. Hard to tell which way the jury leaned.

Just wait until cross. Then, they'll come around.

Kenneth trudged to the stand, even though his legs weren't shackled, plopping into the chair as Baz placed the backup FM-200 canisters at his feet and adjusted the tubing to prevent kinks.

Classic—turning the witness stand into his stage, with help from his attorney. Potentia, indeed.

John turned his head left and right, surveying the scene.

In the first pew by the jury box, Deputy D. Clyde Brothers sat, paying close attention. Behind the prosecution table, Sheriff Parnell sat, elbows on his knees, observant and focused on Kenneth's every move. On the opposite side, Dallas Taggart guarded the side door used by Judge Chapel and the bailiffs.

Under John's suit coat, he gently squeezed his arm against his side, confirming the shoulder holster hanging underneath felt thick with the Smith & Wesson 5906.

All exits secured, and priority targets protected.

Baz asked Kenneth to raise his right hand.

"Do you solemnly swear to tell the truth, the whole truth, and nothing but the truth?"

"I do," replied Kenneth.

John watched the air around Kenneth's head closely, but saw nothing. Annaleigh glanced at him, and he gave an almost imperceptible head shake, followed by a tiny adjustment of his shoulders.

Was he actually admitting to telling the truth? I really expected to see something.

Hoover strode into the well and spread his hands.

"Mr. Atlee, against my advice, you insisted on testifying today. Why is that?"

"Because I'm tired of the lies," he said in an unfamiliar voice, as if trying to hide his regular snarl. "This town—people like her," he nodded at Annaleigh, "think they have me all figured out. Take one look at me and judge for yourself."

"I'd like the record to reflect the defendant was referring to the prosecuting attorney."

Annaleigh shot out of her chair. "Your Honor, the defense counsel makes it sound like this is a victim identification. That's ridiculous."

Hoover shot a sly grin over his shoulder. "If the shoe fits the assailant," he murmured.

Judge Chapel cleared his throat. "Enough. The record will reflect the direction of the witness's gesture, but," he turned to the jury, "the jury will disregard any insinuation of improper conduct by the prosecuting attorney." Chapel returned his focus to glare at Hoover. "That... requires proof. Let's move on."

Hoover leaned against the short wall.

"Mr. Atlee, what do you believe the prosecution... er, everyone, is lying about?"

"Everything." Kenneth leaned in, trying to sound folksy. "Take these." He held up his hands, pulling the tubing tight and knocking over the canister. "Torture devices. Painful. And worthless. I got no powers." Kenneth's head lit up with a lilac glow, then faded.

John extended his elbow about an inch from its resting position on the chair's arm, lightly touching Annaleigh. He expected to do this often. Though surprised by Kenneth's unexpected testimony, they'd already arranged a secret signal to use whenever John sensed a lie in any witness.

"I was in Vietnam," Kenneth continued. "Injured at the end of my first tour. These scars on my wrists? Bad luck, bad timing, and bad memories from a war I can't forget."

Another bump on Annaleigh's elbow.

"Mr. Atlee, the prosecution has presented evidence—or what they call evidence—"

"Objection," Annaleigh yelled, standing up.

"Withdrawn," Hoover drawled, waving a hand at Judge Chapel. "Mr. Atlee, the prosecution presented some documents regarding city contracts. Can you explain those?"

"KRA Industries? Cameron set that up. Didn't even know about it until it was mentioned here in court. Sounds like a shell game to me. It makes sense he'd name it after me, so nobody looked at him."

Elbow.

"But, Mr. Atlee, they showed your signature on some documents?"

"I worked for the guy, but he called the shots. If he said, 'Sign this,' I did it. It's not like I even understand all that legal jargon."

More shimmer, more elbow.

"Everything's a lie," Annaleigh whispered to John from the side of her mouth. "I get it."

"If anyone's pocket got lined, it's his," Kenneth continued. "I may have gotten a few performance bonuses from him, but I didn't know where they came from—"

"Thank you, Mr. Atlee. That's enough—"

"No, I'm up here to clear my name, to tell the truth, like I swore to."

God, he's loving this. He's the center of attention. Was this his plan all along? The main attraction in Coldwater's greatest circus.

"In fact," Kenneth said, "I'm pretty sure almost everyone in the gallery can imagine themselves in my shoes. Taken advantage of, underestimated, heck, undervalued... I mean, I'm the guy who's last at the table and holding the check. That's why I was at that warehouse—I wanted to get caught. So I'd be able to tell my side. That lady lawyer over there has nothing on me. In fact, we're only here because they killed the real criminal back in May in a car chase—"

John and Annaleigh stood up, shouting at the same time.

"Objection!" John hurried back to his seat, letting Annaleigh take control of the situation. Before she could explain her reasons, Judge Chapel made his ruling.

"Sustained, the jury will disregard the last statement by the witness. If you have further questions, Mr. Hoover, I suggest you tread carefully."

Hoover pretended to bow. "Not at all, Your Honor. I think everyone understands what's going on here. No further questions." He sat back down and folded his hands on the table, wearing a smug grin.

"Cross-examination?" Chapel asked toward the prosecution table.

Annaleigh sat and offered a supportive signal to John, who rose and entered the well.

"Mr. Atlee, based on what you've said, it sounds like you see yourself as the victim in this trial. Is that really how you feel?"

"Absolutely. I've done nothing wrong." A bruise-colored shimmer flickered around his head, there for a moment, then disappeared.

"Let's talk about your capture… the night you were finally apprehended after three months of being on the run. You said you *wanted* to get caught?"

"Absolutely. Planned the whole shebang—and drew you in like a moth."

He saw it again. A plum flare, shapeless, radiating outward then collapsing inward, gone.

"Or maybe you were backed into a corner and became desperate?"

Kenneth's exterior shell cracked slightly, maybe not enough for the jury to notice. But John saw.

"All part of my plan," Kenneth lied.

"City Hall records show KRA Industries received hundreds of thousands of dollars for work that was never finished. Many projects never even started. Your company, your signature. Your story is that you were coerced?"

"That's right."

"But, Mr. Atlee, don't you remember? We put Reginald Windermere III on the stand last week. He's the manager at the First Bank of Coldwater, the bank where KRA Industries' accounts are held. Do you recall him testifying that he remembered you signing documents to open the account? And that you were there... alone? Mayor Raith wasn't even present. So, how could you have been coerced by someone who's not even there?"

"Raith's puppet strings. Look at me. I was the muscle. *His* muscle. He was the brains. You saw what he could do. That kind of power doesn't need to be in the same room to be controlling... someone as powerful as that, their presence is the only sign you need to know that you don't mess with them."

The longer Kenneth spoke, the more his contempt showed. John knew the man wanted to tell everyone that he was in charge, that he wielded the power he described.

I just need to get him to say it.

John circled the well, taking small steps to think through his next question. "If I didn't know better, it almost sounds like you're talking about yourself. We've heard multiple witnesses describe how you carried out these so-called orders from Cameron Raith without him ever needing to show up. But, only you were there. You. Each time something needed this power... you were there. That seems awfully suspicious to me."

"Maybe you should call *him* to the stand, then. Oh, wait, you can't. Because he's dead."

"If you think about it, it's pretty convenient for you, isn't it? When all the evidence points in your direction, you point at the one guy who can't answer questions. It sure looks like *you* were the one pulling strings. That *you* were the real mastermind here. Admit it—*you* were the boss, weren't you?"

John realized he had rushed it. He hadn't made Kenneth squirm enough. There's no way he'll fold this quickly.

No matter what he says here, I need to keep hitting him with the evidence. Make him refute every little thing. Then, he'll slip up.

"Fine," Kenneth said with a sarcastic sneer. "I was the genius. Raith was *my* front man."

A purple shimmer appeared around Kenneth's head, as usual. But unexpectedly, it grew brighter instead of fading away. It became more vivid and intense, causing John to narrow his eyes and squint. When the bloom popped, like a light bulb shattering, John jumped back, feeling as if he'd been pelleted by unseen shards.

What the hell was that?

"Mr. Chance, is everything all right?" Judge Chapel's question initially went unanswered as John continued to stare at the now-empty space around Kenneth's head, trying to process what he had witnessed.

The only way to know is to test it.

"Yes, Your Honor, I'm... I'm fine," John lied. He scratched his neck and adjusted his shoulders. "I don't think the court appreciates your humor, Mr. Atlee, although the record will at least reflect you admitting guilt... in your own words." John paused, awaiting another Hoover objection. None came. "Another witness testified to seeing you assault Evelyn Raith. Is it your claim that you never harmed Mrs. Raith?"

"In my experience, secretaries can't be trusted. They're not owners—they're employees. Followers. They do whatever they're told to do. Maybe even what they're told to say. Doesn't matter, anyway. I never laid a hand on that woman."

John peered in, but saw only Kenneth's arrogant grin.

Shit.

"Um... are... are you sure?"

"Sure as I'm sitting here today, *Counselor.*"

Nothing. No shimmer. No haze. No mist.

It's gone. Mid-fucking cross. And it's gone.

The old oak flooring in the courtroom spun beneath John's feet. It felt like heat rose from his head and steamed into the air. He swallowed.

"So… uh, you're saying… did you… I mean, she, um… you haven't… never hurt Evelyn Raith?"

"Objection, Your Honor. Asked and answered. He's badgering the witness now. Or, maybe having a stroke."

Chapel issued a sympathetic ruling. "I'm afraid he's right, Mr. Chance. Sustained. Move along, please."

"One second, Judge," John replied, turning back to the prosecutor's table. He stood with his back to both Kenneth and Judge Chapel, nervously shuffling through papers as if searching for a document. Catching Annaleigh's eye, he swallowed hard.

"You okay?" she mouthed.

He nodded feebly, but he knew she saw right through it. She stood up and addressed the court.

"Your Honor, may I request a short recess to consult with my colleague?"

Hoover jumped out of his chair.

"In the middle of their own cross-examination? Highly irregular, Your Honor. Either finish questioning my client or end it." He looked at Annaleigh, tilting his head. "No timeouts on the playground."

"I have to agree with the defense," Judge Chapel said monotonously. "We'll take a short break *after* this witness. Now, do you have anything else?"

John spun around, hands clasped, head bowed. "No further questions." He walked around the table to his chair.

The courtroom fell silent, unaware of what caused John to suddenly step back from the witness. A member of the gallery coughed. Others shuffled their feet. The judge appeared to let the moment linger.

"Redirect?" Chapel asked.

Hoover, still standing, waved his hands as if holding at Blackjack. He stifled a chuckle.

"No thanks, Your Honor. I think we're good here."

Judge Chapel checked his wristwatch. Then, confirmed again by looking at the large analog clock hanging on the back wall.

"I think we can break and all have a nice, long lunch. The court's in recess until one o'clock."

The gavel's firm thump sealed John's fate. It sealed the town's destiny.

John had just lost the trial.

There's no way the jury could witness a performance like that and believe in any way, shape, or form that the prosecution had made its case.

Kenneth was about to walk free.

23

SHADOWS OF SECRETS

The courtroom cleared out quickly. John couldn't have been more grateful.

Clyde hurried the jury out, urging a quick exit. Once the last juror exited, he and Baz escorted Kenneth through the side door. From across the courtroom, he gave a sympathetic smile at John, then disappeared with Deputy Dallas Taggart to send the defendant back to the county lockup.

At the same time, townsfolk in the gallery quietly left, whispering and shuffling their feet, uncertain whether they should feel sympathy for the attorney who lost his marbles or concern that a suspected arsonist and murderer might go free.

Twice now, they'd seen their prosecutors fall apart.

Cynicism was justified.

Sarah excused herself and went back to their upstairs office, but not before giving a reassuring touch to John's shoulder.

He didn't feel it.

He didn't hear whatever words she said. The incomprehensible murmur faded into the cyclone whirling inside him. The thunder of Judge Chapel's gavel still echoed in his ears.

Annaleigh lingered at the prosecution table, casually packing her briefcase with folders and notepads. He wasn't sure, but it definitely looked like she had already put the same pad in there three times.

John rose, heat curling up his spine. Clenching his fists, he jerked his foot, kicking the wooden chair and causing it to slide across the hardwood floor. It slammed into the jury box with a clatter.

"I blew it. I was complete dogshit."

He moved into the well, the same spot he occupied moments earlier when the unthinkable happened, and the world stopped. When his gift had left him.

To some, having the ability to see lies was unthinkable.

To John, it was losing it.

But none of that mattered anymore. It no longer existed. When he needed it most, his own abilities had betrayed him.

Fingernails dug into his palms. His hands trembled from the pressure.

"One more fucking day. All I needed was for it to be there one more goddamned day. It stopped... without any warning."

Annaleigh walked around the table, spun, and hopped up to sit on it. "At least you got him to admit, under oath, that he was the mastermind," she said, crossing her arms. "That's got to count for something."

He glared back at her. "You've got to be kidding... he was being sarcastic. The record may not reflect those words, but every juror heard it. You saw it. Nobody believed him."

"Then that's something we'll have to cover in our closing arguments. We need to convince them that he wasn't being sarcastic—that he said the words and meant it."

John's pacing led him to the jury box, where he leaned on the half-wall. He gestured to the empty twelve chairs.

"You're going to try and convince them that what they heard wasn't what they heard? Believe your lying ears?"

"I've done it before." She smirked.

"No... " He shook his head. "This isn't on you to fix my screw up—"

"Sure it is, John. I'm the prosecutor. It's literally my job. We'll make this right somehow."

"But... but, I mean, I had him. I was leading him right where I wanted..." He glanced at her mid-sentence. Her expression told him the truth. Maybe he would have gotten there. Eventually. But, he wasn't as close as he thought. He rushed over to her. "Fine, test me. Tell me something—anything. Lie to me."

Her brows lifted, then she quickly rolled her eyes and shook her head.

"John..."

"No! I mean it. Maybe it was a blip. Maybe it's back now." He leaned in, eyes flicking around her head in anticipation of seeing that purple shimmer.

She looked down at her lap, then lifted her chin, and with her face completely drained of emotion, she spoke in monotone.

"You didn't screw up. I'm not worried about the verdict. At the diner, I lied. Sarah told me that she's in love with you. I've decided you can date her, too, if you want to. We'd make a nice throuple."

In the space around her head, he saw... nothing. He winced, rubbing at the back of his neck. Then, it hit him. He had stared so intently at the space around her head that her words didn't quite register.

"So," he said, scrunching his face, "those... were all truths? Or lies? Tell me you're lying about that last one."

"Of course I was, you idiot!" she snapped, storming back around the table and shoving the legal pad into her satchel for the fourth time.

"Wait... so, you *are* worried... about the verdict?"

"Yes, I'm worried," she huffed. "You should be, too. You relied..." She pursed her lips and exhaled. "*We* relied on your little trick to break that monster on the stand. And it didn't work. And we can't call him to the stand again. We can't question him again. Our best chance to put him away forever... is gone. So, yes, John, I'm worried. Because now I have to get twelve people to ignore everything they just heard and saw." She strode to the courtroom doors, pausing at the threshold. "I'm going upstairs to start work on my closing arguments. Put that chair back before you leave."

John closed his eyes, his mind racing. He stood alone in his pity.

His eyes moved over the empty jury box, the witness stand, and the judge's tall, ornate chair. This room represented the one place where justice could be served.

Where wrongs were made right. And victims found their closure.

A victim, like his mother. Someone who that son of a bitch tried to burn alive. And the only thing Coldwater's dogshit detective had to prove he did it was a set of tire tracks in some loose gravel.

He'd failed everyone. He'd failed Annaleigh. He'd failed his mother.

He had even failed as a detective—what kind of detective doesn't gather enough evidence to arrest someone who's apparently committed every kind of crime imaginable in Coldwater?

And, the cherry on top?

He'd failed at being a lawyer. How did he forget how to ask questions? To trap a witness into contradicting themselves?

In law school, cross-examining witnesses was child's play for him in every mock trial. He'd twist them up so badly that they nearly confessed right there and then. One time, he even made one of them cry. Cry! A witness in a mock trial, pretending to be a defendant, cried over something they didn't even do. Because of him.

That's how talented he *used* to be.

He achieved all of that without knowing exactly when someone lied to him. However, when his talents needed to shine, they froze, and he relied on a magic trick—one that vanished right in front of everyone's eyes. He'd turned this place into the furthest place possible from justice.

He righted the kicked chair and tucked it neatly under the

prosecution's table. He passed through the swinging gate and paused once he reached the gallery. He released it and observed it swinging back and forth.

He chuckled to himself.

They call this gate the bar because to become a lawyer, you must pass the bar exam. It's a literal metaphor. You pass through the bar, and then you're allowed to make your case to the judge. After what I did today, maybe I belong on this side of it.

He sank into the front pew of the gallery and folded, elbows resting on his knees, his head in his hands. His stomach churned, and bile rose up, choking him. He swallowed it back down. He rubbed his forehead, feeling its damp warmth as if it had been near a campfire.

From behind him, the door creaked open. Footsteps approached, and the pew groaned as a figure sat down next to him.

John lifted his head and saw the familiar kind eyes of Deputy D. Clyde Brothers looking back at him. He lowered his head back into his hands.

"Clyde, I know I probably could use it, but I don't know if I want one of your pep talks right now. I… I don't deserve it."

"How about just some company, then? We don't have to talk at all. Not if you don't want," he said with a smile.

Clyde had a knack for saying the perfect words. Sometimes, for him, not saying anything was his play. The man had a gift for unpressing whatever button had knocked John askew.

He had stopped John from going too far with Clayden Kendrick at the town hall after Gamble died, then refocused him after the shed fire, while his mother lay wrapped in bandages in the hospital.

In fact, there were many times when Clyde offered a reassuring word or piece of advice—the kind that John needed—that made his first three months as a part-time detective bearable.

"I cheated, Clyde," John admitted. "I've been cheating this whole time. You probably won't believe me, and it may not make sense, but some strange things have been happening. When Wesley's hands blew up, his blood got into me somehow... from being on my face, I guess. Then Foley knocked me out, and when I woke up... I could see when people lie. When they lie, even by not speaking, I don't just know it, I *see* it. I've been using this shortcut when talking to witnesses, in depositions, during this whole trial. First, doc says I have herbicide in my blood. Then it starts to get better. But now, I can't see the purple anymore. So, unless Annaleigh can convince the jury to ignore reality, he walks free. I screwed up everything."

John's rant was free-flowing, chaotic, and heartfelt. He drew a long breath and exhaled quickly.

But as soon as the words left his mouth, he knew it sounded crazy.

Clyde leaned back and folded his hands. "That explains why you froze up there?"

John eyed him without moving his head. "That's all you're going to say? I tell you I have this crazy ability to see when people lie... and you're not going to ask about it?"

"Had."

"What?" John snapped back.

"You said *have*," Clyde said, shrugging. "But, you lost it."

"We're going to devolve into semantics?"

"Not at all, young man. You've had a rough couple of months. It also sounds like you're close to getting a full bill of health from the doctor. That's great news. And 'tween you and Ms. Stanton, I know this trial is only going to end one way—in our favor. Don't sound like losing to me. In fact, seems like you're right on the cusp of a winning streak."

"That's one way of looking at it," John said with a suspicious tone. "You can be optimistic all you want. But I lied. To everyone. I had this secret... kept it from everybody. Even Annaleigh. And now I think she's pissed—I mean, mad at me."

"You fought for what was right... with what you had. Don't

sound too bad to me. But, secrets like that... they weigh heavy. Don't I know it."

John's chin slammed back. "Secrets? You? What do you know about those? You're the most open book I know, man."

"Maybe, but things get hidden in this town sometimes... obscuring is part of this town's history, it's bloodline. It's like the creek flowing through. Always been there. Always will be there."

"For the first time, Clyde, you're the one not making sense."

The kind eyes that were a staple of Clyde's face reddened and glistened.

"A while back, you asked about my name. Maybe it's time I told you."

"Your name?" John asked, perplexed. "It's Clyde. Everybody knows that."

"No, John. My full name. D. Clyde Brothers."

"Oh, that's right. Almost forgot about that part. What about it? Is it embarrassing? Can't be worse than Clyde, no offense."

Through watery eyes, Clyde smiled. "No, not embarrassing at all. In my family, names are important. In fact, we've always had a tradition, of sorts. You see, my daddy's name was Clyde. So, when he had a son—me—he took his first name and gave it to me as a middle name. Look at my family tree, it's that way as far back as we can see. A man's first son takes on his father's name. It's a link in a chain that never ends. It's special."

John's head tilted. "So, your dad's name is Clyde, and you go by Clyde, too? Didn't that get confusing?"

One side of Clyde's lip curled up. "You wouldn't know, but I didn't always go by it. For a long time, everybody called me by my real first name. But, some time ago, I decided to switch."

"So, what's your first name, then?"

"That's what I'm saying, John. I want to tell you about it, if you'd like to hear it?"

"You make it sound like it's some state secret."

"It's not like that, but maybe just as important." Clyde swallowed hard. "John, my first name is... Deacon."

John thought for a second. "But... wait... your name... is Deacon?"

"Yes, John. I'm Deacon Clyde Brothers. And what's your name? John Deacon Chance."

John's lips parted, but nothing exited. His heart pounded.

"John, it's me. I'm your father."

All the air left John's lungs in one quick heave. Inside his head, his world twirled and twisted.

"You? It's you? After all this time? But... why not... I, uh... what the..."

The courtroom doors slammed open with a loud bang, echoing through the room and startling both men. Sheriff Parnell hurried in, gasping for breath and shouting.

"Both of you, let's go. Cadaver dogs hit on something. I... I think we've found her."

Clyde straightened up and wrapped a strong arm around John's shoulders, pulling him to his feet.

"I promise, we'll talk. Long and proper. I'll tell you anything you need."

John nodded weakly, his legs numb underneath him.

All three men hurried from the courthouse and entered separate cars. Still shaky, John's fingers fumbled as he turned the key and started the engine, while he watched Clyde's cruiser pulling away.

Clyde? My father? Right next to me... this whole time?

John's foot slammed on the accelerator, and he sped off toward the Raith property.

Focus on one crisis at a time... in a sea of problems.

Everything needed answering.

24

RACE TO THE FIND

Dane Parnell gripped the wheel. As he zipped along, the concrete town roads transitioned to rural asphalt roads. The convoy he led included the deputies' cruisers of Deputy D. Clyde Brothers and his young detective, John Chance.

He knew exactly where the path led, but he wasn't sure what they'd find when they got there.

If only he'd been more aggressive in searching the property after she was reported missing. Consent and politics be damned.

Textbook domestic violence. It's always the husband, right? Except in this case, it looks like you farmed out the work, Cameron. You coward.

If only someone had followed up on Issabel's statement all those years ago. Could they have reacted in time to save her?

Dammit, Mumber. Could've forced Cameron's hand and fought harder. Maybe then you wouldn't still be trying to heal the burns on your face.

His heartbeat raced as his cruiser matched pace along the winding roads out in the Coldwater outskirts. This was the first time they'd needed to use cadaver dogs in Coldwater. Naturally, he had concerns about pinpointing the remains of a body potentially buried years ago.

Cadaver dogs were trained to detect human remains, the Wayne County Sheriff had told him. "If they hit, it's a virtual guarantee there's a body. And, it won't be animal."

"They ever miss? Ever find animal remains instead?" Parnell had asked. "I dug up a cow or horse on that property with my detective. If there are others like that out there, I don't want to waste anybody's time."

The Wayne County Sheriff cleared his throat. "If they miss, I retire them. They get to live a good life somewhere and never have to sniff for a living again. Then, I get a new dog that don't miss."

"How many dogs have you gone through, then?"

"Still on my first." Parnell heard the man's wide grin through the phone. "Sheriff, my boy don't miss. We'll see you in a few days."

Any doubts about this operation vanished after that conversation. He crested the hill and proceeded toward the Raith driveway.

Years in the making. If it's her, it's the final nail in the coffin of his legacy. Dammit, Cameron. What have you done? What did Kenneth do for you?

He rounded the last corner and hit the brakes, skidding to a stop and digging deep ruts in the gravel. Up ahead, blocking the entrance, sat a duel-wheeled pickup truck and its lowboy trailer carrying the backhoe.

"What the hell is this mess? You were supposed to start digging an hour ago," he yelled, hopping out of his cruiser.

The driver raised both hands, then pointed toward the iron arch sporting which bore the name "RAITH" in wispy letters.

"Height, Sheriff. The trailer's too tall to pass under that arch. We were just about to start taking apart the split-rail fence and take it through the grass."

Parnell shook his head. "Won't work--too much of a gully there. You'll tip that hoe right off," he said, pointing to the dip that funneled rainwater shed off the road. "Back up and let me get in there." He nodded toward a length of loose chain lying on the trailer. "And give me one of those."

Parnell glanced at Clyde and John arriving, signaling for them to hold out on the road. He slipped through the opening made by the pickup, stopping inside the arch. He poked his head out the open window and moved back to align his trunk with one side of the arch.

A few minutes later, Parnell had wrapped one end of the chain around the railing, about halfway up, by standing precariously on his cruiser's trunk lid. The chain's other end rattled as he wrapped it around his metal bumper. The engine revved, and the back tires spat dirt as Parnell gunned the gas pedal.

The iron arch ripped loose from its foundation and clanged to the ground with a satisfying sound. He kept driving perpendicularly to the long driveway, towing it further into the yard and away from the entrance. He waved the pickup through and tossed the unhooked chain onto the trailer as it passed by.

Raith's name in the dirt. Fitting. Evelyn deserved so much more than Cameron. Poor girl.

He pulled the radio from his belt and barked orders.

"Dallas, backhoe is headed your way. Guide it down that hill." John followed the trailer, but Parnell stopped Clyde's cruiser with a wave.

"The kid looks pale," he said, leaning down to the window. "I take it you told him."

"I think it hit him hard," Clyde said. "Was about to explain everything, then you burst in. Almost gave us both a heart attack."

"Sorry, thought things were a bit more imminent here. But, Clyde, if they really found something..."

"I know, it means you weren't wrong this whole time. But, do me a favor. He doesn't understand why yet, so give the kid a break until he does."

"Roger that," Parnell replied. "I'll meet you all down there. Let's close this."

Parnell hurried back in and followed Clyde up the driveway, to the right past the main house, and down the worn path leading to Kenneth's cabin. Several Wayne County cruisers were parked beside a Coldwater Sheriff's deputy car, with Dallas Taggart signaling everyone where to stop.

About fifty feet past the spot where he and John dug up the animal, along the same edge of the forest, the cadaver dog lay in the grass. The Wayne County deputy, the dog's handler, pointed at a spot.

"Let's hope this isn't a retirement party, eh, Sheriff?" Parnell said sarcastically as he approached the Wayne County Sheriff. The man responded with a short grunt and a chin lift. The backhoe unloaded and moved into position, and Parnell gathered everyone in a circle.

"All right, folks. We're going to dig in shallow increments, down to a depth of eight feet, unless we hit something before then. We start here," he motioned to the exact mark made by the dog, "and then move outward as needed. First sign of remains, we switch to shovels and expose what we can by hand. The coroner's on standby in case we find... well, in case we find what we're looking for. Everybody on the same page?" He looked around and got several acknowledgments, except for John. He still looked dazed, like his whole world spun inside his head. He motioned to the operator. "Let's dig!"

The backhoe roared to life, and the operator skillfully scraped a six-foot-long section of earth to a depth of a few inches. Each deliberate pass stopped at the first sign of resistance, allowing Parnell and his deputies to inspect the cause.

At three feet, the backhoe struck a pocket of dense clay. Clyde had hopped into the hole and probed the bottom with a shovel.

"Undisturbed clay, boss. It don't lay like this if it's already been dug through."

As John and Dallas helped Clyde, Parnell signaled to the Wayne County Sheriff. He relayed an order to his deputy, and the cadaver dog began inspecting, sniffing around each edge of the hole and then branching outward. It sat at the corner of the hole closest to the forest.

"Extend the hole in that direction," Parnell ordered.

The operator used the bucket to partially refill the hole and tamp down the loose dirt, helping to prevent a cave-in. Then, he adjusted the position and scraped away in the new spot.

Inch by inch, the operator removed roots, clay pockets, and dirt, dumping it into a pile behind him. Pivoting the backhoe's cab 180 degrees to access the dirt mound took nearly as long as removing the thin layer of earth. On each backswing, Clyde bent over and inspected the hole, looking for anything that didn't belong.

At four feet deep, he hollered and waved to the operator before the next scrape started.

"Whoa! Sheriff, you're gonna want to see this."

Parnell leaned over the breach, peering in. "I'll be damned." As clear as day, the bottom corner of a flowered blouse poked out from the disturbed soil. A button, previously white but now caked in brown dirt, stared at the Coldwater sky for the first time in years. Dark red stains splattered the fabric.

Parnell's eyes welled up with tears. He exchanged a look with Clyde, one that both men understood without saying a word. Clyde patted him on the back.

"You did it, Dane. You found her."

"Maybe. Check and see if she still has it."

Clyde carefully eased himself into the hole, being careful where he stepped. He hand-dug in the direction where a head might reasonably be, taking small scoops and dumping the earth behind him. He reached and picked up an object from the dirt with his gloved hand—a small cross on a thin chain, covered in a light layer of dirt. He wiped it clean with his thumb and held it up.

"Engraved with the initials, E.R.," he said, voice cracking. "It's her, Dane. It's really her."

Parnell swallowed hard. He composed himself and spoke softly.

"All right, let's get this hole cleared out. Shovels, everyone, let's go." Dallas jumped into the hole next to Clyde and worked to remove the remaining dirt. When John tried the same, Parnell raised a hand and pressed it into his chest, stopping him.

"I know I've been a little quiet, Sheriff, but I'm good to dig."

"Understood, but I don't want this broadcast on the radio. I want you to drive to the hospital and tell Dr. Jensen face-to-face. Then, escort her crew out here, code three. Go ahead, son. Get them and bring 'em back so we can get her out of the ground. And let's pray there's something on here we can link to Kenneth. Otherwise, it might end up as a hollow victory."

John said nothing, but panned an unnoticed glance at Clyde, busy clearing dirt in the hole.

"John?" Parnell said, catching up to him after a few steps.

John spun, eyebrows raised. "Yeah, boss? What else do you want now??"

Parnell's brows raised. "Look, I know what Clyde told you. I'm sure you want to know more... to understand more."

"You... you knew, too?" John stammered.

"I did, son, but it wasn't my place. All I can say is try not to be mad at the world. You and Clyde will have that talk. I promise... he promises. But for now, I need you to focus on the problem in front of you. Not the questions you really want answers to. The only thing we need to know right now is whether Kenneth did this to her. If he did, then we can make him finally pay for it."

After a silent nod, John strode back to his cruiser, showing all the telltale signs of being furious.

Parnell understood, but unfortunately, John's situation didn't take priority.

Getting that blood-stained shirt tested was all that mattered.

25

UNPLEASANT PRESENTATIONS

When Judge Chapel gaveled the court into session at nine o'clock the next morning, Coldwater had already packed tight into the court's gallery. Some members stood along the back walls. Harlan did his best to shower those in the aisle with looks of disappointment and urged them to squeeze into any remaining pew space.

Word of a body being found had spread quickly. The tension in the room pressed down on everyone. Whispers bounced, ranging from wondering if they'd bring in a casket as evidence to whether Kenneth would be shot right there at the defendant's table if found guilty.

Judge Chapel's stern expressions didn't help, either. With so many curious onlookers, his uneasiness showed with continual glances at the FM-200 canisters on Kenneth's arms and feet.

Annaleigh rose from her chair, her steady voice cutting through the murmurs behind her.

"Your Honor, the prosecution moves to reopen its case based on newly discovered evidence."

"Your Honor!" Hoover shot to his feet. "This is outrageous—it's an ambush! The prosecution has already rested, and the defense is in the middle of its case. This is highly irregular and most certainly prejudicial!"

Chapel said nothing, but waved both attorneys up to his bench for a sidebar discussion.

"Yesterday afternoon," she began quietly, "cadaver dogs located a body on the Raith property—near the defendant's cabin. Preliminary evidence confirms it is Evelyn Raith, who, as we all know, has been missing for years. This directly supports witness testimony about Kenneth Atlee's assault on her and strengthens the conspiracy and financial crime charges. It also warrants amending the indictment to include the murder of Evelyn Raith."

"This is a fishing expedition," Hoover said loudly, causing Judge Chapel to motion with his hands to lower his voice. "Prosecution is grasping at ghosts to save their crumbling case!" He turned to Annaleigh. "Desperate theatrics, Stanton. Maybe you can conjure up some evidence and try to convict me, too."

She smirked. "Your client left so much evidence of his crimes lying around, we'll still be finding it long after you've left town, Hoover."

"All right, you two. I know there's history here, but my courtroom will not succumb to incivility," Chapel admonished. "I would advise counsel to refrain from accusations of evidence tampering. If you have proof, present it... and not in my sidebar. Return to your tables, and I will announce my ruling."

Both walked back to their chairs, but remained standing.

Judge Chapel spoke loudly and clearly. "The court will allow a reopening to ensure a complete record and serve the interests of justice. The new evidence appears both material and timely. Mr. Hoover, your objections are noted, but I'm not shutting down this trial. Ms. Stanton, you may proceed."

Annaleigh held up a piece of paper. "We seek to amend the charges to include first-degree murder of Evelyn Raith. Forthcoming testimony will show the body was found in a shallow grave near the defendant's known residence, along with visible blunt-force trauma consistent with prior testimony."

"Your Honor," Hoover said, still standing, "this new charge blindsides the defense! We have no time to prepare... witnesses, experts, alibis. This violates the due process of my client—"

"Counsel, the evidence is newly discovered and highly relevant to these proceedings!" Judge Chapel's voice had never sounded that loud before. "The defense will have full opportunity—and sufficient latitude during cross-examination—to rebut newly presented evidence. Continuing this trial serves justice—dismissing it would not." He sat up straight in his chair, face expressionless. "Your implied motion to delay is denied."

More whispers rippled through the crowd. At the defendant's table, Kenneth shifted in his seat, eyes narrowing.

Annaleigh sat down, leaned toward John, and whispered in his ear.

"Foley's here. Sitting in the back row. Did you see him?"

"No," he replied, twisting to look. "That traitor shouldn't be anywhere near here."

"Last row, far side. Make sure everybody knows."

"Of all the days we've been in here, not sure why he picked today. On it." He twisted his shoulders, discreetly waved to get Clyde's attention, and mouthed an update.

She stood. "The prosecution recalls Sheriff Dane Parnell."

After being reminded he was under oath, he eased into the witness chair.

"Sheriff, describe the discovery, please."

"Yes, ma'am. Cadaver dogs indicated strong scent, not far from the defendant's cabin—same general area we searched days ago. The backhoe uncovered a grave about four feet deep. Female remains, decomposed but still intact. No signs of burns or melting. The cause of death was likely blunt force trauma to the skull, consistent with a heavy blow to the head."

She approached the witness stand with a photo. "Sheriff, can you describe what's in this photo, please?"

"It's a picture of a necklace we found buried with the body. A cross, thin silver chain, engraved on the back with the initials, E. and R. For Evelyn Raith."

"And, what's in this photo?" she asked, handing him another.

"This is a photo of former Mayor Cameron Raith, along with Evelyn, from his mayoral inauguration many years ago. She's wearing the necklace in question."

"Thank you, Sheriff. How certain are you, in your opinion, that the body buried on the Raith property, a stone's throw from the defendant's cabin, is Evelyn Raith?"

"One-hundred percent."

She went back to the table, signaling to Hoover. "Your witness."

He stood and stayed at his table. "Sheriff, you found animal bones days ago—what made you see the need for dogs now?"

"I wasn't aware that detail had been made public," Parnell said, brows lowered. "But, dogs don't lie. Dogs have no agenda. They either sniff human remains or they don't. The hit was unmistakable, and it panned out."

"How can we be sure that what you found isn't the body of some vagrant—and you planted the necklace to make it look like Evelyn Raith?"

Parnell chuckled.

"Oh," Hoover snarked. "Is tampering with evidence funny to you, Sheriff?"

"Not at all," Parnell replied calmly. "It's odd that you'd defend your client from Evelyn Raith's murder by suggesting he killed someone else, but not her."

"Objection, Your Honor—permission to treat the witness as hostile?"

"Denied. You asked the question, Counselor."

Hoover slumped his shoulders and sat down. "No further questions."

Annaleigh rose, looking around. "Your Honor, if I may, I'd like to request a brief recess. Our next witness isn't—"

The courtroom's rear doors swung open, and Dr. Jensen stepped through, holding a manila folder and offering an apologetic smile.

"Never mind, Judge. We'd like to recall Dr. Abigail Jensen."

On her way to the stand, she handed the folder to Annaleigh, who quickly studied the printouts.

"You're still under oath," Judge Chapel reminded a nodding doctor.

"Dr. Jensen," Annaleigh began, still looking at the paperwork. "Please tell the court about your actions regarding the discovered body."

"We worked all night to perform the requested tests. We verified the victim's identity and analyzed the blood stains found on the victim's clothing."

"And, you were able to produce verifiable results in such a short timeframe?"

"Yes, you're holding them right now."

Annaleigh held up the results. "Perfect. Now, the last time you testified, you mentioned finding a specific chemical in the defendant's blood. Can you refresh our memories on that?"

"Absolutely," Jensen said, turning to the jury. "Our tests found something called Picloram in the defendant's blood, as well as in former Mayor Raith and his son, Wesley. It's... uncommon, to say the least."

Annaleigh approached the witness stand, pointing to a specific line on the results. "Can you explain what the report means when it mentions *concentration profiles*?"

"Whenever we detect a contaminant in our test—in this case, Picloram—we measure how much of it is present in the blood samples. We refer to this as a concentration profile. Having that profile helps us identify patterns and match different blood samples, if the need should arise."

"You mentioned finding Picloram in those three individuals—the two Raiths and the defendant. How much did the concentrations differ between them?"

"Yes, um, that's right," Jensen replied, briefly glancing at John sitting at the prosecution table. "For the individuals referenced in the report, the concentration profiles we found were unique for each person. It was very easy to differentiate between them."

"Thank you, Dr. Jensen. Now, getting back to the present, what findings were you able to uncover regarding the blood stains on the clothing from the grave?"

"We identified two separate blood samples from the recovered clothing. One matched Evelyn Raith's blood type, and the other matched... to the defendant."

Hoover's chair scraped the floor as he pushed it back to stand. But before he could protest, Annaleigh raised a hand to stop him, causing him to recoil.

"You can't be serious, Dr. Jensen," she said, turning back to the witness. "Surely, you must be making all of this up. How could you possibly match that blood to the defendant? There must be so many people with the same blood type, right?" She twisted back to Hoover, whose mouth was slightly open. "I got you covered, Chadley," she said, gesturing for him to sit down. Reluctantly, he did, red-faced.

"Oh no," Dr. Jensen said, defiantly. "I'm not making anything up. And we didn't use *only* blood type for that particular match. We were able to match it precisely to the concentration profile for Picloram found in the defendant's blood. It's a direct match. No individual in our comparative set showed this exact profile. It's definitive."

Annaleigh smiled, first at Dr. Jensen, then briefly glared at Hoover.

"Doctor, if you had to theorize, how might the defendant's blood be found on the clothing of a murdered woman buried next to his cabin?"

"I'm not in the business of those kinds of theories, Ms. Stanton, but generally, when analyzing blood samples from victims like this, it indicates that the matched individual was present at the time of the murder. In my experience, that often suggests that person is also the attacker, but I'll leave it to others to interpret what that means."

"Thank you, no further questions." Annaleigh returned to her table as Hoover replaced her in the well.

"Even in perfect conditions, say, in your lab, chemicals degrade unpredictably, correct?" Hoover stated, matter-of-factly.

"Every chemical has a specific half-life. I wouldn't call it unpredictable—"

"So, you admit that under imperfect conditions, like being in the soil for years, these chemicals you mentioned, and the blood you found, would degrade to the point of being unreliable?"

Dr. Jensen shook her head. "No, I did not say that. Degradation is quite predictable under controlled conditions. Perhaps, under uncontrolled conditions, there is a lower chance of matching samples. However, even if the samples are less than perfect because they were buried for years, we matched on the specific concentration profile found in the defendant's blood. That match is the match, Counselor. A binary answer. Yes or no. I'd even go so far as to say that no other human on the planet would have this specific concentration profile."

"That's a bold claim, doctor," Hoover snarked. "Isn't Picloram common? Well known?" He raised his hands to the jury, acting as if he were on Broadway. "I'm sure there are many others that could potentially match that, even in Coldwater, much less the whole world!" A deep laugh rumbled from his belly. Members of the gallery joined in, nervously.

Dr. Jensen paused, allowing the extra noise to fade away. "I don't think you understand, Mr. Hoover—"

"Me? You're the one making claims about having worldwide certainty!"

"Picloram is a herbicide, Mr. Hoover. Typically, when it's in a person's bloodstream... that person is dead within days. Weeks, at the latest." Her eyes skimmed to John, then quickly returned. "In most cases."

Hoover leaned in. "And yet, the defendant is sitting right

there. If it can happen to him, isn't it plausible that it could happen to someone else, too? Meaning your match is worthless?"

Another head shake. "It's statistically impossible for two people to have the exact concentration profile. The odds of that happening are greater than the number of grains of sand on all the beaches on Earth. Maybe there are other people out there with this grass killer in their blood, and maybe they're somehow still living with it. The defendant's blood matched *precisely* with the blood found on the victim... I'm sorry. It's science. It's his blood. No doubt."

Hoover exhaled deeply and muttered, "No further questions for this witness."

Annaleigh nudged Judge with her leg. They'd done it. They'd finally found the right mix of witnesses, evidence, and presentation to quiet the great Bradley Hoover.

"The prosecution rests once more, Your Honor. The evidence speaks for itself," she said with a flourish.

Judge Chapel acknowledged her before returning to Hoover, now slumped behind the defense table. He leaned over to whisper something to Kenneth, then stood up.

"Your Honor, the defense requests to recall the defendant for surrebuttal to address these new allegations."

Chapel motioned for Kenneth to rise.

"The defendant may now retake the stand—and he is also reminded that he is still under oath."

Kenneth stood, pushing his chair back with his calves. He looked around the courtroom menacingly, from Judge Chapel to the jury, the prosecution table, and finally across the entire gallery. His eyes paused on the last pew on the right side of the gallery, then he turned back and delivered a line that chilled everyone in the room.

"Absolutely. It's time."

26

A FIERY DEFENSE

Kenneth Roy Atlee plopped into the witness chair, bracing himself with firefighter's gloves against the front wall of the stand. The thermos-sized canisters strapped to his arms—one on each side—created an odd illusion that his arms were even larger than usual.

With squinted eyes, John watched as Baz, Judge Chapel's favorite bailiff, adjusted the tubing and repositioned the backup canisters of FM-200 at his feet. After a cautious glance at Kenneth, he backed away to stand at the wall.

The tension in John's shoulders loosened a little, seeing Kenneth settled into the witness chair. The tightness wouldn't fully ease until the trial was over and Kenneth was safely under lock and key. But every moment that went by without disaster was a good one.

His arms relaxed inward, brushing the empty holster under his left armpit. A cold jolt ran through him.

In the rush to get to court this morning, he strapped on the holster but neglected to fill it with his 5906. He calmly emptied his lungs, eyes still on Kenneth.

Please don't let today be the day I actually need it.

Kenneth straightened against the chair, shoulders back, like a king surveying his subjects. Hoover asked his question from the defense's table, not even bothering to stand.

"Mr. Atlee, would you like to respond to these new and frivolous allegations regarding Evelyn Raith?"

"You're damn right I would." He raised both gloves and shook them at the jury. "She was family. Knew her for years. I was best man at her wedding, for cripe's sake. I'd never hurt her."

"And what about the evidence they claimed to find on the body?"

"Oh, that necklace? That they *found* in the ground?" He once again raised his gloves to air quote his words. "Planted to frame me, same as everything else in this circus."

"What about the pseudo-science and talk of these... concentration profiles? They sounded pretty confident—"

"Anyone can be confident if you practice enough. Or, if you believe the lie."

"If you could convince the jury of your innocence, what would you say?"

Kenneth's face softened. His grumpy scowl softened into a sympathetic expression, something John didn't think possible.

"I would say, 'I'm not a monster.' I would tell everyone that I'm like you, someone who's lived here their whole life, trying to live a good life. A regular, upstanding member of the community."

A random spectator in the gallery stifled a laugh, covering it with a gentle cough and a throat clear. Whispers floated in the sticky air. Kenneth continued, unaffected.

"If that body truly is Evelyn, and it isn't, by the way, because I watched her drive off out of town, then I'd say it's a shame. Maybe she had second thoughts and came back, maybe she fought with Cameron about it. Maybe *he* killed her and buried her on *his* land. Yes, that would be a terrible shame. But, do you know what else?"

Kenneth's eyeline shifted from Bradley Hoover and drifted across the gallery, finally settling in the far-right back of the room as he kept talking.

"I think it's a shame that we're all here, in this stuffy courtroom, spinning like *records*, round and round, getting nowhere. The prosecution has got nothing. When it's her turn, she's probably going to ask what my favorite color is. Or maybe, it'll be even more ridiculous, and she'll have me guess a number between eleven and thirty?"

Eleven and thirty? Those are oddly specific numbers.

John craned his neck to scan the gallery, trying to find the target of Kenneth's leer. Nothing appeared unusual. The rear doors were closing, as if someone had recently left, probably to use the bathroom or grab an early lunch at the diner. All other eyes were fixed on Kenneth up on the witness stand, except for a few that looked at John in response.

His testimony was a car wreck that stole everyone's attention.

Hopefully, this one doesn't jump the roundabout, too.

John spun around to refocus, then did a double-take at the last row of the gallery.

The place where Foley had sat... was empty.

Did he leave? In the middle of questioning? Why now?

"Here's a serious question I have for the prosecution," Kenneth said, his voice lowering and turning sinister. "If I had the abilities you say I have, do you really think these silly tubes and gloves would stop me? Someone with that kind of raw power sounds unstoppable. Like they could go anywhere—and do anything—they wanted."

Then Kenneth glared directly at John and Annaleigh at the prosecution's table.

"You don't catch power like that. It lets itself be caught. Against someone with a *gift* like that... what hope do you have of proving anything he's done? It's like trying to convince an ant what the airplanes are doing when flying overhead."

His scowl reappeared, directed straight at Sheriff Parnell.

"And, with someone like that, even if you thought you could bring proof of anything... what makes you think he'd let you?" He eyed Hoover. "And, imagine what somebody with that kind of power would think about a lawyer who couldn't do his job as expected?"

The entire courtroom held its breath. They weren't sure what they were actually hearing.

Threats? Stories? What-ifs?

To John's left, Hoover tensed up. A small tremor ran through his shoulders, and the smirk on his face vanished.

I thought they were on the same page. Hoover knew who he was dealing with, didn't he?

In a blink, the tension left Kenneth, and his face went blank again. "But, that's not me." He shrugged, trying to show sympathy. "As I said, I'm not a monster. And I don't think anyone's fake science reports can prove otherwise."

Hoover rose and gestured toward Judge Chapel, who sat still, mouth slightly open. "No further questions, Your Honor."

The time had come. Their second chance to make Kenneth implode—and not explode—on the stand. John leaned into Annaleigh, watching Hoover as he sat, gripping the wobbly sides of his armchair to steady himself.

"Keep an eye on those gloves," John whispered to her. "You got this. But don't get too close."

Overwhelmed with mixed emotions, this was the right move. He might have had an edge when he could tell if a witness lied, but Annaleigh taking over the cross-examination made sense.

More experience for the most crucial point in the trial.

"Don't worry," she replied softly, gripping his forearm. "I've got this."

She pushed out of her chair and shrugged off her navy suit jacket. She draped it over the back of another chair without breaking eye contact with Kenneth, exposing a simple sleeveless, white button-down tucked neatly into her dark slacks. A crisp look, almost military in its precision—no frills, nothing to get in the way of performing the ugly task of whatever came next.

She shrugged her shoulders once and stepped into the well.

John felt his chest tighten again with each step that brought her closer to the witness.

"Mr. Atlee, let's talk about Evelyn."

"Second bite at the apple, and you're focusing on these add-ons? These trumped-up charges? The ones you didn't even start with? Can't prove what I did with plan A, so you're throwing a Hail Mary?"

"Is that an admission of guilt for your initial charges, then?"

"Hardly."

"So you're saying you don't want to talk about her?" She turned around and pointed to the jury and gallery. "This place is packed. They're all here for you. Don't you want this opportunity? The... *limelight?*"

He shifted in the witness chair.

"Fine. You want to waste everyone's time, go for it."

"Is it your contention that the body we found is *not* Evelyn Raith?"

"If you want to say that's Evie, fine. I'm only saying I didn't put her there."

"That's an interesting turn of phrase, Mr. Atlee. Almost sounds like you're admitting to the murder, not the burial?"

Kenneth's eyes flicked to Hoover, expecting an objection. None came. Instead, Hoover bored a hole through the table with a glazed look, as if he wasn't even paying attention.

"You're twisting my words, Counselor."

"But, you were there, weren't you? Your blood is all over the clothing she was wearing?"

"Y'all got my blood when I was in jail. For all I know, you put it there after digging her up."

"Your story now is that we extracted your blood, aged it to match Evelyn's buried clothing, and then, what? Sprinkled it over the grave you dug by your cabin?"

Kenneth again looked at Hoover, silently expecting an interruption to Annaleigh's question. Hoover remained distracted. Kenneth's scowl deepened.

"Sounds like you've thought about how you'd plant evidence, Counselor."

"Some of Evelyn's fingernails were broken, suggesting a struggle. After you struck her at the church and put her in your vehicle, is it fair to say she regained consciousness and fought back? And that's when she drew your blood?"

"You can say what you want, and so can that church lady. No matter how many times you repeat it, it's still a lie."

"All this power you claim, Mr. Atlee, what if the domino that topples your so-called empire... is simply your loss of temper?"

"I keep telling you, this entire story is fabricated."

"So, everyone's out to get you? There's some big conspiracy revolving around you... all to secure a guilty conviction?"

"If you say so."

"Why do you believe everyone is out to get you? Could it be related to all the thousands of dollars—hundreds of thousands—you stole from taxpayers?"

"No," Kenneth growled.

"Or, maybe the Sheriff's Department is targeting you for colluding with the former mayor's son by setting those fires last May? Those fires hurt multiple people and even killed one of the Sheriff's deputies."

"Pigs do tend to play in the slop, Counselor."

"Spoken like a real upstanding community member, Mr. Atlee."

"Is that a question?" He again side-eyed Hoover, who stayed seated. "A competent lawyer might object to that."

Annaleigh glanced toward the defense table, then turned back to Kenneth. "Even rats flee a sinking ship, I guess." No response. Only a growing smirk and a flick of his tongue against his cheek. "You mentioned before that prior witnesses only sounded confident because they believed their own lies. Is that why, perhaps, you're so confident right now, Mr. Atlee?"

"I don't know what you're talking about. I didn't say that—"

"Sure you did, Mr. Atlee. You said anyone could be confident enough if they practiced. How long have you practiced that 'I am not a monster' speech?"

"I—I didn't... you're twisting my words."

"I don't think so, Mr. Atlee. You said those exact words and then went on some demented, hypothetical rant. If anyone listened closely enough, it sure sounded a lot like a confession."

He straightened in his chair, leaning toward her, a grimace on his face growing.

"I didn't confess to anything."

"You said someone with that kind of power allows itself to be caught, didn't you?"

"That was a figure of speech—"

"No, that's exactly what you said, sir. I can ask the court reporter to read it back for you if you'd like. I believe your words were: 'you don't catch that power, it lets itself be caught.' Isn't that what you said?"

"Maybe."

"Yes or no, Mr. Atlee. Weren't those your words?"

"Yes, but—"

"So, someone with that kind of power has no chance of being caught by law enforcement. If someone has this so-called gift, they can only be caught if they want to be caught."

"Yeah."

"But, isn't that exactly what you did, Mr. Atlee? Your first time on this stand, when my colleague was questioning you, you admitted to *letting* yourself get caught. Phrased it as, 'I drew you in like a moth'?" She grinned and crossed her arms. "It's starting to sound like your words weren't so hypothetical."

Kenneth swallowed as his cheek twitched. He panned over the jury box and saw twelve angry people looking back. He dipped his head and bounced his chest as he chuckled to himself. He looked at Annaleigh through his eyebrows, raising his gloved hands in a slow surrender.

"Fine, Counselor. You win."

He drew a long, deep breath and exhaled, glancing at the back wall, then to his lap, as if calculating in his head.

"It doesn't make much difference now."

His eyes again drifted to the back wall—looking somewhere above the gallery.

John craned his neck and looked in the same direction. No person or thing in his line of sight, except a clock hanging on the back wall. It read 11:27 am.

Almost time for lunch. And Kenneth is getting cooked already.

Kenneth lowered his hands between his legs and leaned forward.

"Lady, I've decided it's your lucky day. I'll confess. Which crimes, exactly, would you like me to explain to you?"

"All of them, Mr. Atlee. This town finally deserves the truth."

An eerie smile stretched across his face.

"Your wish is my command. In fact, everything that happens in this dump is under my command. You all have it wrong. Cameron Raith wasn't some mastermind. He was an idiot. A good talker, sure—good enough to get himself elected by all the morons in the gallery, but barely enough intellect for anything else of value. I thought to myself, 'Finally, the dolt has made himself useful.' You called him Mayor... I called him my puppet."

Gasps echoed through the crowd as Kenneth kept going.

"That's real power, Ms. Stanton. To control whatever you want and never let anyone realize it's actually you pulling the strings. That ends today. After today, no one will forget who really runs this town. It ain't the mayor. It ain't the Sheriff."

His voice lowered as he lowered his chin, looking at the room through his brows.

"It's me," he growled.

Annaleigh waved him on. "That's a fine story, Mr. Atlee, but it doesn't sound like a confession. If you can't provide details, everyone here will continue to think you're an old fool... not controlling fire, but blowing smoke."

Kenneth's cheeks flushed red. "You still think a confession

will fix anything? You can't prevent what's coming, no matter what I say."

"So, it's blowing smoke then—"

"You're out of your depth here, little girl. You don't even see half the picture. Fine, you want facts? You can have 'em." He looked around her and stared directly at John. "I burned your mama, Detective. Torched that crappy little shed. It was supposed to send a message. Not my fault you can't take a hint to stop looking into us."

Sarah yanked on John's arm, stopping him from rushing out of his chair. Annaleigh subtly patted the air behind her, signaling for calm.

"So you admit to arson, Mr. Atlee. Don't stop there—this town would love to know what you've been responsible for over the years."

"City contracts? Pure cash grab. This town is full of idiots—lining up to throw money our way. If they didn't pay up, we'd burn them down. They would take their insurance money, too. Had them in quite a pickle. Joke's on them. Got that money hidden where y'all can't touch it, and it ain't in no stupid bank."

He chuckled and jostled his hands, still hanging low, in between his knees.

Annaleigh gestured again toward the gallery. "The town would love to hear more, Mr. Atlee. Anything to add? Ready to confess to murder, too?"

He grinned. "You think a dead woman and some stains mean anything? When she found out what I had Cameron doing, she freaked out. Said she was going to the cops. She was on her way to you, Dane. So I handled it." He glared around the room. "Made Cameron dig the hole, though. He needed to be kept in line, and boy, after he tossed her body into that grave, he never did backtalk me again. Played his part well, until the idiot killed himself."

"Embezzlement... arson... and now, murder. You're on a streak, Mr. Atlee. Anything else you want to get off your chest?"

"I love how you think this changes things," he snarled,

glancing again at the back wall. "We've talked a lot about my words, haven't we? I fear that everyone's forgotten it. So, let me say it again. *Potentia.* It's not just a word. It's a statement. It's a promise. A war cry."

"Well, Mr. Atlee, it's a shame you couldn't finish off your testimony with a flourish and show us those powers of yours. With multiple armed personnel in attendance today, we could have found out whether some flames from your fingertips would also have made you bulletproof. It's too bad those gloves you're wearing prevent all of that."

"You mean... *these* gloves?"

He stood and threw the gloves onto the ground at Annaleigh's feet, raising his hands from his sides with palms facing up. The canisters strapped to his forearms fell with the gloves, clanging as they hit the ground.

Annaleigh's eyes widened.

John sprang to his feet, hand reaching into his empty holster.

"You all exist," Kenneth yelled, "because I *let* you. It's me. I am... *potentia*!"

An explosion shook the room.

27

TRIAL BY FIRE

A deep, bone-rattling boom rolled through the courthouse. Windows shivered in their frames. Plaster dust sifted from the ceiling like dirty snow. For one heartbeat, everyone froze—then the screams began.

Through the east-facing window, City Hall resembled a torch—orange flames eagerly burst out into the fresh air from every lower-floor window. Black smoke billowed into the autumn sky.

City Hall has just been bombed.

Kenneth stood at the witness stand, hands empty and restraints removed.

No shackles. No gloves. No hiss of suppression gas. The backup FM-200 canisters tipped over and clinked against the ground, their roll only stopped by their tangled tubes.

John's contraption, built solely to restrain Kenneth's unstoppable power, had failed.

A low, subsonic thrum sounded, as if coming from everywhere.

John felt it more than heard it—a pressure pounding against his chest. A vibration in his teeth. The noise felt familiar, but the sight... wasn't.

There was no white-hot glow in Kenneth's hands—nothing like Wesley Raith's hands had emitted months ago.

Is his power different...? No... God no, this can't be happening.

Kenneth extended his palms to his sides. The air around them warped—heat distortion rising in invisible waves, bending the light like a mirage over summer asphalt. The gallery's collective breath caught.

His eyes had turned dark—pupils swallowing the irises until only black remained. When he spoke, his low, almost intimate voice echoed through every corner of the room.

"You wanted to see power?" he growled. "Enjoy the show."

Red light glowed deep in his palms—vibrant, smoldering, like embers beneath ash. It intensified until twin spheres of fire hovered over his skin. He flexed his fingers once, almost gently.

With a swift motion, he raised both arms. A line of flame erupted along the well—initially knee-high, then rising to chest level, and higher, in a roaring curtain. The fire split the courtroom in two: the judge's bench, the witness stand, and Annaleigh on one side; the prosecution and defense tables, John, Sarah, the gallery, and the law enforcement on the other.

Smoke billowed upward, thick and choking, transforming the barrier into a shimmering veil.

Parnell, Dallas, and Clyde, although positioned in different parts of the room, dropped low behind the gallery's rail as if moving together, pistols raised. The smoke and flames, however, made shooting impossible, or at least too risky to aim without a good chance of hitting Annaleigh, Judge Chapel, or one of the jurors.

Seen only through spurts, Kenneth twisted and outstretched a hand. A fireball left his hand in a shallow arc—red, almost liquid—in the direction of the defense table.

It skimmed off the table's surface and slammed into Bradley Hoover's chest.

A choking sound erupted from him. His arms flailed. He slumped forward onto the wood, body limp, suit jacket smoking.

The second fireball struck the jury rail. Plasma splattered outward, igniting chairs, seat cushions, and note pads. Jurors dove to the ground. Screams escalated into panic. Townsfolk crawled over benches toward the exits, while jury members scrambled over the half-wall into Clyde's grasp, avoiding smoldering pieces of wooden chairs.

The third headed for John, just as he flipped the prosecution table with a grunt and dragged Sarah behind it.

"Stay down!" he barked. She nodded, eyes wide, clutching files like a shield.

Another fireball streaked overhead, close enough that heat singed the hair on John's arms. He risked a glance toward the witness stand over the table's edge. Annaleigh had been right there, maybe ten feet from the prosecution's table and only five feet from Kenneth—way too close—when the chaos erupted.

She was nowhere to be seen.

Fireball after fireball thudded against the back of the table, each one shaking the wooden shield and threatening to topple it. John pressed his back into it, keeping it upright. He felt every hit land. And the heat... he felt it with each impact through the inch-thick wood.

This shield wouldn't last forever.

He peeked around the edge—only for a few milliseconds—trying to catch a glimpse of Annaleigh. His attempts were unsuccessful until the fourth try.

Through the haze and between wisps of flames, John glimpsed a body.

Lying prone on the other side of the fire, the form sprawled in familiar dark pants and a white shirt, with fabric blackened by the flames along its arms. He couldn't see a face, and the fire's smoke obscured a way to identify it from this distance.

It's not her. It's not her. Can't be her. Got to get to her.

With his back still against the table, he scanned the gallery to find Parnell. If they could coordinate, even nonverbally, maybe Parnell could draw Kenneth's attention while John slipped around the side to help Annaleigh. His heart kept telling him that the body he saw wasn't hers.

His gut feeling wasn't so sure.

He thought he saw a glint of a badge through the haze, alternating between popping up to help gallery watchers out the rear door and ducking from incoming fist-sized fireballs. John yelled, but caught no one's attention.

Off to John's left, Clyde sheltered behind the jury's half wall. Fortunately, he was out of Kenneth's view but visible to John. When Clyde would reach up and help pull a juror over the barricade to safety, he'd attract Kenneth's attention before diving down to the temporary safety of the short wooden separator. Yells in his direction went unanswered, too.

Dallas Taggart, on the far side to John's right, had been sitting past the defense's table. John looked past Bradley Hoover's slumped body but couldn't see the young red-haired deputy.

With a relentless barrage of projectiles coming their way and John unable to return fire, his worst fears kept racing through his mind.

We're all going to burn up in here. I'll never get to hold her again.

When the angle at which each plasma ball hit the table changed, John's focus snapped back to the courtroom's front. Previously, each thud felt like a direct shot, straight from the witness stand. Either Kenneth's power waned... or these glancing blows signified something even more terrifying.

Kenneth was moving.

"Parnell!" he yelled blindly. "He's moving! Take the shot!"

John heard a shouted response amidst the screams, though he couldn't make out most of the words.

Then, the thrum fell silent, and the fireballs stopped. The curtain of flame guttered but refused to die, still blocking the well.

John twisted and poked his head around. Kenneth's large, unmistakable silhouette moved calmly and unhurriedly toward the side exit.

"Far side!" John yelled. "Take him down!"

Parnell fired once. The shot struck the doorframe.

Another shot hit the wall next to the door from Clyde's gun. Another miss.

"Taggart! He's headed your way!" Parnell shouted, voice cutting through the chaos. "Stop him!"

The anticipated gunshots were never heard.

A large shadow appeared in the side doorway, obscured. They were too late. Kenneth stepped into the smoke and disappeared.

Heart pounding in his chest, John lunged from his cover and faced the line of fire blocking access to the witness stand—and Annaleigh.

Have to find her. Need to find her.

He gasped for filtered air through his sleeve and jumped through the flames. The heat scorched his face. His pant legs caught fire as he flew through the air. He landed hard on the other side, rolled, and quickly wiped the embers off his shins with his palms.

He dropped beside the figure. His hands shaking, he turned the body over.

Baz—face blackened, eyes open and sightless—looked lifelessly up at John. His crisp white uniform shirt burned away in patches across the chest. His blackened, slag-like arms told of a heroic act gone wrong. He tried to restrain Kenneth... and paid the price.

But where was Annaleigh?

Relief turned into horror. John's throat clenched. She had to be somewhere. Had Kenneth taken her?

"Annaleigh!" His voice exited him raw and desperate, but the roar of fire and screams swallowed it. He scanned through the smoke.

Something moved. It was slight, but a flash of white material shimmied behind the jury box half-wall. He rushed into the jury box, knocking over chairs as he landed. Annaleigh crouched there, alive. Coughing, but alert.

"Annaleigh!" Tears welled in his eyes as she scrambled toward him on hands and knees. He enveloped her in his arms, pulling her close. "I thought I'd lost you."

She gripped his arm, eyes half-closed and face covered in soot.

"I'm okay," she rasped. "I dove as the fire went up. For a second, I thought I had died and gone to hell."

"I'd have come down and brought you back," John panted. He held her tight against his side as the courtroom burned.

Flames climbed the walls, and smoke filled the air. Outside, one block east, City Hall roared like a furnace. The sound of approaching sirens offered them little comfort.

He poked and prodded, checking her for injuries until she swatted him away.

"I'm fine, John. We have bigger problems now."

They were alive, coughing, and furious.

Through the flames, the vacant doorway where Kenneth had vanished mocked them.

"He's out there now," John said, voice hoarse. "And he proved he can burn this town down whenever he wants."

The fire agreed with a hungry crackle.

28

COUNTING THE MISSING

The fires had waned, but the courtroom still reeked of ash and melted hardwood when Toby pushed through the double doors with his small team of firefighters, each carrying thermos-sized canisters.

FM-200 hissed and smothered the stubborn flames along the jury rail and the judge's bench. White fog rolled across the scorched hardwood like a cold front, dissipating once it hit the walls.

John stood near the overturned and scorched prosecution table, arms crossed, watching the firefighters work. Annaleigh and Sarah had already gone upstairs to check their offices and files.

He hadn't followed.

He needed answers.

Toby pulled off his mask, face streaked with soot.

"Didn't expect to deploy this stuff in a real courtroom so soon," he said, voice rough from smoke. "Hell of a test run."

John managed a thin smile. "You have no idea."

"More stories for us to share over that beer, for sure."

They walked together to the witness stand. Kenneth's restraints were discarded on the floor—gloves untouched by the fire, FM-200 canisters dented, but unbroken.

And silent.

Toby crouched, carefully picking through the remains with his gloved hands.

"Tubing melted," he said, lifting a section. "Bypassed the wick completely. That... wasn't supposed to happen."

John knelt beside him. "We built it to take extreme temps. Why wouldn't the wick have melted before the tubing?"

Toby removed one of his gloves and rubbed his forehead.

"Maybe it wasn't that extreme."

"What the hell are you talking about? You weren't here—there were fireballs, Toby. Fucking fireballs!" John pointed at Bradley Hoover's lifeless body prone on the ground. The sheet covering the corpse had a single blood stain leaking through it—a six-inch hole mid-chest. "That guy took one straight through his chest, melted him inside down to his spine. Died from a goddamned fireball. Believe me, there was extreme heat."

"That's not what I meant, man. We assumed it would go from ambient room temp to over 135 and melt the wick." Toby pointed to the straps. "Look here—the thread we used to stitch the Kevlar straps to the glove melted too. Even if the tubing hadn't melted, the gloves would've slipped off like butter after the straps gave. Another flaw."

John's stomach twisted. "I still don't get it. Why wouldn't the wick have melted?"

"That's what I'm trying to explain, but I'm figuring it out on the fly. The tubes weren't rated for prolonged heat exposure—we expected the wick to melt, the spring to trigger, the gas to flow instantly. If he... somehow," he thumbed his soot-stained chin. "I mean, if he knew to heat the gloves hotter than expected... or maybe if he knew the right spot to melt through without tripping the wick, that would have disabled the whole kit."

"There's no way he could've known that. No way. We didn't even know that... did we?"

Toby shrugged. "You gave us the specs from what you saw. Seems like this guy's abilities are different. Better, even."

John dipped his head and clenched his fists. "Dammit! I should've known something like this would happen."

Toby looked up. "Listen, we were all working with what we knew back then. Heck, when Shep suggested the thread—he said it'd hold up. We all thought it was smart... at the time."

Parnell approached alone, dusted with ash, face grim.

"Judge Chapel is furious, by the way. He's outside getting checked by paramedics, but he keeps repeating 'it was supposed to be safe' like he's playing it over in his mind on a loop. I have a feeling we won't be in his good graces for a long time."

"Where'd Clyde run off to?" John asked. It wasn't the right time for their talk, but he got a strange feeling when Clyde rushed out of the courtroom.

"Sent him to City Hall. Assess damage, secure what's left." Parnell rubbed his jaw. "As for here, everyone but two is accounted for. Some bumps, smoke inhalation, nothing fatal, thank the Lord. Kinda amazing, if you think about it. One is Deputy Taggart. No sign of him."

John's gut clenched as he grimaced. "Hostage?"

"Maybe." Parnell's eyes hardened. "Or worse."

"Let me guess, Cason Foley's the other one."

Parnell nodded. "Clyde told me you saw him in the back row. That boy was supposed to stay far away—"

"He slipped out of here during Kenneth's testimony. I remember Kenneth said something weird, and then Foley was gone."

Toby's radio crackled. He stepped aside, listened, then came back. "I've got some updates from City Hall, Sheriff. But first, and I'm not sure it's related, one of my guys is missing too. He reported to the firehouse this morning—got a call, then vanished. When the alarms went off for us to come here, had to leave without him."

John's pulse kicked. "Who on your crew is missing?"

"Shep."

John looked around at Toby's crew—familiar faces, but indeed, no Shep. "You sure he's not over at City Hall?"

"Positive. He rides in our truck."

"Well," Parnell said, stroking his mustache, "your man going A.W.O.L., combined with my deputy being taken... the timing certainly is suspect. We need information before we can do anything else. Tell me about City Hall."

Toby's face darkened. "An incendiary device detonated in the records room—deeds, contracts, whatever was in there... everything's gone. Blew a hole all the way through to the mayor's office. We believe the signature's a clue—it's someone who knows fire pretty dang well."

John's mind raced. "Seems like we've had a few suspects recently with fire as their M.O., eh? But Kenneth was on the stand. Couldn't have triggered it. That's one down."

"Unless the charge was already placed," Parnell said. "And on a timer." He turned to Toby. "Did you all find anything like that?"

"Not yet, but they're still looking."

Parnell rubbed his ear and then turned back to John. "When Foley left, what was it that he said that sounded strange? You mean that Latin word?"

"No, it wasn't that. To be honest, it was a couple of things. The way he talked about records spinning—he said it with this extra emphasis. And his little numbers game. Who picks numbers between eleven and thirty?"

Toby's face went pale. "Eleven thirty? He said those numbers? Those exact ones? Then all hell broke loose?"

"Yeah," John replied. "Why?"

"The explosion at City Hall went off at precisely 11:30 this morning."

Parnell's eyes widened before he tongued his cheek. "Hot damn, he was barking orders from the stand. And I didn't even pick up on it."

"Foley!" John snapped. "That's why he left. It was right after

Kenneth told him where and when. It would have been enough time for him to get there and set off the bomb."

"I don't know about that," Toby said. "Crafting a device like this one, don't think that's in Foley's wheelhouse. Not the way my guys described it over the radio."

John looked at the gloves and tubing on the floor. "How much do you trust your man, Shep? He helped build those... the gloves Kenneth somehow knew exactly how to escape from. Big coincidence he decides to disappear today."

The accusation lingered between them like smoke on a windless day.

Toby looked back at John. John thought he might swing at him for even suggesting that a fellow firefighter could be responsible. The smoke-eater looked down, kicked a smoldering piece of hardwood, and shrugged.

"I don't know. I trust him in a fire. Not sure what kind of crazy he gets into off-shift."

Parnell pursed his lips. "So, we've got a few POIs... Foley and your guy, Shep. Dallas, too—"

"No." John knew he'd said it too quickly. "Dallas was with us at the warehouse arrest—he had overwatch the whole time. He's not... he wouldn't. Kenneth must have overpowered him..."

But doubt crept in. Hostage or traitor. Both end badly. Besides, praying that someone was a hostage, instead of the alternative... there was no good option. He looked at the ruined stand.

"They were inside. Moles. Nested everywhere."

Toby shifted. "If Shep helped design the flaws... maybe he told Kenneth how to beat it. Melt the tubing, melt the thread—bypass everything."

John's hands clenched. "We built the damn cage. But he had a key the whole time."

Parnell looked into his eyes. "All right, this got a lot worse. We have missing people, missing records for the whole town, and a man who burned his way out of a contained courtroom. We're not finished here."

John straightened up. Time to put away the law books. This town needed him back in a different role.

Detective mode.

He looked at Parnell, then Toby. "Kenneth's loose, but he's not invisible. Not yet. His trail is fresh—and we're on it, no matter how many traitors we have to go through. Let's go."

Parnell nodded. "Clyde's already at City Hall—might find something in the rubble."

Toby shouldered his canister. "I'll check Shep's locker—see if he left anything we can use."

John cast one last glare at the charred witness stand. The courthouse lights flickered once—then stabilized. Outside, the sirens continued wailing. It was Groundhog Day. With a twist.

"Time to go hunting again," he said. "But, this time, I'm not going to arrest him."

29

BACK TO THE HUNT

The overhead lights in the Sheriff's Office bullpen buzzed softly in a mostly empty room. John pushed through the door, still carrying the faint smell of smoke on his clothes.

A deep feeling in his gut caused his temperature to rise as he looked around. Unmanned desks dominated the room.

Was this department cursed?

Sheriff Dane Parnell had only one deputy remaining and a part-time detective who had recently graduated from law school.

What an operation.

The department's liabilities vastly outweighed its assets.

Deputy Amos Hinkle, killed months ago in the line of duty as Wesley Raith escaped from custody.

Former Detective Hollis Mumber, newly retired after sustaining critical injuries.

Deputy Cason Foley, suspended for his actions, not only potentially for aiding in Wesley's escape but also for mistaking John for a fugitive and attacking a fellow law enforcement officer.

Deputy Dallas Taggart, the shaggy red-haired new hire, was missing — either taken as a hostage or... John shuddered.

The department's latest fiasco saw Kenneth Roy Atlee abscond from the courtroom in a literal blaze of fury, accompanied by a synchronized explosion at City Hall—the biggest instance of unrest Coldwater had ever seen.

The last *biggest instance*? A mere three months ago, when Wesley nearly burned this station down.

Before that?

Over thirty years ago, a detective was killed while investigating a series of suspicious deaths.

Thirty years had passed between major incidents. Until a new power emerged from the ashes. And then, two terrible events in three months, with bodies falling everywhere.

If there's a next one, the entire town might fall. Maybe it already has.

Dane Parnell sat at his desk, sleeves rolled up to the elbows, with a county map spread out under a desk lamp. Clyde leaned against a filing cabinet, arms crossed, badge catching the light. When John entered, Clyde's eyes flicked up—longer than usual, steady, searching. The deputy's kind eyes bore through him, more deeply than ever.

John felt it like a hand on his shoulder, a warm, fatherly hug he had waited his whole life to feel.

"We can rule out the Raith property," Parnell said, not wasting time. "Too obvious, too hot. He knows we'd check there first. There's no way he'd go back."

Clyde nodded. "Public places too—bars, motels, stores. Nobody would risk hiding him—not after today. Broden Reed did it once at Three Pump, but I doubt he knew what Kenneth really was. The whole town's scared now. They'll turn him in the second he shows his face."

John stayed near the door, his hands in his pockets. "What if he's got more followers? More than Foley and Shep? Those can't be the only two."

"Don't have time to vet everybody in town," Clyde said calmly. "So, we'll need to figure out the next best route. If we don't catch him today, we might never get another chance."

Parnell nodded, his finger tracing invisible lines across the map.

John quietly moved toward Parnell's desk.

"What's the latest from City Hall?"

Clyde exhaled. "Records room's completely gone. What little they'd entered into the computer remains, but all the paper burned up. Deeds, contracts, blueprints—you name it—it's all ash. The mayor's office suffered collateral damage. Thank goodness he was out to lunch at the time. If not, could've needed yet another special election. That place has nothing usable left."

Heavy silence followed. John felt Clyde's kind eyes on him again—quiet, patient. Not now, John thought.

Find Kenneth.

Save Dallas.

Parnell rubbed his jaw. "So where? He's got no safe houses we know of. No friends left standing."

John moved over to the corkboard where a pinned photo of Kenneth's photo hung next to a rough sketch of his suspected escape route from the courthouse. "He doesn't need friends. People like him don't make friends anyway. They have subordinates. He needs cover. Somewhere remote, defensible. Somewhere he's already been. Somewhere he knows."

"We've checked every inch of Raith's land," Parnell said, frowning. "I know for a fact he's got no more buildings on that land."

"What about before he moved into that cabin? Where did he live? What about his parents? Did they have a place here?" John asked.

"He's lived at that place ever since he returned from 'Nam. His parents died while he was deployed, and their house was sold. He came back to nothing. That's why Cameron took him in."

"You make it sound like he was a poor little orphan," John said, head tilted. "The man admitted to being the mastermind of every bad deed that's happened in the town for probably a decade or more. I don't think we should dismiss it as sarcasm."

Clyde shifted. "Even still, we've got nothing at City Hall. No documentation of land parcels, no old deeds. Everything we'd use to look for ownership went up in smoke in that blast. Only thing I can think of is we hit the streets and start asking questions."

John's stomach twisted. He trusted Clyde implicitly, but that idea sounded horrible. It would take forever, and it wouldn't solve the nagging pit he felt in his stomach. He looked at Parnell.

"I need to confess something, Sheriff. About Foley."

Parnell's eyes narrowed.

"I knew he was dirty. Weeks ago." John's voice stayed low. "Not suspected. Knew. Confirmed. I followed a lead, and it turned out to be his dad's auto shop. On the way out, his sister admitted that Kenneth had been there that morning. And that Foley had been in touch with him. That was how I knew Kenneth would be at the warehouse." He paused long enough to observe the frozen expressions on Parnell and Clyde before continuing. "I confirmed Foley's place in all of this during Reed's deposition. You're not gonna like this, but I put Foley in a photo array, and Reed picked him out." John raised both hands, acknowledging fault. "When I confronted Foley later, it caught him off guard. But I told him he needed to come clean. He laughed. Said if we lost another deputy, the department would fall apart. State Troopers would move in and take over everything."

Parnell leaned back, chair creaking. "Ah... so that's what's behind the two of you fighting in the grass? First off, he's lying. Not gonna happen. Troopers and I have a history. Still stings... but they're not coming here unless I call them. Now, with Foley..." He exhaled through his nose. "I've kept an eye on him since Wesley slipped away. Knew he was dirty and in cahoots with the Raith boy, helped him escape. But partnering with Kenneth? Gotta say, that wasn't on my bingo card."

"We all missed the clues," Clyde said softly.

John caught the tone—gentle, almost paternal. It hit differently now. He didn't look up, but nodded once.

Parnell studied him. "Still, you should've told me the moment you knew."

"I know. Thought I could handle it. I was wrong."

Silence lingered.

"There'll be time for sorries later," Clyde said. "Did the sister, by chance, say anything else helpful? Think hard."

John squinted, reaching back into his memories. "She was reluctant, didn't want anyone to know she was helping us." He rubbed his forehead. "She complained about Kenneth... thought he was a creep... wait." He dipped his head, staring at the floor, trying to remember the exact words.

Then, it hit him.

"Broden."

"What's that, son?" Parnell asked.

"Broden Reed," John replied. "At the deposition, he used a phrase... 'at the forest.' That was something Kenneth and Foley would say to each other at Three Pump," John said, leaning in. "Foley's sister used the same exact phrase. *At* the forest. Not *in* the forest. They both said *at*. It's gotta mean something."

"The same as him talking about spinning records and picking numbers—it's all a code," Clyde said with a smile. "Nice job, John."

John straightened. "So, if forest isn't trees, then what is it?"

Parnell frowned. "Could be a lot of things. A business, a street, a—"

"Property?" John shrugged. "People have all kinds of nicknames for their land... like so-and-so ranch, this-and-that farm."

Clyde's brow lifted. "Makes sense. But the records we'd need to check are gone."

John smiled as the answer materialized in his mind. "Not all of them. Listen, if you two could check the map and whatever we have here to find street names or businesses with the word *forest*, I've got a crazy idea."

He grabbed Parnell's phone and dialed Annaleigh at the courthouse. She answered on the second ring.

"I'm on my way to pick you both up," he said. "I know where to find another set of property records, and I could use some extra eyes."

A beat of silence. "I'll be ready."

John hung up. He looked at Parnell, then Clyde—meeting his father's eyes for the first time since the courtroom confession. The look held—long, unspoken.

Parnell nodded once. "Go. We'll hold the fort—keep us updated on what you find."

John turned toward the door. The growing weight of the day settled more heavily on his shoulders. But something else arose beneath it.

He stepped outside into the cooling afternoon.

Time to find the forest for the trees.

* * *

JOHN PULLED the ugly brown Caprice into his mother's driveway as sunset threatened to fade from the autumn sky.

Annaleigh sat shotgun, still in her white shirt and dark pants, sleeves rolled up. Her jacket was long gone, left burning on the courthouse floor when John tipped the table and toppled the chairs for protection.

Sarah rode in the back, clutching a small stack of files from the upper courthouse offices. "Never know what we might need," she reasoned before climbing into the backseat.

None of them spoke much during the drive. The silence wasn't tense—just heavy.

As his boots crunched on the gravel driveway, he patted the roof of his Dart. "Don't worry, girl. I haven't forgotten about you."

Annaleigh strolled over and whispered in his ear. "First, you cheat on me with Sarah, and now... your car, too?"

"I don't know *what* you're talking about," he joked. "That

throuple you wanted includes this beauty, or the deal's off." He brushed off a pair of fallen leaves from the hood.

"I'm not even going to make you unpack that one."

Bonnie met them at the door. She'd been watching from the window and gripped both John and Annaleigh in a tight embrace. Her eyes flicked over the three of them—taking in the soot smudges, the exhaustion, the unspoken weight—and shook her head.

"The two of you are some kind of concoction, that's for sure. Explosive and messy," she said softly before her lips twisted into a devious smile. "But, I love you both and wouldn't have it any other way." She looked to Sarah, who stood meekly behind them, arms still clutching her files. "Same goes for you, dear. It's good to have you here. Come on, everything is this way."

Stacks of MLS printouts, color brochures, and old listing sheets already covered the kitchen table—years of Bonnie's real estate career spread out like a paper quilt.

"I set out everything you asked," she said to John, her voice steady.

Annaleigh slid into a chair, already reaching for the top stack.

"I can't believe you kept all this."

Bonnie offered a small, tired smile. "Realtor habit. Never throw away a listing. You never know when yesterday's dead-end might turn into tomorrow's sale."

"Is mine in here?"

Bonnie reached over and gave Annaleigh a firm side-hug on her shoulders.

"Oh, no, honey—that one's framed in the hallway. My favorite sale for my favorite girl."

Annaleigh smiled. "Is it really, though? Since you wouldn't let me pay you commission?"

Sarah sat next to Annaleigh, eyes wide but focused. "Where do we even start?"

Bonnie grabbed a fistful of printouts and laid them in front of her.

"Wherever you can, dear. Start flipping through 'em, you'll get the hang of it."

They dove in. Pages turned. Coffee mugs appeared, full to the brim, although John's was filled with hot cider.

Bonnie moved between them like a conductor—pointing out abbreviations, warning against outdated information, and quietly correcting Sarah when she misread a parcel name.

John watched his mother work and felt something loosen in his chest. She hadn't changed—still methodical, still the one who knew the location of every little piece of data. He caught her eye across the table. She paused, her hands on a stack, and gave him the smallest smile.

When Annaleigh and Sarah were buried in a pile of 1980s brochures, John stood up and moved to the kitchen counter. Bonnie followed a step later, pretending to refill the coffee pot.

He kept his voice quiet. "Clyde told me."

Bonnie didn't flinch. "I figured he might."

"You and Clyde... how is this going to work, now that I know?"

She set the pot down and looked at him—really looked.

"It's not about me. Are you happy knowing?"

"I think so, Mom," he said, surprised at how real it felt. "I really think I am. But I want to know more. I want to know everything."

Bonnie reached out and rested her hand on his forearm. "He will. When the time's right. But you should know—he called me while you were in college. Law school, too. He wanted to know you were okay and hear what you were up to. I think he was waiting for the right time... but, you came back, then everything happened, and it's never really stopped, has it?"

John's throat tightened, and he nodded once.

Behind them, Sarah's voice broke in.

"Wait—I thought of something. I'm pretty sure my great-grandpa's name was Forest. What if we're looking at it backward? What if it's a person, not a place?"

Annaleigh looked up. "Properties owned by someone named Forest?"

Bonnie's eyes lit up. "Smart. All right, we need to review everything again. The owner isn't usually listed, just the agent. But sometimes, if I knew who it was, I'd write it in the margin, along with a phone number if I had it. Look for handwriting on the edges."

They tore through the stacks again. John flipped pages faster now, his heart pounding. Not all had names, but many did. The common names blurred together—Smith, Johnson, Boone, Sutton. A few also stood out—Gamble, Raith.

Then—

"Willard Forest," he said aloud.

The shuffling of papers stopped as the room went silent.

Bonnie leaned over his shoulder. "Parcel 75-07-24. Used to be an old logging camp, on the western edge of town, other side of the highway."

John's pulse pounded. He stared at Annaleigh. Her eyes responded, unblinking. He jumped up from the table, grabbed the phone, and stretched its long, spiral cord to the kitchen. He dialed Parnell and held the receiver between his ear and Annaleigh's.

Parnell picked up on the first ring. "You got something?"

"Willard Forest. Property owner of a chunk of land, west of 76 off of 504. Check the system."

A pause—keyboard clacks. Then Parnell's voice, flat, dejected.

"Nothing. No record of a Willard Forest in the county database. Not even a driver's license."

John exhaled. "It's an alias. It's gotta be him. Probably forged the property sale... he's been hiding in plain sight." John relayed the exact location, then pressed on. "We need to crash it, Sheriff. But... I'm a lawyer. I appreciate that you gave me some leeway to lead at the warehouse, but you need to take this one. It's too important."

Parnell hesitated, though John heard a breath. "With Dallas

still missing, I don't think the three of us can do this and be successful. I don't like the thought of it, but..."

He didn't finish. Didn't need to. John said it for him.

"Call in those troopers, Sheriff."

Another beat. "Agreed. I'll make the call. We'll establish the staging area, let's see..." John heard thumping sounds, as if Parnell were tapping the map on his desk. "We'll set up east of the place... yeah, here. State Road 504 and Cobblestone Lane. I'll have the troopers meet us there. We go in hot, so make sure you've got your gear in your trunk. After what happened at the courthouse and City Hall, we need to expect resistance."

"I'll be there in 10 minutes, Sheriff," John said as he ended the call.

Bonnie watched him. "Be careful. Make good choices, you hear me?"

He met her eyes. "I will."

"We're coming with you," Annaleigh said, standing.

Sarah nodded. "Yeah, let's ride!"

John looked at them—three women who'd stood with him through the fire, the trial, the secrets. Though comprised of both new and familiar, he felt a shift inside him.

He had no power. But, he had them. *They* were his power.

And he had to keep it that way.

"Don't get mad, but not a chance in hell. If I'm going to be out there, I need to know that you all are safe in here." He looked at Annaleigh. "No extinguishers this time. Go get the guns out of the safe. Lock the house and shoot anyone who tries to get in, even if they knock. The next person that comes through that door is me. Just me."

He hugged his mother, high-fived Sarah, and gave Annaleigh a long, passionate kiss.

Then he shut the door behind him, popped the trunk of his brown Caprice, and reached for his gear.

Dusk had settled in, cold and clear.

Somewhere, out there in the dark, Kenneth waited, with God knows who beside him.

And Dallas—alive or not—was running out of time.

30

CRASHING THE COMPOUND

One half mile from the Forest parcel, Coldwater's finest waited in a gravel pull-off—no houses in sight, only a symphony of pine trees and moonlight.

Three cruisers sat nose-to-tail, lights off. Parnell leaned against his hood, arms crossed, watching the road. Clyde stood beside him, quiet, rifle slung low. John paced, trying to burn off the adrenaline still buzzing inside him.

Headlights pierced through the darkness as three Missouri State Highway Patrol cruisers rolled in—matching models in a dark slate gray that the moonlight turned into hints of green. No lights, no siren.

Silent. Purposeful.

They parked in a neat line, and three troopers stepped out, heavy vests, rifles already in hand.

The lead trooper—thirty-ish, with dark skin, short black hair, and a face as solid as granite—walked directly to Parnell.

"Dorsey," Parnell drawled. "Thought you got reassigned to the Ozarks."

Dorsey's mouth twitched—almost a smile. "Changed back. Heard you needed help. Rounded up who I could." He jerked a thumb at the two troopers behind him. "Franklin. Beck. Tell us where you want us."

Parnell raised his chin. No handshake, no warmth. Only recognition. He motioned for everyone to gather around his cruiser's trunk.

"Plan's simple," Parnell said, pointing to a map and a crude hand-drawn layout of the property. "Long drive in from the road—gullies on both sides, which limit maneuverability. Main residence is straight ahead at the end of the drive. A barn past that to the right, and no other structures we know of. We go single-file: me lead, Clyde, you two, then John, and you covering the rear. We believe our fugitive is somewhere on the property—Kenneth Roy Atlee." He raised a photo and showed it to the trooper. "Consider him armed and extremely dangerous. Doesn't matter if he has a weapon or not... his hands are the weapon, and I'm not talking about boxing."

Dorsey looked at his fellow troopers, then back to Parnell.

"This is... that guy? The fire guy?"

"Is that going to be a problem?" Parnell asked, brows high.

"No." Dorsey didn't hesitate.

Parnell eyed the other troopers, who silently nodded in agreement. He held up another photo.

"This is my deputy, Dallas Taggart, presumed to be a hostage and alive, Lord willing. We breach, clear structures, then secure. No heroics. Be prepared for anything. Got a good feeling we'll encounter opposition. Protect yourselves and each other, so we all make it home tonight. Any questions?"

Dorsey studied the map Parnell unfolded on the hood. "No air support?"

"Don't really have a chopper lying around, Dorsey."

He pointed at the drawing. "If that's accurate, isn't that driveway going to create a bottleneck for us?"

"No other way onto the property, unless we want to drive through the woods."

"Is that an option?" Dorsey asked, free of sarcasm.

Parnell stared back, squinting. "No," he said. "Ditches beside the main road are only a foot or two deep. If you need to cross it, approach at a shallow angle, and you get to the other side without much trouble. Hit it too straight on, and you'll be kissing your front bumper goodbye. *Limited,* not impossible."

"Warrant?"

"Exigent circumstances—hostage, armed fugitive, fresh murder charge."

Dorsey grunted. "Good enough." He looked at John for the first time, sizing him up. "You're the prosecutor?"

John met his eyes. "And detective... and the one who lost him." He shook his head, regaining confidence. "I'm going in with you."

Dorsey gave a brief nod. "Hey, it's your rodeo. We're backup. I know Parnell wouldn't let you in the field unless you've passed the training."

John nodded, slipping his thumbs into the corners of his bulletproof vest. It had been the first time anyone of consequence had truly questioned his duality.

"He's a better shot than me, Dorsey," Parnell said, winking. "Maybe even you."

Dorsey cracked a half-smile. "Doubt it."

Clyde stepped into the group's center and clapped once.

"Any other questions, gentlemen?"

Heads shook.

They loaded up, and the engines purred to life. Parnell led, Clyde behind him, then Dorsey, Franklin, John, and Beck. Single file. Lights off. Tires whispering on gravel.

John gripped the wheel, heart thudding.

Dallas. Please be alive. And still on our side.

Parnell made the turn onto the property, with the other five following behind him. They crept in, eyes alert for danger. Three-quarters of the way up the driveway, the moonlight revealed a problem—a pale yellow pickup truck angled across the road, blocking access.

"Yellow pickup up ahead, possible obstruction," Parnell called out over the radio.

"That's Kenneth's," John replied.

"Eyes up," Parnell warned the group.

The gap narrowed to a hundred feet.

Seventy-five feet.

Fifty.

Thirty.

Twenty.

"No sign of a driver... whoa—" The transmission cut out as Parnell's brake lights flared red.

Flashes of light burst ahead, accompanied by the faint sound of popcorn popping.

Gunshots.

Clyde's cruiser veered left and stopped, pointing down into the gully. Dorsey swerved right, hitting the ditch at a shallow angle, then popped up onto the grass on the other side. He turned the wheel left and hit the brakes, fishtailing into a sideways protective stance.

Franklin jutted his cruiser behind Clyde on the left, but turned too hard and entered the gully wrong. He buried his grill into the dirt, causing his rear end to lurch upward slightly.

John slammed the brakes and ducked under the dashboard.

Bullets whistled past, punching metal and smashing glass.

Parnell's door flew open. "Lights! Lights!" he commanded over the radio.

In unison, headlights and rooflights lit up. The post-mounted spotlights shone on the yellow pickup ahead, shielding the deputies and troopers from the attackers' view.

John opened the door and scampered out, pistol already in hand. He sprinted behind the scattered police cruisers and reached Trooper Franklin's car door.

Franklin, dazed and sporting a fresh red welt forming on his forehead, had slammed into the steering wheel on the unexpected impact. John helped him out, stayed low, and positioned him on the ground behind the rear tire.

Bullets whizzed past each other in the air. The pickup gradually became riddled with holes as tires blew and pockmarks appeared in the door and bed panels as if by magic.

John peeked around the back of Franklin's cruiser and saw Parnell and Clyde scrambling behind Parnell's cruiser, firing back. To John's right, Beck had moved in with Dorsey behind his cruiser, guns blazing.

Muzzle flashes illuminated the night like strobes.

A yelp erupted through the pops from John's right. He snapped his head in that direction and saw Trooper Beck rolling on the ground, clutching a bloody ankle. Dorsey shoved Beck against the tire with one hand, while his other hand fired blind cover shots over the trunk.

On a reload, Parnell twisted and caught John's eye across the gap, then jerked his head. He straightened his palm and pointed it to John's left.

John understood.

Flank. Woods.

John didn't hesitate. He rushed past Franklin's cruiser, hidden behind the bright lights focused on the pickup. He ducked and sprinted across the knee-high grass, slipping between the pines, boots silent as he dodged fallen leaves and branches.

Bullets zipped by—some sounded close, most were wild. He didn't know if they were aimed at him or wild sprays.

Didn't matter.

Keep moving.

He circled wide, breath shallow, heart pounding. The pickup appeared from the side. He couldn't see faces—only shapes. Some movement.

Two, possibly three shooters. Hard to tell with the shadows behind the truck.

They all huddled behind cover, popping up to fire and then retreating to safety.

John watched for a few seconds, trying to analyze the situation. He couldn't wait long. Every bullet fired from behind the pickup could hit Parnell.

Or a trooper.

Or... my dad.

He realized there were four shooters when three stood to shoot, but a fourth remained crouched, either unwilling or unable to fire. As one hunched back down, and light caught metal—a badge.

John's stomach dropped.

The fourth shadow, nearest to him, turned and pointed at John.

John's hands did not shake. He'd prepared himself for this possibility. There was only one way to stop more tragedy. He raised the pistol, sighted, and exhaled.

Two quick shots.

The shadow dropped into an unmoving heap. Another one spun around at him, rifle raising—John fired again. That shadow fell too.

As soon as the second body hit the dirt, the remaining two bolted around the truck's far side—right into the sights of Parnell and Clyde. Four raw cracks sliced through the evening air, two at a time. Almost simultaneously.

And two more bodies hit the ground.

Silence settled quickly as the echoes faded into the forest.

John moved forward, weapon still raised, sweeping the shadows for more threats around the pickup. The air smelled of gunpowder and blood—bitter, metallic, cutting through the pine scent. Parnell and Clyde closed in from the other side, rifles up, boots crunching gravel.

The two shooters John had hit lay sprawled in the dirt behind the smoking pickup. One face-down, blood pooling under his chest, the other on his back, eyes staring blankly at the stars.

He stepped closer. John trained his weapon on the body, nudged his foot under, and rolled it.

He instantly recognized Broden Reed, the bartender from Three Pump. The man's greasy hair and beard had become matted with dirt and blood. Painted on his face, John saw a familiar scowl, as if he'd just been asked a stupid question. The man had once helped Kenneth escape arrest, so it made sense he'd be here yet again.

Based on his reluctance to shoot like the others, whether he was here on his own volition made no difference. He was no longer valuable to Kenneth anymore. Just meat in the gravel.

The other man could also be identified easily. With his head cocked to one side and legs splayed at an unnatural angle, Cason Foley's rifle rested loosely in his lap.

John relaxed the grip on his gun and drew a deep breath.

He almost threw up.

The killing shot had hit the disgraced deputy above the left ear and, when it exited the other side, took a quarter of the man's skull with it. Now, his flesh, bone, and what little brain Foley had left leaked into the earth.

A traitor who had threatened John, lied to his face, and played both sides. The disgraced deputy who wanted to be with Annaleigh. Stalked her. The one who laid John on his back with a cheap shot right to the face.

And the one who somehow kick-started John's venture into gaining temporary powers of his own.

John stared. His hands trembled on his pistol. He'd aimed for the center mass. Foley must have turned, moved somehow, making the bullets land elsewhere. Turning them even more deadly than intended.

John had pulled the trigger to stop the threat. He had no choice in the dark, amid the hail of bullets. But now, in the quiet of the aftermath, it suddenly hit him.

Wesley Raith. Back in May, John shot him in the shoulder—disabled, not killed.

Deliberate.

Clean.

No blood on his soul.

This was different. Two men. Dead by his hand. His first kill.

And his second kill.

Am I a bad person? Did I make good choices?

The question kept circling, relentless. He'd sworn to uphold the law and solve cases, not end lives. But out here, in the dark, with bullets flying and friends at risk—had he crossed some invisible line? Become the animal he hunted?

The 5906 felt heavier. It now carried the weight of those bodies.

He couldn't move or look away. The world shrank to those two still figures and their blood seeping into the dirt.

A hand clamped his shoulder—firm, grounding. John flinched and spun. Clyde stood there, rifle slung over his shoulder, face shadowed beneath his hat brim.

"Easy now," he said softly. "This part's done."

John's throat clamped. He swallowed deeply to fix it. He glanced back at the bodies.

"I... I killed them."

Clyde's grip tightened. "You did it to stop them. They were firing on us. He would've shot us. Would've shot you, too, if given the chance. You saved us, John."

"But—" John's voice cracked. "Last time... Wesley. I... I didn't kill him. I could've. But... I didn't. Didn't want to. But this..."

Clyde nodded once, eyes steady. "Part of the job, son. The most horrible part. Not everyone walks away clean. But the point is that you walk away... alive. And so do the people you're protecting."

The words seeped in, like rain on parched ground.

Not absolution.

Truth.

Clyde gave his shoulder a final squeeze. "Come on. Let's check the others."

John plodded behind him and rounded the tailgate.

Two more bodies lay there—sprawled where Parnell and Clyde's bullets had dropped them.

The first sported a jet black beard with no mustache. Face pale in death, Shep's yellow turnout gear lay half-zipped and stained red.

John flinched as Parnell kicked the ground inches away, sending gravel out into the grass. "Why, kid? Why?" he repeated.

A quick glance at the fourth body and John realized the reason for Parnell's outburst. Bushy red hair and beard. Wearing a bloody badge that still shone in the headlights.

Deputy Dallas Taggart.

John's heart sank yet again. His mind teleported to Scoops—when he stumbled on Dallas and his girlfriend, Tammy, sharing a sundae and kissing in a back booth.

Did she know who Dallas really was? Did we?

Clyde knelt beside the red-haired body, checked for a pulse, and shook his head once.

John stared. "Jesus, Dallas... what did you do..."

Clyde's jaw clenched. "Not hostage, boss. Sorry."

Parnell stood, adjusting his hat. "That explains all those signals in court. Shep built the bomb, and Foley set it off at the right time, in the right place. God only knows what Dallas' part was in all of this."

"Probably getting word to Kenneth on how to break out of my restraints going to and from court," John said, nodding blankly.

The conspiracy was truly larger than anyone expected.

"So," Clyde asked, "the question now is... was this the entire inner circle? Or the first layer of defense?"

Parnell stood and gripped his rifle. "Let's find out. Secure those weapons. We clear the house and other buildings."

Dorsey stepped up. "Sheriff, my man thumped his head on entry. Beck took a ricochet to his leg. They'll both be fine, but I need to stay behind with them. I'll secure this drive and will head your way when backup and an ambo arrive."

Parnell nodded. John looked toward the main building. Its dark windows showed no signs of movement. The wooden barn they had seen in the MLS photos sat eerily on the woods' edge, as if trying to slip into the trees.

Kenneth had to be here.

Somewhere.

And now they knew—he hadn't run alone.

He'd had help.

And there was no way to know if more trouble would be waiting for them.

John tightened his grip on his weapon.

He stood beside Clyde and Parnell, and what remained of the Coldwater Sheriff's Office marched into the darkness.

31

ALWAYS, BOSS

The main house on the Forest property sat a hundred feet beyond the bullet-ridden pickup. Its dark windows and sagging porch greeted them. Over the front door, a single bulb burned like a dying eye.

Parnell, Clyde, and John crouched behind the thick trunk of an old oak in the front yard, their breath beginning to fog in the chilly evening air.

"Bad news," Parnell said, pointing into the darkness. "MLS listing photos showed two structures. They must have been out of date, because I see a third one, too."

Clyde squinted past the house and barn. "I see it now. Looks small, though. Might just be a shed, Dane."

A head shake. "It's farther away. Could be bigger than it looks. Still gotta clear it."

John turned, barely able to see the new building Parnell described. A barn tucked at the back of the property, half-hidden by pines, its roofline barely visible in the green and orange leaves of the darkened forest. He looked to Parnell.

"Three searches. Three of us. Math works out."

"No," Parnell said gruffly. "We clear each structure together. Kenneth's too dangerous one-on-one." His eyes flicked to Clyde, then back to John. "I promised to get you home tonight. Somebody important still owes you a talking to, young man."

John shook his head. "And while we're all in that house, he drives off in some vehicle stashed in one of those barns? I can handle myself, Sheriff. We can't let him escape again. Especially now that we know exactly what we're up against."

Parnell looked at Clyde, then nodded. "Alright, here's the plan. Clyde," he said softly, voice low. "You clear the house." Clyde shifted next to John, rifle cradled across his chest. Parnell peeked around the tree once more, studying the layout a little longer. "John, you've got the first barn—the closest one. I'll take the back building and sweep the woods around it, then circle back around to you both. Clyde, I know you'll be out of sightline, but do your best to keep an eye on John's barn. Watch his back as best you can. Clear the house quickly, then head his way."

Clyde met Parnell's eyes. "Might take a minute. Lots of rooms and a basement to clear." He turned to meet John. "But, I always got my eye on him, boss. Always have. Always will."

The words landed heavier than they should have. John felt them settle deep inside. His mother mentioned this back at his house, but it hadn't really sunk in.

Clyde had been watching his back his whole life, even when John didn't realize it.

"Move quietly," Parnell said. "No radio traffic unless it's urgent. If you see him, don't engage alone. Call it in."

He rose first, low and smooth, and slipped toward the distant barn as his shadow melted into the forest.

Clyde turned to John. For a second, neither spoke.

The night pressed in—some crickets, a distant wind, the faint hiss of the bullet-ridden tires from the pickup down the drive.

Clyde's soft voice pierced the dark. "I know now's not the right time, but... before we split... maybe I should tell you what you want to know. About me. About why I stayed away. In case—"

"Don't." John's interruption sounded both firm and gentle at the same time.

Clyde's jaw tightened. "John—"

"If you start now, it means you think we might not get another chance." John looked directly at him—his father, still so strange to say, even in his own mind. "We're getting another chance. We find Kenneth, we come back alive, and then you tell me. All of it."

Clyde looked at him for a long moment. A flicker of relief or gratitude passed through his eyes.

"I like that plan. First round's on me."

John exhaled, the knot in his chest loosening enough to breathe.

"Didn't realize you actually drank. If that's the case, all the damn rounds are on you."

"What did I tell you? Cussin' don't make you cool, son."

Clyde clapped him once on the shoulder—brief, solid—then headed toward the house, rifle raised, silhouette fading into the gloom. John's thin-lipped smile stayed with him until he vanished completely.

Focusing back on his own goal, he checked his pistol—magazine full, round chambered—then moved toward the barn, zigzagging from tree to tree.

Every step sounded louder than it should.

He told himself it was nerves. He told himself Kenneth had heard the gunshots and probably knew they were coming.

Maybe he'd fled already. Or perhaps he was never here in the first place. He left his lackeys to cover his tracks and buy time for his escape.

But deep down, he knew better.

Kenneth had always been one step ahead. The fire-throwing brute had a plan. Tonight, the shadows belonged to him.

And John hoped the iron in his hand was strong enough to get him through the night.

32

CLEAR THE BRUSH

The barn assigned to John had an unusual layout, much different than what he expected.

To him, a typical barn was a simple, wooden building. Four sides. Big door in the middle.

This one was larger than anything he'd ever seen and featured an open drive bay on one side. With its own roof and corner supports, the bay looked like an aftermarket addition, but it reminded John of the covered drive-up areas at upscale hotels where you park your car and then go inside to check in.

This old place is no hotel. It might be a hundred-year-old hiding spot for a mass murderer.

He approached the barn from the side.

From this angle, the drive bay resembled a large porch, without the floorboards, serving as the barn's front. Moonlight slanted across the gravel, reflecting off the rusted sides of an old pickup parked inside—faded paint, tires flat, windshield cracked like spiderwebs.

Behind it sat a flatbed trailer, tongue down, loaded with nothing but darkness and a few rotting pallets. The dilapidated pickup mostly hid two large, wooden doors, which John believed led to the barn's interior.

He paused at the bay's edge, his gun held in a low-ready grip.

The barn smelled of mildew, old hay, and motor oil. No lights inside. No sounds except the faint creak of wind moving through the pines overhead.

First things first. Clear the bay for threats.

He circled wide, keeping the engine block between him and the open bay, then crouched down to check underneath. Nothing but weeds and a few scattered oil cans.

No legs. No boots.

He rose, eyes fixed on the cab. The pickup's slightly open driver's door drew his attention—enough to worry him. The antique also sported a dirty windshield—so covered in grime it was impossible to see through—and wooden planks leaning against the sides.

Stacks of one-by-twelve sheathing boards, gray and splintered, with some still holding nails. One good bump and they'd come crashing down loudly, alerting anyone nearby to his presence.

On the passenger side, the planks completely blocked the door and window, making it unlikely anyone had used that entrance in a long time. On the driver's side, the stack mostly spread across the back fender, with only a few boards draped over the door.

Only need to move a couple to fully open that door.

John reached out with his free hand, fingers brushing the top plank. He lifted it carefully, muscles tense, and gently set it down. The wood scraped softly against metal. He froze, listening.

No footsteps inside the barn. No rustling. Only the night breathing.

He exhaled through his nose and reached for the second plank. This one weighed more. Closer inspection revealed it was nailed to a broken pallet behind it, secured with a few ancient, square fasteners. He worked it free bit by bit, and halfway through, the nail popped with a sudden metallic ping. The plank shifted—then slipped.

It crashed down in a clatter of wood and dust.

John dropped flat against the pickup's fender, heart pounding. He held his breath, ears straining.

Silence.

No creak of floorboards. No shifting shadows.

He waited thirty full seconds—long enough for his pulse to slow—then got up again. If Kenneth was nearby, he wasn't responding to loud noises.

Maybe this location is empty after all?

He snailed open the driver's door with his free hand, holding the barrel with the other.

An empty cab. Nothing but dust.

One last check. The flatbed trailer.

John moved to the rear and swept the pistol underneath in a quick arc. More weeds, dead leaves, and a couple of old logs half-rotted in the dirt.

He straightened, wiping sweat from his warm palms onto his pants. The barn doors loomed ahead—double-wide, wood warped and gray, with one panel hanging crooked on rusted hinges. A narrow vertical crack of darkness showed between them.

John moved forward carefully. He reached the seam, pressed his shoulder against the left door, and nudged it open with the muzzle of his gun.

The hinges groaned—deep and hesitant.

The door swung open a foot. Then two.

Blackness waited inside.

He listened for movement, waiting until his eyes adjusted.

It's time.

John gulped one more steadying breath, then crossed the threshold.

33

BARNSTORMING

John eased the barn door shut behind him. The hinges squealed, but if he heard that sound again, it meant someone had entered behind him.

The darkness welcomed him first—thick, smelling of old hay and rotting wood. He caught a whiff of hot metal. Then he saw the light.

A handful of old incandescent bulbs hung along the rafters, their weak yellow glow barely reaching the floor. A few fat candles burned on a workbench to his left, flames steady in the still air, but too dim to have leaked out through the cracks from outside.

Doesn't mean Kenneth is in here... could have been one of the other traitors, before the ambush. Keeping looking. Don't die.

John stepped forward, floorboards squeaking softly. The same type of one-by-twelve wooden planks that were stacked outside had been used for the floor inside.

The barn's inside was even bigger than it appeared from the drive bay—two stories with open rafters, wide enough for tractors or threshers when the place still operated as originally intended. Now, it lived a second life as a metalworker's dream shop.

Forging equipment dominated the center—an anvil bolted to a heavy stump, a rack of hammers and tongs, and an old grindstone wheel leaning against the wall. Leather strapping hung from nails in neat loops—thick belts, harness pieces, straps that could bind anything, but probably used to wrap knife handles. Tools lay scattered across workbenches—files, punches, a small lathe, a drill press. Machining gear for blacksmithing.

Oddly, though—no forge. No coal bed, gas burner, or crucible.

John's mouth quirked despite himself. Kenneth didn't need a forge. He was the forge.

He moved further in, scanning the corners. An antique power hammer stood against the far wall—cast iron frame, exposed flywheel and belts, motor humming faintly even though it wasn't running. No safety guard over the belts or pulleys.

That's an OSHA violation if I've ever seen one. Big one.

The thought nearly made him smile. If the situation weren't so horrible and if he hadn't just killed two people, that machine would be exactly what he'd joke about staying away from.

He kept the gun raised, sweeping in arcs, checking behind machines, and peering intently into the darkness. The candles flickered as he moved past, casting long shadows that danced across the rafters, merging into the one at the edges of his periphery, making things infinitely worse.

Why do I keep forgetting a flashlight?

A shape burst out from behind a tall shelving unit. It moved quickly, fast, and was larger than him. John had half a second to recognize it—Kenneth, angry, arms tucked, eyes wild and dark.

Shit.

Kenneth hit him hard like a linebacker.

One massive hand grabbed John's vest edge, and the other slammed into his ribs. The pistol flew from his grip and skittered across the floorboards. The radio on his vest tore free, antenna snapping.

John twisted and tried to bring an elbow up, but Kenneth had already lifted him. He felt his feet leave the ground—then he flew.

He landed on a nearby workbench, tools clattering, pain jolting across his back as he slid off and hit the ground.

Kenneth bent down, picked up the 5906 as if it were a toy, and pointed it in between John's shadowed eyes.

When John stared down the barrel, tunnel vision kicked in—everything else blurred.

The muzzle filled his world like a black hole, steady and unblinking. He couldn't look away. This was it.

Would he see the flash of light? Would he feel the bullet? How would Parnell tell his mother about his death?

And Annaleigh? She'd be furious he'd gotten himself into this mess.

Kenneth's next move caught him off guard.

His other hand closed around the barrel, and he switched his grip until he cupped the gun within his palms. Between his hands, a bright white light flashed—sudden and blinding. The gun's metal shell changed from matte black to dull red, then to cherry orange within seconds.

The slide warped. The grip bubbled. Molten steel dripped between Kenneth's fingers, sizzling as it hit the wooden floorboard. He opened his hands. The gun became a shapeless lump, still glowing faintly.

Kenneth dropped it. It hissed on the floor.

"I don't need a gun to kill you, boy," he taunted. "You've interfered for the last time. This way will be more fun for me... and more painful for you."

A smirk spread across half of Kenneth's lips, and he refocused on John. Then, he reached for John's throat.

John instinctively ducked under the grab, rolled, and swept Kenneth's legs with everything he had—heel hooking behind the knee, driving his body weight through. Kenneth's balance broke. He staggered, arms windmilling, and crashed backward into a set of metal shelves.

The shelves buckled.

Tools rained down.

Kenneth's hand, still glowing, landed on a patch of oil — and flames immediately licked up, hungry, consuming everything in their reach. Rags, toolboxes, and Kenneth's clothing all fed the fire.

He shook his fists, and his own fire sputtered as he patted his pants and shirt to smother the rogue flames.

John scrambled up.

Kenneth rose too, but reached his full height dramatically slower. His eyes appeared to burn brighter than the growing fire next to his feet.

John threw a jab. Just A quick thrust to test the older man's reflexes.

Kenneth blocked it and countered with a left hook that grazed John's jaw. Pain flared white-hot. John ducked the follow-up and then drove a fist into Kenneth's ribs. The feeling of flesh and bone met John's knuckles.

Kenneth had no reaction. He didn't double over in pain. Instead, he laughed.

Low. Ugly. Perhaps it was a growl.

"Nobody fights me and lives," he snarled. "You think you'll be the first? I'll kill you with my bare hands, then burn what's left of you to ash. They'll have to identify you in a dustpan."

Kenneth swung again, but John slipped it and responded with a knee to the gut. This time, Kenneth grunted.

Sensing an opening, John pressed again. A jab, a cross, two hooks. Kenneth caught the last one on his forearm, twisted, grabbed, and threw John sideways.

John struck the edge of the workbench hard, knocking his breath out. His eyes fell on a pile of small metal scraps—offcuts, punch-outs, sharp-edged pieces. He grabbed a handful, spun around, and threw them at Kenneth's face.

Kenneth flinched and raised his arm to block. The scraps uselessly clattered off his sleeve, as hoped.

A distraction that worked to perfection.

John followed up with a mid-height, hard kick—like busting

through a door. His foot slammed into Kenneth's abdomen, causing him to gasp and stagger backward.

His balanced shift as his arms flailed—and crashed against the antique power hammer.

The machine jolted to life.

A deafening clang rang out as the flywheel engaged. Belts slapped, wheels spun, the hammer head dropped once—fast and brutal—then rose, only to slam down again. The whole frame shook.

Kenneth pushed himself away from the machine, eyes wide for the first time.

John froze, chest heaving.

The power hammer cycled—clang, rise, clang—steady and relentless, like an iron heartbeat.

Kenneth stepped back, firelight flickering on his face. He flashed a toothy, bloody grin.

John watched him across the growing flames, eyes narrowing.

The barn burned around them.

And the hammer kept falling.

34

FLAMES OF FATE

The power hammer's relentless rhythm beat like a giant iron heartbeat, echoing off the rafters.

Sparks flew from the flywheel every time the head dropped, lighting up the barn with stuttering flashes. John backed away from the machine, chest heaving, eyes fixed on Kenneth.

Kenneth wiped blood from his lip with the back of his hand. His breathing had degraded to ragged now, eyes narrowed to slits.

"You've knocked me down twice," he said, voice low and dangerous. "That's two more than most men get." He drew a long, deep breath, hands clutching his stomach, as if begging for his diaphragm to work properly. "You won't get another chance."

John didn't answer. He circled left, his boots slipping on dirt and scattered tools, searching for a different angle.

Kenneth lunged—quick, too swift for a man his size.

But John saw it coming. He feinted with a low kick, the same move that had worked before.

The same move he knew Kenneth would expect.

Kenneth twisted to the side, arms dropping to block the anticipated strike. That eagerness to prevent another fall left his jaw wide open to attack.

John pivoted on his heel and landed a right hook straight into Kenneth's face. The crack of knuckles hitting bone echoed loudly against the barn's walls. Kenneth's head jerked to the side. He staggered, knees buckling as he hit the ground hard, groaning, one hand clutching his jaw.

John scanned the nearest workbench, looking for a tool, a weapon, anything that would even the fight. He glimpsed a length of rebar leaning against the leg—rusty but sturdy. He grabbed it with both hands and swung it in a quick, brutal arc across the back of Kenneth's skull.

Kenneth grunted once, eyes rolling back. He slumped forward, unconscious, with his face scraping the old plank floorboards.

John stood over him, breathing hard, rebar still raised.

For a long second, he thought about bringing it down again.

And again.

And again... until nothing moved except for dead nerves triggering spastic flinches.

But he didn't.

Instead, he stepped back, chest tight.

"You're lucky that's not who I am," he muttered.

He didn't care if no one heard him. He spoke to an unconscious Kenneth, to himself, to the empty barn. Anyone who would listen and hear that he's not a killer.

He looked around. The candles still burned on the workbench, somehow spared after John was thrown into it. The leather straps still hung on the wall—thick, dark, oiled.

John grabbed a handful. He moved fast, unsure of when Kenneth might come to.

He knelt, rolled Kenneth onto his back, and individually wrapped each wrist—tight loops, double knots—then crossed them with even more knots and strapping.

The leather creaked under his fingertips. But it felt firm. It didn't have to hold forever. Just long enough.

John stood, wiping sweat from his eyes, and waited. He

glanced at his radio, shattered on the ground. Useless now—and he didn't dare leave to get help and risk Kenneth losing sight of him.

He considered yelling for help, but the machine's noise would drown him out.

He'd have to wait for Parnell or Clyde to come to him.

Maybe they'll hear the hammer and come running. I'll bet it's loud enough to be heard all the way from the ashened courthouse.

Kenneth stirred. He groaned.

He rolled onto his side and gradually pushed himself up to a sitting position, his head lolling. He blinked and noticed his bound hands, letting out a low, rasping laugh.

"Surprised you didn't finish me," he said, voice thick with blood and mockery. "Could have swore you had it in you."

John kept the rebar ready. "I've killed enough for tonight."

Kenneth curled his fingers. "Pity."

A thin, blue-white beam of fire jetted from his fingertip—precise, surgical, like a laser. The leather instantly smoked, blackened, and split down the middle. The strap snapped with a dry crack.

Kenneth shook his wrists. Long, charred remnants dangled from each arm—smoke wisps curled upward. "Same trick I used on your stupid firefighter gloves," he said, standing. "Minor inconvenience."

He opened both palms. Red fire bloomed, bright and hungry. The dangling leather straps caught—edges glowing, then smoldering, thin trails of smoke rising like incense.

John tightened his grip on the rebar. He shifted his stance—feet wide, knees bent, hands choked on the metal like a batter waiting for the pitch.

Kenneth advanced as firelight danced across his face. John swung—hard, level, aiming for the temple.

The brute caught the rebar mid-arc with one flaming hand. The metal glowed instantly—red, then orange. It softened, sagged, dripped in molten droplets onto the dirt.

John dropped the useless stub and backed away, eyes darting to find something else.

Nothing in reach.

Kenneth stepped forward to close the gap, reaching out, hands blazing, fingers spread to grab John's throat.

John reacted on instinct. He raised both hands and caught Kenneth's hands with his own.

He braced. He squinted. Then, he closed his eyes.

He waited for the searing pain.

The next logical sensation he'd experience would be the distinct odor of his own cooked flesh. Then he'd feel his grip slide away as his skin, muscles, and tendons melted. And, once his hands were dripping piles of goo, he'd have no proper way to defend himself.

John had already cheated death a few times. Hell, he'd just stared down the barrel of his own gun. But there are only so many times a man can get lucky before the reaper's scythe fully swings through him.

What happened next... stunned John.

The barn did not fill with the smell of burning flesh. The first pains that would drag John down the road to his death never started.

He felt the pressure of Kenneth's hands pushing against his. He still felt the grip of his fingers, staving off his enemy.

Somehow, John still had the strength to push back.

He opened his eyes. And wished he hadn't.

His hands were on fire.

Flames consumed his fingers, his palms, his forearms—red and steady, nipping at his shirt's dirty and bloody cuffs. Like smoke rolling across the water, the fire coated John's skin.

Dancing and fluttering.

Playing and wisping.

There was no pain. No burn.

Kenneth's eyes widened as he pulled his arms away. He withdrew a step, unbelieving.

John stared at his own burning hands.
Then back at Kenneth.
His brows furrowed, and he gave the smallest of smiles.
The fire was his now.
This fight just evened out.

35

BALANCED SCALES

Flames flickered across John's palms, curling around his fingers like living silk.

No pain. No blistering skin. The solid burn of power he'd never asked for.

Kenneth stood frozen, eyes wide, mouth slack. The same fire that had consumed everything Kenneth touched now flickered on John's skin.

"Time to give you something you've never had," John said. "A fair fight."

Kenneth howled and lunged again—hands blazing, rage peaking.

John met him halfway. He slapped Kenneth's wrists aside with open, burning palms, the impact sending sparks scattering like fireflies. Kenneth staggered off balance, surprise flashing across his face.

John struck again before Kenneth could right himself.

He drove a right jab into Kenneth's ribs—hard and precise. Kenneth grunted, doubled over slightly, his shirt sparking. John followed with a left hook to the jaw. Kenneth's head snapped to the side, and he stumbled backward. Burnt flesh filled the air.

More.

Jab. Cross. Hook.

Again and again.

Each punch landed with the weight of something greater—every lie, every burned body, every time Kenneth had smiled while the town bled.

A jab for Doyal Gamble.

For Amos Hinkle.

For Hollis Mumber.

For his mother.

With each strike, Kenneth groaned and retreated, arms raised, desperate to block. Not accustomed to a fair fight, his flames flickered uselessly as John's own fire met and matched them. The repeated blows further sent Kenneth into a hazy rage, unable to mount any coherent defense.

Kenneth's back slammed into the workbench. Tools clattered. He pushed off and swung wildly—John ducked, then came up with another uppercut that cracked Kenneth's teeth together.

Kenneth stumbled backward—toward the power hammer. His back foot reached out to brace himself, inches from the hungry machine. The motor thrummed, its flywheel spinning frenetically, belts slapping. Kenneth didn't notice how close he was. Too busy snarling, trying to summon a fireball.

John feinted left—Kenneth overcommitted, stretching to block.

John stepped in close and slammed a straight right into Kenneth's solar plexus. John felt the man's sternum give way, and Kenneth folded, air bursting from his lungs.

He staggered back another step, and his heel caught the power hammer's base.

And he fell, arms reaching high for leverage.

The straps—charred and dangling from his wrists—whipped out as he went down. One caught the exposed belt.

The flywheel grabbed it like a hungry mouth. A sickening snap—then a yank. The motor groaned as it yearned for more.

Kenneth's right arm jerked backward. He groaned and tried

to pull back to safety. He reached with his left hand to free his right, and the momentum of those straps—still looped around his left wrist—caught next.

The machine began to eat that one, too.

Kenneth's arms were trapped, straps caught in the engine and pulling him in. His back slammed against the spinning wheel. The belts and gears ground into him—cloth, flesh, muscle, bone, spine.

He wailed—high and animalistic.

His palms blazed as he tried to burn the straps off his wrists, but the leather fought back. Flames roared outward and to his elbows, encasing his entire arm in white-hot heat, scorching the air. The heat only fused the leather tighter to the belts.

The motor didn't care. It kept turning. Little by little, his wrists inched toward his face.

Kenneth's eyes widened in panic. He thrashed, screamed, flames erupting from his hands in wild arcs—but the machine was stronger. Unyielding.

John could have easily freed the man. He could have found a way to turn off the power hammer.

Instead, he watched as Kenneth was moments away from melting off his own face.

Just as his palms pressed against his cheeks, a bright white light shone, and the leather straps finally gave way with a snap. Kenneth's arms hung limply as a bloody, charred smile appeared on his face. He looked at his hands, the glow reflecting in his pupils.

And then he looked up at John, squinting, blinking, and breathless.

"My turn."

Kenneth groaned and climbed to his knees, intent on standing, but never made it that far. He'd only taken his eyes off of John for a second, but the young lawyer didn't waste the unexpected advantage.

John's knee connected with Kenneth's chin. Splintered ivory

flew out from Kenneth's mouth as he exhaled hard, spitting blood.

Kenneth's arms dropped from shock as John swung with rights and lefts. Flaming knuckles met toughened skin as the man drooped to his knees. With a fierce grab of his shirt, John twisted the cloth in his left hand and kept the man from collapsing all the way onto the floor.

He clenched his right hand, and the flames grew hotter and brighter. These were no longer wisps. It no longer danced.

It roared.

And he wailed away, pouring every emotion inside him into Kenneth's face.

Anger was a familiar feeling to John—but this... this was different. It was rage.

Every insult hurled at him by Cameron Raith. By Welsey Raith. Hoover. Kenneth. The feeling welled up inside him, urging persistence. Almost as if a voice whispered in his ear.

Cheering. Celebrating.

Keep swinging, the voice whispered. *Deliver punishment. Mete out the kind of justice one remembers for the rest of his shortened life.*

John finally had the power to fight back. To give the revenge he so deeply desired. The power was his.

His cheek muscles tightened, twisting his mouth into the beginnings of a smile.

It flowed through him, from his fingertips down to his toes. And it felt... good.

Kenneth was no longer fighting back.

Hell, the man might not even be conscious anymore.

It didn't matter. Every one of John's punches landed deeper. Perhaps the brute's blue and purple skin was finally giving way.

He drew a deep breath, and a jarring roar tore from his throat. His hand flared, and its light radiated everywhere, washing out the bruises on Kenneth's face.

John's right arm drew back, and through gritted teeth, he

swung forward, driving his fiery fist deep into Kenneth's cheekbone.

Except John's fist didn't encounter resistance.

It didn't bounce off bone.

It sank in.

John's fiery fist entered Kenneth's skull and liquified it from within. The flares shone out like spotlights from Kenneth's dead pupils.

A blinding orange flare bloomed—brighter than anything John had seen—and an inferno roared outward from Kenneth's lifeless skull.

John yanked his hand back, eyes wide. He released the grip on Kenneth's shirt, and his body went limp, sagging to the ground with a dull thump against the power hammer's motor.

John's mouth dropped open.

His temperature spiked. His eyes fluttered. A black hole formed within his stomach.

Wha… what just happened? What did I do?

The left side of Kenneth's face had vanished, replaced by a hollowed mask—skull exposed, bone blackened and melted, eyes flattened and matte. The macabre scene was eerily reminiscent of Prosecutor Doyal Gamble's death.

Nothing but a husk, hollow and empty.

John stood frozen, breath ragged, hands still burning. The power hammer kept its rhythm—apathetic, passionless.

Voices approached from outside the barn—Parnell shouting, Clyde calling his name.

John looked down at his burning hands. The fire rippled around his hands—bright, alive. Panic surged.

They can't see me like this. No one can. Ever. Not after what I've done.

John clenched his fists, then loosened his fingers and shook them as if trying to shed sweat.

The flames obeyed.

They dimmed, then disappeared. His hands were normal again—red, raw, bloody, but unburned.

John stepped back from the body—from what had once been Kenneth Atlee.

He wiped his face with a trembling sleeve.

If the trial wasn't over before, it certainly was now.

And something new had arisen within him.

36

SILENCE AFTER FIRE

Aside from the faint crackle of dying flames and the steady, mechanical thud of the power hammer, the battle inside the barn was over.

John stood over what remained of Kenneth Atlee and stared at his own reddened hands. Some residual heat curled up his fingers, as if it belonged there.

He hated it.

That he used it to win the fight.

And, for a split second... that he enjoyed it.

The same fire that had terrorized the town for months now burned on his skin. And he had... what? Gotten some kind of thrill, using it to end Kenneth's hold on everyone?

But what if I can use it differently? To protect people? To protect my family?

That same power had taken lives, melted metal, and turned men into hollow skulls. No matter what kind of man John was before, the fire had already changed him.

Kenneth's corpse testified to that.

Was he powerful enough to control it?

Or would it control him?

The fire longed to maim. It longed to kill. It fed on chaos.

Pushing it deeper, or burying it within, may not suppress this kind of power. It killed Cameron Raith when it finally broke through. Maybe even pushed Wesley and Kenneth across the veil into death.

Whether he liked it or not, that power now flowed through his own veins.

He needed to ensure a different end result for himself and not let the rage win. John's shoulders curled inwards, trying to disappear into his own chest.

The hinges on the barn door screeched, and Parnell's voice pierced through—muffled, urgent.

"John! Call out!"

Parnell and Clyde burst in—rifles raised, sweeping the corners. Parnell spotted the power hammer and yanked the cord, killing it. The machine wound down with a long, dying whine, and silence swallowed the space.

Clyde reached John in three quick strides, hands grasping him. "You hurt? Talk to me. Son, did he hurt you?"

John didn't answer. He couldn't look away from Kenneth's remains.

Parnell knelt beside the body, grimacing.

"He's gone. I'd check for a pulse, but he's missing half his face." He craned his neck and looked John in the eyes. "What the hell happened in here? Why didn't you call for backup?"

John exhaled—a long, shaky breath. "Power hammer... got him. He fell... head... got crushed..."

Parnell studied John, then focused on Kenneth's face, and looked back at John's bloody fists. He raised an eyebrow at the hammer's bloodless base, then cast a curious glance at Clyde.

"He's in shock, Dane," Clyde urged. "I think he's had enough trauma for the night, don't you think?"

Parnell responded with pursed lips and a slight nod.

"Agreed. Nothing more to do here. Get him out of here."

John's knees buckled. He caught himself on the edge of a workbench, fingers digging into charred wood.

Clyde's grip tightened. "Easy, now."

Parnell stood, dusting ash off his knees. "Come on, let's get you checked out by the medics. We need you alert and responsive. We'd hate to be the ones to explain all this to Ms. Stanton."

John's head snapped up. "Explain... what?" His voice cracked. "What... did you see?"

Clyde's hand stayed firm on his shoulder. "Nothing, John." A pause. "Is there something else we should know?"

John looked at Clyde's face—then at Parnell's.

A deep breath. A head shake. A long exhale.

Clyde squeezed once, then released his grip.

"Alright, it's all over now," he said quietly. "But Bonnie might insist we lock you in the holding cell for your own protection. You've shed more blood in four months than we have in thirty years."

"Trouble seems to follow you, kid." Parnell paused, squinting. "Or maybe you're really good at finding it."

John looked at his bloody hands and shrugged. Normal now. No fire. No glow. Only red, stinging skin remained.

Mixed with Kenneth's blood and brain matter, and the faint smell of char. He gulped and managed a thin-lipped smile.

"Gotta be good at something."

Outside, sirens wailed closer—more troopers, fire crews, probably the coroner. The night was far from over.

But inside the barn, the power hammer was still. The flames had died.

And Kenneth Roy Atlee would never burn again. John made sure of that. In his throat, a lump grew. He was sure it wouldn't go away anytime soon.

John turned toward the doors.

Clyde fell in beside him.

Together, they walked out into the cold, clear dark.

37

NO MORE SECRETS...?

A few days later, the kitchen at Bonnie's house smelled like cinnamon and fresh coffee, the warm, lived-in scent that had always signified safety to John.

Balloons floated near the ceiling—red, white, blue, inexpensive and joyful—and a crooked sheet cake sat on the table, with blue icing spelling out "First Trial Win!" in Genie Glitter's distinctive loopy handwriting.

The small gathering had a smattering of close friends—and new family. Even as guests entered through the reconstructed front door, John whispered complaints to his mother.

"People died, Mom. The courthouse is a crime scene. I still don't understand why we're eating cake."

"Even with messy circumstances, a milestone is a milestone," Bonnie responded. "I'm proud of my son. That's what matters. Plus, the cake may be for you, but the celebration is for all of us. This town has earned it."

She moved to the kitchen and bustled between the stove and the sink, alternating between preparing and washing dishes.

Annaleigh leaned against the counter, arms folded, smiling at something Sarah said. Sarah—still in her courthouse clothes, though the jacket was off—held a paper plate, nursing a generous slice of cake. Parnell sat at the table nursing a mug of black coffee, looking more relaxed than John had ever seen him. Clyde stood near the window, quiet, watching the room as if he were still on duty.

Abigail Jensen and even Toby dropped in for a bit, laughing and drinking with the rest of the crew.

Genie Glitter swept in with a tray of fresh pastries, her hair streaked with pink and purple, apron tied over a sequined top.

"A win is a win!" she declared, setting the tray down with a flourish. "I mean, no matter how unconventional, you went to court and got the bad guy. Now try these and tell me you love them."

John managed a tired laugh. "The trial didn't actually finish, Genie. The courtroom ended up in flames."

She waved a well-manicured hand. "Details, precious. You survived. We all survived. Come on now, eat up. This party is also an unofficial taste test for my new bakery. I swear, though, if anyone complains there's too much sugar, I promise I'll just go and add more."

A laugh rippled around—soft, relieved, the sound of people who'd been holding their breath for too long.

John inched himself through the kitchen and slipped out the back door. The cool night hindered nothing. A multitude of stars shone perfectly overhead.

He slumped into the nearest wicker chair, staring at the dark yard and nursing a beer. The ache in his hands had dulled to a low throb, but the memory of fire still lingered beneath his skin.

The screen door creaked open, and Sarah stepped outside, now barefoot, a plate of cake in her hand. She sat beside him without a word, pulling her chair close enough for their shoulders to touch.

She placed the plate on his lap. "I'm glad you're still alive," she said softly.

John nodded. "Thanks. Me, too."

A long silence. Crickets. The hoot of an owl.

Sarah drank in the crisp, Coldwater air. "Look, I know this might sound weird coming from me, but maybe... maybe you should think about giving up the detective stuff."

John looked at her—really looked. Her eyes were wide, worried, and honest. He exhaled through his nose. "You think so?"

"I've been here long enough to see what working both jobs is doing to you, John. You can't keep dividing yourself and expect to feel whole."

"I don't think Annaleigh is paying you enough to be that smart. Because that sounded pretty smart."

She giggled. "See? This is why we need you as a lawyer. Laughs. We've been missing that for a while now."

He tilted his head, raising his brows. "It's probably more because she thinks—thought—that I was cheating on her... with you."

She scowled. "No offense, but... I can do better." She elbowed him, laughing.

The door opened again. Annaleigh stepped out.

Sarah looked up and then quickly stood. "I'll leave you two to talk." She moved toward Annaleigh and paused beside her, voice gentle. "I'm sorry if the way I acted with John caused you to worry. I care about him, but not in that way. I want you to know I'd never be disloyal to you, either professionally... or personally."

Annaleigh's mouth curved into a small, genuine smile.

"Thank you, Sarah. I know. I mean, I should have known, and I should have trusted you." She tilted her head. "Why don't we get drinks sometime. Coffee, maybe—but not three sugars in mine."

Sarah's face lit up. "Ooh, I'd like that. But we deserve something a little stronger. We're gonna do shots!" She slipped back inside, missing Annaleigh's eye roll.

Annaleigh walked over to the wicker chairs and sat beside John—close, but not touching. Whether intentional or not, she had subtly shifted the chair slightly away.

She said softly, "Clyde told me everything."

John's stomach dropped. *How much did she know?*

"That he's your father. That you killed two people at that property. That you fought Kenneth—hand to hand—and that you..." She hesitated. "That you're the one who made it out."

John stared at the yard. "I think you could have figured out that last one on your own."

Annaleigh turned to him and placed her hands on his. "Do you want to talk about it?"

His sarcastic smile vanished. He didn't answer right away.

He couldn't.

Instead, he leaned sideways—shifting his chair in small increments—and rested his head on her shoulder.

Annaleigh said nothing. She wrapped an arm around him, pulling him close. Her hand rested on the back of his neck, fingers tender in his hair.

John closed his eyes.

Silent tears rolled down—hot, quiet, soaking into her shirt.

She held him tighter.

The night shielded them.

Inside, laughter drifted through the screen door—Genie telling a story, Bonnie scolding someone about seconds on cake.

Out here, it was just the two of them.

And for the first time in a long while, John allowed himself to stop running.

* * *

BEHIND THEM, the screen door swung open again.

Clyde stepped out onto the back porch, hands in his pockets, shoulders squared the way they always were when he had something heavy to say. Annaleigh looked up, met his eyes for a quiet second, then squeezed John's arm once.

"I'll be inside," she said softly.

She slipped past Clyde with a small nod—respectful, not cold—and disappeared into the house. The door clicked shut.

Clyde didn't sit right away. He stood, feet away, by John's chair, staring into the darkness as if still scanning for threats. He moved in front of John and grasped the empty wicker chair with a firm grip, turning it to face him. Then he lowered himself into it, leaving a careful foot of space between them.

Then, he simply let the moment be.

John looked at his hands—still slightly red from the barn, but ordinary now. Not enough for anyone else to see, thank goodness. But, more importantly, no fire.

Clyde broke the silence first. "Best I start at the beginning, I guess."

"I'll take it," John said softly.

"I met your mom while we were in school. Scoops was our favorite place to go. After a while, it just didn't work out. Nothing either one of us did, things like that just happen. Time wore on, I met someone else, and we got married," he said. "She's a good woman... I hope you'll want to meet someday. She and I had a life planned out—house, kids, the usual. Then, your mom... well, she came back into my life."

John didn't lift his eyes. He listened.

"Bonnie's always been... different. Bright. Beautiful. It was like life was brand new again. She made me laugh in ways I hadn't in a long time. She made me see myself differently." He paused, looking at the stars. "It wasn't planned. It wasn't right. But it happened. And she got pregnant."

Clyde's voice stayed even, but there was a crack under it—old guilt, worn smooth by time.

"I loved them both, in different but real ways. But I tried to be honorable and keep my promise to Ellen. She eventually forgave me. It was tough, and your mom... she handled every minute of it with grace. Never asked me to leave, never blamed me. She raised you. Alone. Told me she'd keep it quiet. And... I let her."

John swallowed hard, the words he wanted to say weighing like an anchor around him. He finally found the courage to speak.

"Am I a mistake?"

Clyde turned to him then—full, unflinching.

"No," he said. "Not for a second. You were never a mistake, John. You were the best result that could have ever come out of my mess. You know... times were a lot different back then. Coldwater's a small town. People talked. They judged her. I thought staying quiet protected all of us. I know now that I was wrong."

John's throat tightened. "Why give me your middle name, then? Deacon. Always hated it growing up, never knew why I had this name that felt like a preacher's kid. If you were trying to keep everything so quiet, why the name? Wouldn't everybody figure it out at some point?"

Clyde gave a small, sad smile. "Family tradition, John. And... you're family. *We're* family. One night, I asked her if she'd be okay with it. She asked me the same question. I told her it felt right. So that you'd carry a piece of me."

A confused look washed over John's face.

"I still can't believe you changed your name. For me."

"I started telling everyone to call me Clyde—did it relentlessly until no one even remembered my real name. I told them I was doing it to honor my father, and no one questioned it. That way, when you came along, no one would be too curious."

"Not too curious? In this small town?" John managed a light chuckle. "But... all those years. You never said anything."

"I called all the time. Checked in with your mom, asked how you were doing. While you were away. College. Law school. No matter how small, she told me everything. I listened. That was all I let myself have."

John rubbed his face with both hands.

"I don't even know what to feel."

"I understand, this is tough for both of us, believe it or not. I've been ashamed for a long time. Not of you, but because of how I treated you and your mother. I don't like the man I used to be, but if you give me a chance, I'd like to be part of your life, John. I want to be there for you."

John exhaled—a long, shaky breath.

"You don't have to decide tonight," Clyde said. "Or even tomorrow. You can be mad... you can stay that way for however long you want. Just... know I'm sorry. And I'm here. If you want me to be."

John bit at his lips, unsure of a response.

"What I know for sure right now... is that if it had to be anyone in Coldwater," he glanced at Clyde's kind eyes, seeing them differently now, "I'm happy it's you." He paused as those same kind eyes welled with tears. When the silence became too much, he shifted the conversation. "I also know you still owe me those drinks."

Clyde let out a low, surprised laugh—a rough sound.

"I do. More than a lot, in fact. A *shit* ton, pardon my French."

John managed a small, crooked smile. "Cool... what if we space them out? Say, one at a time, for at least the next twenty-four years?"

Clyde grinned. "Deal."

They sat there a while longer.

John extended his hand across the space between them.

Clyde looked at it for a long second—then reached out.

John felt his callused and warm grip. The grip of a man who'd waited a lifetime to hold on.

Neither spoke.

They didn't need to.

* * *

MOONLIGHT SLIPPED through the half-open blinds of Annaleigh's bedroom, painting silver stripes across the floor.

She and John lay crooked on the bed, pillows knocked off and sheets tangled around their legs. The ceiling fan's downward breeze cooled the sweat on their skin as their heavy breaths slowed.

John lay on his back, one arm behind his head. Annaleigh curled against his side, cheek resting on his bare chest, fingers tracing lazy circles over his heart. He felt her smile before she spoke.

"You normally aren't that noisy," she murmured. "I liked it."

He huffed and turned his head to see her face in the dim light.

"I love you," he said. The words came out steady—simple, genuine, true.

Annaleigh stilled. Her fingers paused on his chest.

John kept going, his voice even softer. "And I'm a horrible boyfriend for not saying it back when you told me. I should have said it right then. I felt the same way, then... and now. I just... those three words are hard for me."

She lifted her head, eyes searching his. Then she leaned in and kissed him—once on the lips, then again on the corner of his mouth, his jaw, the pulse under his ear. Everywhere and anywhere she could reach.

"I love you too," she whispered between kisses. She slid on top of him, straddling him, and buried her face in his neck. "I'd say it took you long enough, but I don't care. You said it. I don't care when you did."

He touched her face gently in both hands, pulled her up to him, and kissed her back—deep, long, passionate. He had to make up for lost months. When she pulled back, he didn't let go.

"There's more," he said.

She raised an eyebrow, playful yet curious.

"More? You're... ready again?"

"You and your one-track mind," he said, shaking his head. "It's something different. Better, maybe. Well, maybe not better." He smiled, letting the suspense linger. "I'm going to turn in my detective's badge."

Annaleigh blinked, then rolled off of him and bolted upright. The sheet that had been covering them slipped to her waist. "Oh my God, you're serious?"

"Yeah." He exhaled. "Being in the courtroom with you—prepping, arguing, winning—that's where I belong. I'm done splitting myself in two. No more chasing leads in the dark."

She studied him. "Is it because of the fight? Because of what happened?"

"Partly." He glanced down at his hands. "When my power left me in the courtroom, I didn't know what happened. I couldn't read him. Couldn't catch his lies. Then I realized—I was a fraud. Leaning on something that wasn't earned... wasn't a skill. I trusted that purple glow more than any law book I'd read. I know I've got a long way to go before I'm a great lawyer. I want to get there the right way."

Annaleigh's expression softened, and she leaned back into him. "That's a big step," she said against his lips. "I'm proud of you."

"There's actually... something else, too."

She kicked her legs out and settled onto her stomach, propping her chin up with her elbows.

"Don't stop, now. I'm curious about what comes next."

"We said no more secrets, right?"

"Right..." She swallowed and nodded, a small, hesitant smile tugging at her lips. "Where's this going, John?"

"I want you to know, this is brand new... and you're the first one to see it. But, true to my word, I have no more secrets from you."

She sat up, grabbing at his chest, playfully pushing him.

"Just tell me already."

He raised his right hand between them, causing her to recoil an inch.

"Can't tell you. Need to show you."

He snapped his fingers and a bright red flame ignited in his palm—steady, controlled, and dancing like it had always belonged there. He curled his fingers, and the fire drifted between the tips. From the center of his palm, a bright white light grew and illuminated the entire room, chasing away the shadows.

Annaleigh gasped and scrambled backward, sheets tangling around her, eyes wide as saucers. The mattress dipped hard, and she half-fell, half-tumbled off the edge, landing with a muffled thump on the rug.

For a heartbeat, only her hands were visible—gripping the edge of the bed like she was clinging to the side of a cliff.

Then her head popped up over the mattress, hair wild and cheeks flushed.

She stared at his hand, squinting into the flames.

Her voice cracked with shock and disbelief, loud enough to bounce off the bright walls.

"What the *fuck*, John?!"

THANK YOU

Thank you for joining me on another exciting journey through the stories of Coldwater, Missouri.

Each story in this anthology series will capture the charm of this small southern town across different eras and genres.

This has been Book Two of the main storyline. Don't worry, Coldwater has many more stories to share.

I look forward to sharing them with you. Stay tuned for more adventures!

For book and series info, updates, and more, visit *www.drywrites.com*

www.ingramcontent.com/pod-product-compliance
Lightning Source LLC
LaVergne TN
LVHW020704110826
845149LV00012B/2101

* 9 7 9 8 9 9 3 1 4 1 0 2 2 *